Other Books by Christopher Keene

Dream State Saga
Stuck in the Game
Back in the Game
"First in the Game"

GHOST IN THE GAME

CHRISTOPHER KEENE

Future House Publishing

Ghost in the Game

Future House Publishing

ISBN: 978-1-944452-83-4 (paperback)

Cover image adaptation by Brad Duke
Developmental editing by Emma Hoggan
Copy editing by Stephanie Cullen
Proofreading by Alice Card
Interior Design by Emma Hoggan

Dedicated to Liam Delaney. Still reading my stuff after a decade.

Chapter 1
THE LAST CONDITION

Hand over hand, I climbed the ladder in the stale darkness. If I never had to do this dungeon again it would be too soon. Struggling with the weight of the hatch, I pushed up at the old wood and light suddenly invaded my eyes. It wasn't so different to the first time I had entered the Dream State tutorial over two months ago. I gasped as the dusty air from inside Apollo's Lookout became the fresh air of the sky. Of course, being in a Dream Game, the air hadn't really changed; even something as trivial as the wind was an illusion here.

Climbing up onto the surface just below the Dream State's blazing sun, I sighed in relief. There didn't appear to be anymore Chaos Engine monster-generators up here. If there were no more monsters I had to face, it meant I had finally completed Wona's final condition for working with them. I was officially the leader of Catastrophe.

I walked out onto the rooftop and looked around. The gap in the railing I had created after being hit by FranktheTank's cannonball was no longer there, probably refreshed when the game designers had gone over it after my first attempt to beat this place. I spun to the black plinth where the sword, my Wakizashi encoded with the video of the beta testers' drug overdoses, was supposed to be. It hadn't been there since my failed first attempt to complete this cursed dungeon.

During that attempt, I had stabbed the Wakizashi into the plinth to load the videos into the game and was then blasted over it by Frank's cannon. Why she had done it and why the Wakizashi was missing seemed to be connected. Siena had obviously shared with her what Brock had told all of my friends: that I had betrayed them. I'd explained exactly what I had to do to become Catastrophe's leader and yet she had acted to stop me.

She must have it.

If this was true, and Wona was still willing to give me a second chance, it meant that they hadn't picked up everything that had happened on their feed. If Wona found out that someone not employed by them had an item encoded with those incriminating videos, all of this would be for nothing.

Out of the corner of my eye, I noticed a dark cloud suddenly appear behind me. Sneaky. The last Chaos Engine was a hidden one. A giant, clawed hand shot out from it and I whirled to avoid its reach, but its claw still tore a chunk out of my red Captain's Coat. It took a quarter of my Hit Points, but that was to be expected. Tertiatier monsters were not to be taken lightly, even by someone like me.

It looks like my mission here isn't complete after all.

I faced the massive beast as it stumbled out of the hidden Chaos Engine, a much stronger monster than the one I had fought last time. The thing was massive, humanoid but hunched, with dark gray skin and ragged wings that looked no good for flying. With its fangs and horns, the closest comparison I could give the creature was a demon.

I grinned in amusement, seeing that it was big enough that the rooftop of Apollo's Lookout could have been a mere perch for it. "Demons don't belong in Heaven."

It swung out another claw at me but I jumped, accessing my Key Triggers and casting three spells in quick succession. First, I spun in the air and raised my hand, then swept it to the side. The gestures were for the spells Illusion and Wind Blast. The next time the demon tried to rake me with its claws the giant hand passed right through me.

Wind whipped at me and I fell after my Wind Blast shot me around the Demon. I avoided it but flew too far out and was forced to use another blast to make sure I didn't clear the roof entirely. As I landed, I saw my illusion flicker and then blink out. A shiver ran up my spine as I remembered the image of Sue doing the same in Rubik's Castle after Sirswift had used the illusion spell to embed her image into the game and trick me. I ground my teeth.

He still hasn't paid for that!

The Demon rounded on me, but it was too late; my Graviton spell warped the air above it and descended, making the Demon shake in the realistic strain that it took for it to move. Gravity spells didn't last long, but they both slowed your opponent and also made their downward strikes twice as powerful. Considering one of its blows had quartered my health, I knew I had to be quick enough to avoid another.

My Mana reached the last third as I cast Rush on myself—the second level of the Speed Amp spell. Instantly, my movements became quicker and I easily dodged around its next striking claw, spinning as the Ruby and Sapphire Edge swords flashed into my hands. The Color Blades shone from the sun above me, and as I continued to dance around the beast, bright arcs of energy shot toward it every time I swung them.

The Demon growled but could do little as my Shockwaves rocked it back—blue and then red and then blue again. Before long, I had evened the odds on the creature and then surpassed the Hit Points it had taken from me. However, when I saw that my Mana was running out, I knew I would have to get up close and personal again. I dashed in, cutting and then dodging away. When my Graviton spell had worn off, so had my speed and I was forced to time my strikes more carefully while letting my Mana regenerate.

I had learned two things in the time I had possessed my Plasma Beam ability: the first was that I needed at least a quarter of my Mana to use it, and the second was that it was my most powerful single-enemy attack and more than enough to take away the Demon's remaining Hit Points. As I flipped back from another blow that caught my ankle and took my health down to the halfway mark, my Mana had finally regenerated enough for me to use it.

Backing up as it advanced again, I balled one hand at my side until it glowed a bright blue and then pointed my finger at the monster. Just as its last strike was going to lower my health into the red zone, the Plasma Beam cut through its hand and then its chest. It stopped suddenly, its claw dropping to its side limply and then it fell forward, its head mere inches away from flattening me.

I was tempted to put my foot on its head and make a victory pose, but before I could, the particles that made up the Demon began to explode and drift up into the air. After killing a normal monster, it would fall and then simply fade away, but this Demon's death was more dramatic. It was more akin to fireworks, just like when killing a boss.

When it had vanished entirely, the realization struck me. Granted, it was the first dungeon I had completed in the new area called Heaven, but this was also a Tertiatier dungeon, meaning that was a Tertiatier level boss. I had just killed a Tertiatier boss on my own. I did form a victory pose then, lifting the Color Blades up into the air to let the nearby sun shine through them. A banner then unrolled in my vision, saying:

—— DUNGEON COMPLETE ——

It wasn't the banner that crushed my joy, but seeing the dual blades raised above me. I knew that without them I wouldn't have been able to accomplish such a feat, but I also knew that if I were to keep my promises, I would have to eventually give them up. Although Siena had said she would fight me and win her Ruby Edge back fair and square, I would've returned it to her even in the unlikely chance that I won. The Sapphire Edge belonged to Data, and even if he did give it to Brock in order to fight me, I still didn't want any animosity between us—not while we were working for the same company.

I lowered my swords and spun back to the hatch leading down to the tower's top floor. A player could not simply summon their mount and fly down, nor could they pad their landing with a Cyclone spell as I learned to my chagrin on my second attempt to finish this cursed dungeon. To complete this dungeon alive, I would have to trek all the way back down the stairs to the bottom, and considering how big the place was, it was a long, arduous affair.

This place is still being designed. Maybe I could point out to Windsor that forcing players to do this ruins some of the fun.

Opening the hatch, I climbed down the ladder. The place seemed darker after having been out in the bright sunlight up above, and brought me back to yesterday's meeting.

M ere minutes after Frank had blown me off the roof of Apollo's Lookout, the Wona Company van had picked me up right outside David's apartment. They'd driven me to a giant, window-walled facility, where some men in suits had taken me straight to the office of Windsor Wona. The place was clean, organized, and about as large as a boardroom, with the only personal effects being a single picture of two men posing for a photograph.

He was waiting for me inside. With my body still weak after being paralyzed for a month, I was relieved when he offered me a seat across from him. Even though we had taken the elevator to the twelfth floor, I still felt out of breath.

Windsor Wona, the Asian-American boss of the most popular VR game in the world, didn't look all that different to his in-game avatar. He had the same childish smile with the same exuberant air, although his Dream State avatar had his crow's feet removed. The man was in his fifties after all.

"Well, Noah Newbolt, I think the first thing we should do is make sure your family knows you are alright." He raised an eyebrow at me, as though trying to imply how foolish I was for not contacting my mother after my escape from their asylum. "After not hearing from you for a good part of two weeks, I feel they might be worried."

I raised an eyebrow back. "You do realize that for the longest time I thought your nephew was trying to kill me, right? I was on the run, and who do you think was the first person they would go to to find out where I was?"

Windsor grinned and nodded. "Of course, of course. However, I have been getting very harsh phone calls from your mother and the police believing that you were kidnapped from the facility and that it was *my* fault."

Not so far from the truth, even if I was kidnapped willingly.

"So, what lie are we going to tell her?"

"Ah!" Windsor winked at me. "Very good question. I was thinking for both of our sakes that there was a bit of a miscommunication."

My brow furrowed. "A miscommunication?"

Windsor rolled his wrist. "You were merely moved to another of our facilities. We tried to send a letter to your parents but the post office messed up the address and it was lost in the mail." He picked up an envelope. "Despite email being the chosen form of communication these days, there are still some businesses that prefer snail mail to prevent being spammed. This just happens to be an apology letter from the postal service for losing the letter I sent your mother about the transfer."

I couldn't help but grin. "You bribed them to lie for you. Isn't that just more corruption?"

He inclined his head. "On their part, yes. For us, it's simply collusion. Nothing too major considering they accepted the bribe."

"Another nice little bow to tie everything up, huh?"

"Not entirely." Windsor's eyes caught mine. "You've yet to complete your end of the contract."

"But I thought I only had one chance to meet the conditions."

Windsor raised a hand to stop me. "Did the contract say you only had one chance to complete the dungeon?"

My memory returned to fighting my friends in the lighthouse. "You want me to go through all that again?"

Windsor shrugged. "Noah, I'm the type of person who likes to complete multiple tasks at once. By sending you up Apollo's Lookout to give us those videos, we weren't only giving you a chance to show us your loyalty, but like many of our employees, we were also getting you to beta test that dungeon before Heaven is open to the public, to see what bugs someone with all the motivation to win and all of the resources to do so might run into."

"And?"

"And you showed us one of those bugs. Imagine how frustrating it would be for a player to beat every boss in the dungeon only to be blown off the roof at the very end! Hah!"

I ground my teeth at the humor in his tone. "I don't have to imagine."

"Exactly!" Windsor pointed at me. "We thought that by removing mounts from Heaven we would make it so no player could cheat and just fly to the top. Now we know that even if they make it to the top by foot, they can still be blasted off its roof. After seeing you play, we have made it so that propelling weapons like that cannon used on you cannot force a player through the barricade. That would give an unfair advantage to Heavies. Do you understand me, Noah? The game needs to be balanced to give everyone a fair shot so that skill can prevail and not some insignificant option chosen in the tutorial."

It made sense. After all, I had tilted the balance of the game in my favor by combining Crystal Blades with the gravity and speed spells. He was trying to avoid something like that from occurring in Apollo's Lookout.

"So, you want me to check to see if it's balanced?"

Windsor nodded. "This is your baby, Noah, the same as with the players beta testing the other dungeons in Heaven. I don't want any defects before it's released to the public, and the only way to find out is to put everything against a player and see if they can still win."

I felt a little twinge of anger after hearing this. "And for me, that was my friends?"

Windsor raised his hands. "Each different Niche was there. Besides, I thought you needed a chance to explain yourself to them."

I looked down, realizing his motives weren't what I thought they had been. "A lot of good it did."

"It did do a lot of good. You even managed to hire—" He stopped and pressed a button on the terminal on his desk. "You can send her in now."

The doors opened behind us and I gasped. By my reckoning, I had known Chloe for a few months now, but not once had I seen her in real life.

Windsor raised a hand out to her. "I would like to introduce you to your new teammate."

Although her Range avatar had altered her height, it had still been going off of her look and body type. She still had the dark brown hair and the jawline of a supermodel, but her eyes were no longer as cold, the coyness in her expression doubled from being in my presence.

"Noah ... I ... hi." She waved nervously.

I smiled at her. "Hi, Chloe. When did you get here?"

"I was picked up about an hour ago. They showed me around the place, and even gave me one of their suites."

Windsor threw something and I caught it by instinct. The fact that I managed this showed that my body was on the mend. When I opened my hand, I saw it was a plastic swipe card on a key ring. "Chloe, would you mind showing Noah to his room? It's on the same floor as yours, just across the hallway."

Chloe nodded, her gaze beckoning me before turning to leave. I followed her out of the office toward the elevator, still slightly speechless. It wasn't until the doors opened and she pressed the button to the eighth floor that I finally found my words.

"So you've really signed on with them?"

She caught my eyes. "You were *very* convincing."

From her sarcastic tone, she didn't sound very convinced.

"Then why did you join?" I asked.

She didn't answer.

The elevator chimed and the doors slid open. I followed her out into a long white corridor with several doors, all numbered with gold figures. She stopped outside room 8-5 and gestured to the door. I swiped the card on the electronic lock on the frame and the door clicked open. We stepped inside and I froze, stunned at the layout of the place. It was the size of an apartment with a wide lounge leading into a master bedroom with a bathroom en suite. The leather couches and glass tables were nicer than any furniture I'd ever owned before. I knew I would have to bring some of my stuff in and leave some dirty clothes lying around before it truly felt like home.

"Not bad."

Chloe nodded, appearing unimpressed. "We'll have to work for this. In fact, I have to go beta test one of Heaven's dungeons today. I should go."

She went to leave but I grabbed her arm. "Chloe, please tell me. Why did you really decide to join Wona? It couldn't have just been because of me."

She sighed, not even turning to face me. "Let's just say it has something to do with my brother and leave it at that for now."

Brother? I didn't even know she had a brother.

I let go and she left me alone in my new suite. I turned around in awe of the place. That this was my new home didn't seem real. It almost felt like I was still in the Dream State.

Although it had only been a day ago, so much had occurred since then that it felt like a week had passed. I walked out onto the last dusty floor of Apollo's Lookout and sighed when I reached the door. It was finally over. There was nothing else the Lookout could throw at me, which meant I had completed my contract with Wona. Now they would have to uphold their end of the bargain. I pushed the doors open and looked around at Heaven.

As always, the floating city was bathed in sunlight. It filled my heart in only the way a masterpiece could. The place was so peaceful with airships and bright clouds drifting lazily overhead, a steampunk version of the American Dream, colorful and cheerful and yet completely unobtainable.

"Alright, I'm done!" I called.

There was nothing for a moment, but then an eerie whisper spoke up in my mind. *"Congratulations, Noah."*

I looked around, noticing a flicker of darkness out of the corner of my eye but seeing nothing when turning to face it. "Hello? I'm ready to find the nearest Gateway."

My comms window popped up and the unfamiliar voice replied, *"I wasn't going to call them that, you know."*

I frowned. "Who is this?"

A contact request appeared on my comms feed, and although it didn't show any connection to the voice I was hearing around me, when I saw the name *Sirswift*, I froze.

"I... once worked for Wona."

It didn't sound entirely like Samuel, the guy who had crashed into my car and had started all of my problems in this world, but I also knew that voices could be altered in the game so you didn't sound like yourself.

I ground my teeth. "You bastard. Your uncle said you're going to be arrested as soon as I come back. You're going down, you piece of—"

Another sudden voice appeared over my comms, breaking my line of thought. It was Dice. "You don't need to find a Gateway to log out now that you're Hero rank, you know. There should be an option in your Key Triggers that can cause the prompt stimulus to wake you up."

I looked down to my Key Triggers menu to see a new option simply called: Wake-Up. I returned my gaze to the contact window but saw that only Dice's communications window was up.

Why is Sirswift still able to play in the Dream State after I signed the contract that meant he would be arrested? Is Windsor going back on our deal?

Balling my fists in anger, I resolved to confront Windsor about it as soon as I awoke. I raised my finger to the Key Trigger at the bottom right of my vision, and as soon as I touched it, I felt a sudden warm jolt and everything went black.

Chapter 2

GLITCH

The first thing I heard was the whirring of gears as the recliner I was lying on tilted me up into a sitting position, like a bed transforming into a La-Z-Boy and then into a regular chair. The neon lighting blinked in my eyes.

—— NotThatNoah LOGGED OUT ——

I pulled my helmet off and it retracted into the opening above me. I looked around the Gamer Chamber, where Wona employees would use the top of the line Dream Engines and DSD to log into the Dream State, and where they did most of their work. It was all so new to me that I even had trouble thinking that I was one of them now.

The Gamer Chamber—or GC—was a circular room, dimly lit and with a dozen chairs placed along the walls that would recline into cubbies to become beds. The cubbies themselves were darkened even further to assist the hypnotic chemicals of the DSD. Dream Engine helmets hung above their indents that players would wear after taking the standard dose. Although it didn't taste very good, one could put it in a drink, preferably non-caffeinated so that the effects lasted longer. Between the chairs were cabinets and monitors that allowed you to see what was going on in-game even after you had logged out.

I shook the blur from my vision and rubbed my head. I hadn't used the waking prompt so soon after taking the drug before, and wasn't used to how the tiredness lingered. Like most sleeping pills, the sleep caused by the DSD wasn't as refreshing as natural sleep, but still went deep enough that the dreams you had under it felt real.

All too real.

Shaking from the effort, I pushed myself to my feet and walked through the chamber toward the exit. The facial recognition sensor above me blinked, and with a hiss, the metal door slid up into the ceiling. I staggered through, determined to confront Windsor about Samuel. No way in hell was I going to let him renege on our deal to get Sirswift, Sue's murderer, convicted.

I made my way down the corridor, looking down the hallways that branched out, leading to the dozens of other GCs in the facility. My brain whirled when thinking of how much such a place must have cost to build. Although I was still new to the facility, I knew exactly where I could find Windsor. Most of the president's time was spent in his personal GC where he could access the Dream State's debug room, a place where he could easily invent and play around with ideas that other game designers under him could put into the Dream State's next expansion.

When I finally came to the corridor leading to it, I saw someone standing outside the room. From the way he stood with his back to the door and his arms crossed in front of him, my first thought was that he was part of Windsor Wona's security team. However, a closer inspection made me rethink this assumption.

I eyed the skinny young man. His hair was shaved to his scalp and he looked to be of Asian descent.

"You don't look like a security guard," I said.

He squinted at me. "And you don't look like you should be out of the hospital."

I grinned, realizing the hypocrisy of thinking him skinny when I was still eating my way back to becoming more than just skin and bones. The aches and pains in the dungeons were beginning to measure up with those of my real body. I was still recovering from the atrophy I had suffered while stuck in the

Dream State the first time, after all. Living with David and his fast food habit afterward had turned out to be a terrible way for me to start putting on weight. My body needed proper sustenance and Wona's personal trainer had been helping me with this whenever I wasn't busy in-game.

I gestured to the door behind him. "How long has he been in there?"

"A couple of hours. He's putting on the final touches to a few of Heaven's newer dungeons." The young man shrugged. "Didn't want to interrupt him."

"I don't share that sentiment; let me through."

The young man nodded and stepped aside. The door slid up automatically and I walked in. In the room, there were only two recliners, and I could see Windsor's shoes poking out from the right one. Beside the door was a panel with two red buttons that could be used to communicate with players in the game. The specialized Dream Engine Wona had given me while I was paralyzed had allowed my mother do the same thing.

I pushed the button. "Windsor, I want to talk about the conditions of our contract."

Holding down the button, I heard a reply. "Just a second, I'll be right out once I can—damn! Why won't you …" I heard him sigh. "Alright, fine."

There was the same buzzing of gears as the recliner lifted his head from the darkness and he pulled off his Dream Engine. He was obviously much more accustomed to waking up from the drug than I was, for he didn't even look drowsy as he rose.

"Noah, couldn't you see I was in the middle of something and …" He paused and gave me a confused look. "Oh, you look mad. What's wrong?"

"What's wrong? You were supposed to have your nephew arrested after I signed the contract, and yet he just spoke to me while I was in-game." Taking my finger off the button, I looked around. "Could he have been in the GC with me?"

Windsor rubbed his head. "No, he couldn't have."

"How do you know?"

He smiled up at me and then rose. "Don't believe me? Alright, I'll show you."

He walked past me, through the door and down the corridor. The young man who had been waiting outside went after him and I followed on their tails as Windsor led us to an elevator. He pushed the button and the arrow above the doors lit up with a *bing*. We walked in and he rubbed the back of his head again.

"I was working on making a new Niche when you interrupted me. Just like a dungeon, it's difficult to make them balanced so they don't break the game." He jolted up then, seeming startled when he saw the other young man was in the lift with us. "Holy mother, when did you get here?"

"I was waiting outside your GC," he replied nonchalantly.

"Next time say something."

"Who is this guy?" I asked.

Windsor raised a hand. "Noah, meet Vega. Vega, Noah."

"Oh, so you're NotThatNoah," Vega said, as though everything made sense to him now. "I've heard of you."

I grinned. "No, I really am that Noah."

Windsor put an arm around Vega's shoulders. "This guy's our new specialist."

I eyed him. "Specialist in what?"

"Games," Windsor replied.

"What kind of games?"

Vega grinned at me. "*All* kinds of games."

The elevator stopped and we came out into an office interior with a soft carpet and glass walls revealing people working on computers and shuffling paperwork. I knew that a games manufacturer needed more than just designers and players, but the marketing and legal side of things always helped to remind me that this was a job I was working now and not just my own crusade.

Windsor continued talking as we came through the corridors. "After you took over as the leader of Catastrophe, I decided we needed some new blood, so I sent out scouts to see what they could find. Vega was their highest recommendation."

I caught Vega's eyes. "Well, I'll look forward to seeing what you can do. How much experience do you have in the Dream State?"

"Before this week?" Vega shrugged. "None."

"None?" I barked.

Vega nodded without another word. I shook my head in disbelief. I had to survive in the game for a month to be noticed by Wona. I couldn't imagine what this guy had done to get their attention when he hadn't even played for a week. *What kind of freak is he?*

We finally arrived at Windsor's office. Opening the double doors, he walked around his desk and pulled up the monitor of his laptop.

"Take a seat. I'm going bring up the feed."

"Feed of what?" I asked.

Windsor nodded. "I figured you wouldn't trust me when I said I would put my own nephew in prison so I managed to persuade the prison security to give me a link to the camera outside Samuel's cell."

His laptop monitor must have been on a pivot, for he spun it around to face me. On the screen showed a black and white video feed of a familiar young man facing the bars from the inside of his cell. I recognized him. He was the young man who had hit my car, killing Sue and paralyzing me: Samuel Wona. I nodded, satisfied by the sight. The murderer was finally facing justice.

"He'll be staying in here until he goes before a judge. Believe me now?" Windsor didn't wait for my answer but just continued on. "I told you, I don't take murderers lightly, even if they're my own family."

I nodded again, more forcefully. "Okay, fine. It still doesn't explain why someone called Sirswift was talking to me in-game."

I noticed Vega briefly glance in Windsor's direction but it seemed the president's mind was already racing ahead.

"I suppose this will be the best time to tell you both. Heaven is going to be having its grand opening in two days and we want Catastrophe to oversee everything in-game to make sure it goes smoothly."

I nodded, the announcement taking my mind off Sirswift. "What are we supposed to do?"

"Observe. My Heroes have tested most of the dungeons and have confirmed that they are playable and balanced; however, beta testing can only do so much before real experience will be able to tell us whether or not a second edition will be needed. Noah, you, Chloe, and Dice will be the eyes and ears of this event while several others will be watching on the screens to see if there are any *glitches*."

"Shows how much confidence you have in your designers and beta players if you expect there to be glitches," I said.

"I used to have more faith in them ..." Windsor trailed off as his eyes lowered to the desk. "There hadn't been any reports of bugs for so long that I thought we had fixed them all, but there have recently been accounts of players who have been logged out of the game involuntary. Each time they have reported witnessing avatars dressed in full Silver Armor, but moving as if their weight wasn't affected by it. Each account has reported the same thing with multiple accounts from The Hall of Doors. The commonalities are an armored player, a deafening scream and then waking up in a sweat without the need of the prompt. Because of the piercing screams the players hear right before they wake up, people on the forums have started calling these armored avatars *Screamers*."

Screamers... sounds more than a little suspicious.

"*Screamers?*" Vega asked incredulously, sounding confused about why Windsor used the plural. "If they're all wearing the same armor, why would they think there's more than one of them?"

"Good question." Windsor pointed a finger his way. "The only differing testimony in each case was the size of their avatars, meaning that they were using different Niches. I first thought that someone might have been changing their Niche so I checked the trans-houses in each district. There was no record of anyone with that armor having visited them between the times of the attacks."

"So we're to keep a careful eye on anyone moving quickly in

Silver Armor regardless of their Niche?" I nodded to Vega. "What about him?"

"Do you really think it would be smart to bring a newbie into the game with you for something as important as this?" Vega gave Windsor another look, but he just smiled and waved us off. "You've already used up more time than I have right now. I have to make sure everything's ready, so if you wouldn't mind."

We turned to leave, but I stopped and turned back to him.

"I would also like to note that the top of Apollo's Lookout has the same weakness with wind magic as it does with cannons. You should make sure to deal with that so Spellcasters don't have an advantage there either."

Windsor cupped his chin in thought. "A barrier should fix both problems and stop the need to ban mounts in Heaven as well." He nodded and grinned. "Heck, what's the point of being up that high if you can't fly around and explore the place anyway. Yes, good work, Noah, that's what I like to hear!"

"Just doing my job," I replied and exited the office.

Chapter 3
CLOUDY PATHWAYS

I spent the next day exploring Heaven with Chloe. After her best friend Keri—a supportive Spellcaster—had beaten her in Apollo's Lookout, she was determined not to show her weakness again. I guess that's why she asked me if I wanted to try the Primatier Heaven dungeon she'd been assigned to beta test.

"It's seriously fun!" she called as she waved me on across the floating bridge.

"Listen, Chloe, I get you want to show off your new dungeon to me, but why are we heading to the market district? Aren't most of the Gateways on the outer rim of the city?"

She spun and rolled her eyes. She still wore her duster, slacks, and cowboy boots, her waist belted with bullets and dual guns in their holsters. "Trust me, Noah. I know what I'm doing. We need an item before we can go up there."

Up there? We're in Heaven, there's nothing above us but sky.

We eventually came to the rotating stores of the Synth Square she had been leading me to, but before we stepped off of the platform she stopped me.

"I'm giving you some items, usually to complete the dungeon you have to farm them in the first area before going on to the next, but I've already earned more than enough for both of us to get what we need."

I nodded and she passed me what looked like a pile of goose down.

—— ACQUIRED 'LIGHT FEATHER X20' ——

I remember Brock received a feather when we had completed Ayer's Rock and wondered if this was the same kind of item. I had my doubts as I looked at it in my inventory. The feathers were white, where the one Brock had gotten was black.

"Now go into the materials store and get them to synth those feathers into Icarisandals."

"Icarisandals?" I asked, feeling that something in that name sounded familiar to me.

"Just go!"

As soon as the rotating shops had come to the materials store, she shoved me over the bridge into the store. I waved my arms to balance myself as I felt the store lift me up like I was on a Ferris wheel. Steadying myself, I walked over to the female NPC behind the desk. Another rotating inventory appeared behind her and I found the item when I looked at what the Light Feathers could make.

I chose the Icarisandals, knowing that I could afford them with the infinite Moola afforded to Hero rank players. I felt that maybe Chloe had been having her own spending spree like I had after being let loose in Heaven. The NPC passed me the Icarisandals. After they disappeared into my inventory, I looked at their stats. They didn't look anything special until I came to the downward pointing arrow that represented a player's weight. It read zero.

Zero?

I equipped the winged sandals and took a step. My whole body seemed to lift as the rotating shop began to descend. I nearly hit the ceiling before I unequipped them and landed with a thump against the wooden floor. I turned and waited for the platform before stepping out to meet Chloe.

"Cool, huh?" she exclaimed.

I nodded. "I have the feeling I know what the dungeon we're going to be doing is like."

She smiled and grabbed my hand before pulling me back in the direction we had come from. "Wait and see."

Together, we made our way back across Heaven's floating islands before coming to the overreaching platforms of the outer rim's launching pads. However, instead of helicopters or planes, each bridge ended at a glowing circular Gateway. Each one was a different color and each one led to a different dungeon.

I nodded. "If they're this easy to reach, they must be Primatier dungeons. I'm starting to wonder what barriers they're going to have to put in front of Apollo's Lookout to make entering it more challenging."

"Apollo's Lookout is challenging enough already. Oh wait, it's this one." Chloe pointed and we approached the yellow Gateway.

Following her, I noticed the option to go to 'Cloudy Pathways' appear in my Key Triggers. I selected it and with a flash from the Gateway we were suddenly standing on a rock platform floating in the middle of the azure sky. I came to the edge to see only the ocean and thick white clouds below.

Chloe appeared next to me and gestured to the inner circle of the platform. "Stand in the middle; it's a lift."

I stepped closer to her and the stone circle in the middle of the platform began to glow and then rose higher, lifting us toward the clouds above. As we ascended through the white mist, I noticed that the ones around me had a kind of structure to them, like pathways leading this way and that through the sky. Along with the name of the dungeon, my suspicions of what the boots were used for were confirmed.

"Isn't it incredible?" Chloe called.

I was about to agree but then nearly bit my tongue when the lift stopped with a sudden jolt, coming to a larger platform above the clouds. From it, there were two paths. The one off to the left was wide and made of stone, but went away from the clouds. The one to the right continued further up into the clouds like the scaffolding around a winding tower.

"Now you see why I had you synth those sandals." Chloe pointed to the goose monsters diving down on the platform. "Otherwise you have grind for a few hours against those birds that appeared on that platform to get enough feathers."

I recalled my time with Brock at Ayer's Rock. "I've fought enough birds during my time here."

Chloe grinned. "My thoughts exactly. So what say we equip the footwear and fight some fallen angels up this pathway instead?"

The giddiness behind her words triggered my own excitement. I reached out and slid my hand up the back of her neck, running my hand up her scalp, wondering if she would let me do that to her in real life. She blushed, equipped her boots and drifted up out of my grip.

"Wait, Chloe." I looked around. "How do we change direction while we're floating along the pathways?"

"Shouldn't it be obvious? Everyone who could make it to Heaven would have some form of spell or attack that could push them in one direction or another... or at least they should be able to get one at this point."

"Oh, right."

I checked my inventory and equipped the Icarisandals. They flashed onto my feet, revealing again the wings on the outer edges of them that flared out. They were the kind of sandals that the Greek god Hermes would have worn.

Following Chloe, I stepped out from the platform onto the thicker cloud. Although I could step over it like it was a normal bridge, the lack of weight made my steps slow and clumsy.

"Don't try walking, use your wind magic." I looked up to see Chloe shooting ahead of me. "Come on!"

I nodded and swept my hand out behind me to cast Wind Blast. Not only did the force of the spell allow me to catch up with Chloe, but it also blew a few of the clouds away behind me.

I see. So, this part of the game is like a platformer. You can use magic to both move around and alter the surroundings.

A sudden confusion came over me as I saw Chloe ahead of me shooting from cloud to cloud. Then I noticed that she was pointing her guns in the opposite direction that she was flying.

Ah, magic bullets. Clever.

I used a few more Wind Blasts to catch up with her, the freedom of flying making a thrill of excitement shoot through me.

"Are those specialty wind bullets?" I asked.

"Yup! Now watch this!" she called and aimed her guns behind her.

She pulled both triggers and blasts of air shot from each barrel, propelling her forward and then up into the wide funnel of clouds ahead of us. I gazed up as small, winged forms flew through the funnel.

"Noah, it's the Cherubs. Hurry up!"

I used one blast to shoot me forward and then another to launch me up into the funnel. I then noticed the small winged, baby-like monsters firing arrows as Chloe shot her regular bullets back at them. Seeing the way normal bullets didn't send her backward made me think that fire attacks didn't affect a player's position. I raised my hand at the Cherubs and began throwing Fire Balls at them.

The fat little things were quick. As soon as I fired at them, the Cherubs took off, dodging out of the way of fire and hiding in the clouds. They started firing arrows my way instead of focusing on Chloe. A few hit, taking a small chunk of my health. I used a Wind Blast to move some of the clouds away but they just flew off to hide in another place.

"Chloe!" I called up at her. "Have you got any Mana booster bullets on you?"

"I think so, why?"

I grinned and put the palms of my hands beneath me. "Because after this, I'm going to need one."

I rolled my hands around one another and as soon as I did, my Cyclone spell flew out from them, the force of the wind rocketing me up between their arrows and above the swarming angels. I then spun and flung my straightened arm out from my chest. Wildfire turned the clouds below me orange as the Cherubs' wings burned up in the fire before they fell from the sky.

"Hah, see that?" I asked, like a demon on Satan's warpath.

"You killed all of them?" She almost sounded disappointed. "You couldn't let me show off for once, could you?"

She pointed her gun at me and fired. The bullet made a blue

light wash over me, causing my Mana bar to regenerate much quicker than passive regeneration would have alone.

I raised my palms. "Alright, alright, I'll let you have the next lot."

She beamed at me. "Good!"

We continued along the cloudy pathways. I was glad I gave Chloe the go-ahead. The way she jumped from cloudy path to cloudy path, firing at the different angelic monsters on her way, made me think she had done this dungeon about as many times as I had done Apollo's Lookout. Frankly, I was a little envious. The Cloudy Pathways dungeon was far more fun to play around in than climbing a Chaos Engine-filled tower where anything could jump out at you.

After she had cleared the area of the winged creatures, she returned to me, grinning in exhilaration. "I told you this place was the best!"

"Do you think Keri would want to try it out?"

Chloe's eyes lowered then and I realized the mistake I had made.

"Sorry, I didn't …"

"It's okay!" Chloe cried out. "You know, even before what happened in the tower, Keri and I weren't as close as we had been in high school. Ever since she and my brother …" She trailed off and I suddenly remembered the look Keri had given me when we were in the Tranquil Grotto.

"Your brother?" A suspicion boiled over in my mind and I couldn't help but ask, "Did the two of them used to date or something?"

Chloe nodded. "Yeah, for a little while anyway."

She kicked her legs like she was swimming instead of flying. A remaining angel snuck out from behind one of the bridges and aimed up its bow. Not wanting it to interrupt us, I launched a Plasma Beam at it. From the amount of them I'd been using, I wasn't entirely surprised when a window popped up saying:

—— **LIGHTNING UPGRADE: 'PERFECT STORM'** ——

A window then revealed a white avatar lifting one finger high into the air as though it were a lightning rod, and bolts of electricity rained down from the sky all around him.

As cool as that is, NOT NOW!

"What happened?" I asked as I tried to remain focused on Chloe's story.

Chloe's voice became solemn. "You wouldn't understand. You might even hate me for it."

"I might be confused if you don't explain it, but I doubt I would hate you for it. Just give me a chance."

Chloe looked down as she continued to drift. "I wasn't surprised that you turned on everyone. I also knew about Brock and the beta testers long before you told us."

I nodded, remembering her exclamation when I first told her that I was friends with him. She was also the only one who never questioned Brock's claim. Despite her words, I remained perplexed but still waited until she was comfortable enough to continue.

"Keri never knew... but my brother was one of the betas who was brain damaged by Wona's second set of DSD trials."

The silence that came after she said this felt deafening.

"You see! I told you you wouldn't understand!"

Honestly, I was still registering what she had said. It made no sense. Why would Chloe be working for Wona if that's what they had done to her brother? Aside from that, I had spent time in their asylum myself. I might have even met the guy.

"Is he in one of their homes?" I asked to make sure.

Chloe shook her head. "We don't know where he is. Lucas went missing nearly a year ago, along with five others. One of the reasons I decided to work for Wona is that I wanted to see if I could find out what happened to him."

A few things seemed to line up in my memory then. I recalled what Keri had told me after we had finished the Tranquil Grotto together.

"We all get lonely sometimes."

That's why she didn't want our relationship to be complicated.

After she had been with Chloe's brother and he had just vanished from the face of the earth like that, it's no wonder she wanted to be sure.

"Man… I guess it makes sense."

"Don't tell Keri," Chloe said.

"Yeah… I understand. Let's just finish this dungeon first, and we can clear all this up later, okay?"

She nodded. "Okay, I'm ready to kick some ass!"

After defeating several more Cherubs and fighting a larger angel called Uriel wielding a fiery sword, which I managed to beat with my Color Blades, we flew up into the stratosphere, an area surrounded by heavy clouds with the wind as strong as any hurricane. In comparison to the serene clouds below, the wide area was more like a screaming, stormy hell of a furious wind god's domain.

As though the thought of a wind god was a call of summons, a giant feathered, serpent-like dragon appeared from above. A scroll unfurled to show the boss's name: Quetzalcoatl. Although larger than most, it looked about as dangerous as the other bosses I had fought in the Dream State. But having just defeated a Tertiatier boss on my own, I felt I could handle it.

"Don't attack it!" Chloe called as we were pushed to edges of the area.

I raised an eyebrow at her. "Why not?"

"It changes the wind. See how we're on the outside of the hurricane?" She gestured to the fact that we had been pushed to the outer clouds and I nodded. "Anything you throw at it will just be blown back at us. You have to wait for it to change the wind so it sucks us in and then we can attack at close range."

Good thing I didn't throw the first punch.

A sudden gust of air hit us, its whiplash taking away a few Hit Points before I could call, "How long will it take?"

Suddenly the serpent that had been flying around in the distance flew into the center of the hurricane and then reared up in a vertical line within the eye of the storm. That's when I felt the wind pull us in.

"Attack now!" Chloe cried and began popping off round after round from her revolvers into Quetzalcoatl.

I was glad she had told me of the wind's effect. I hated to think of the damage all of our firepower being turned back on us could've done. My own strikes would have taken us out in a few seconds. Still being a fair distance from the monster, I summoned my Color Blades and began sending Shockwave after Shockwave toward it until the effect of the wind reversed again and we were blown back toward the clouds.

"Okay, stop!" Chloe called.

I stopped and noticed that Quetzalcoatl was once again circling outward from the eye of the hurricane, coming right up to us. Up close, I could see that it had a long lightning bolt-shaped horn sticking out of its forehead.

"I think it's going to attack, try to dodge it!"

I slashed my hand at Quetzalcoatl, my Wind Blast blowing me back as the dragon waved its horn at us. It was in range now, but I knew that whatever I attacked it with would be blown to the edge of the hurricane. *Unless we were on the inside.*

"Chloe, let's finish this thing off! Get on its inner-flank," I called and watched the confusion on her face become understanding.

She used her specialty wind bullets to dodge another blow from the boss, and then oriented herself so that she was facing it on the outside of the hurricane. I flew to her side by using my Wind Blasts. We caught each other's eyes and nodded.

"Take this!" she screamed.

Bullets and Shockwaves rushed into it. As weak as most Primatier monsters were at our level, it was incredibly cathartic to watch her lay into it with guns ablaze after what I had just made her talk about. After several more blows, it returned to the center of the hurricane. By this point, its Hit Points were already so low that all it would take was one more bullet to finish it off.

"Would you do the honors?" I asked and Chloe gave me a hellish grin.

"So kind of you," she replied, and not taking her eyes away from me, fired the last shot as soon as the wind changed.

Quetzalcoatl stopped writhing within the eye of the storm and the circling wind and clouds began to dissipate, revealing the vastness of the empty sky all around us. It was shocking, the very size of the empty blue world rendering me speechless. As we began to drift down, we watched as Quetzalcoatl broke apart into particle effects before it, too, dissipated into the air.

—— DUNGEON COMPLETE ——

"This is the best part. We're currently as high as you can get in the Dream State. Unequip your Icarisandals!"

I did so and together we plummeted toward the ocean. As we fell, she angled herself down toward me. When we were close enough, she grabbed hold of my hand, drawing herself closer still. She then said one thing in my ear that made the falling all the more thrilling.

It was two simple words: "Hold me."

Chapter 4

LUCAS NIX

That night in my apartment above the Wona facility, sitting on my new king bed and facing my new pristine en suite, Chloe told me her brother's story. After what Brock had told me, it seemed like a very familiar tale.

Her brother, Lucas Nix, was a VR and game enthusiast signed up to be a beta tester of the Dream Engine in hopes of being one of the first people to try a dream-based VR game. Of course, the tests went badly, he lost his mental faculties, and was assigned to Wona's asylum; the consent waivers he signed prevented Chloe and their parents from taking any legal actions against them. A few years later, he and five other betas had gone missing.

Up until the point of him getting brain damage and being shipped off to the asylum, he's almost the same as Brock.

An apprehension rose in me as I continued to listen.

"We tried to hold Wona responsible for losing him, but you know Wona: they always have some legal loophole to get away with things."

"I still don't get it." I turned to see the scorn in her eyes. "Why on earth did you join Wona if they did that to your brother?"

She looked down. "You weren't the only one who sold their soul to the devil, Noah. In return for mine, I asked to be allowed to look through their employee records. I've since found out that after the beta tests failed, Wona fired two individuals, but their names had been blacked out and removed from the records. I tried asking Windsor who they were but he said everything he knows is in those records."

Windsor was more than willing to hand over the evidence needed to convict his nephew. What on earth could be so damaging to his company that he would be hiding something like this?

My mouth dropped as the memory of reading something on Brock's old blog came back to me. "Windsor Wona had nothing to do with the creation of DSD. Do you think it was a chemist who pushed the drug through before it was ready?"

She nodded. "I've had that suspicion for a long time. It's the reason I chose to come over to Wona with you. I don't think the company itself is responsible; I think something went horribly wrong and that they tried to cover it up, and I think it's one of the people who was fired that did it. That's the real bad guy."

Sounds like a theory, but what proof do we have? To convince the others, we have to find out more. I think I remember reading something about this.

I smiled at her. "Looks like we have a mystery to solve."

She grinned back, her expression fierce. "A witch-hunt."

"We'll tackle this together, but in the meantime—" I paused, swallowed nervously, and her brow knitted together in confusion. "Ah… would you like to stay the night? You look like you don't want to be alone right now."

She smiled and grabbed my hand on the bed sheet. "Not tonight, Noah."

I shrugged. "I wasn't suggesting anything weird."

She let go, stood up, and made her way to the door. "I don't mind a little weird… just not tonight."

She opened the door and left.

Can't blame me for trying, can she?

The next day, Dice supplied us with a map that showed the locations of every Gateway to and from Heaven, although we wouldn't be able to explore all of the buildings in the time before the opening.

"We're also given a counter of the people inside and whenever someone accesses one of the Gateways," Dice said. "Because none of the public has been here before, no one should be accessing Heaven with Transfer Orbs either."

My brow furrowed.

Dice met my eyes, appearing to notice my confusion. David's guess had been right: the man was Japanese. We had made a pretty decent team when fighting the Dark Warrior on the first floor of Apollo's Lookout, and I was relieved when Windsor told me that Dice held no grudges against me for not helping him in his fight against Siena.

"If anyone enters Heaven by means other than the main entry or the Gateways, it means that someone is using a glitch in the game to get inside and there's a good chance they'll be one of the Screamers," he clarified.

I simply nodded. Chloe and I each sat down on one of the recliners in the GC and pulled down a Dream Engine.

"Our target," Chloe said. "Should be fun."

"All we need is their player I.D. codes. After that we should be able to track them unless they know of a way to hide it."

I wouldn't put it past them. Brock knew how to hide his, I thought while taking a dose of DSD and letting the recliner lower me into the darkness of sleep.

We decided to scout Heaven to find out all of its accessible areas. We explored the buildings that players could access, pointing out light-heartedly the many pre-nuclear Americana and religiously influenced details in their interiors. So many of the buildings had homes with pianos and long mahogany dining tables.

There was a barbershop with a shoeshine stand. We visited a bar with old-fashioned record players, checker-tiled floors, and wall scrolls of the over-lording patriarch. I always thought that was a bit on the nose considering how much it looked like Windsor.

He really put a lot of himself into this place ... maybe too much.

There were other reasons I wanted to get an idea of the many locations within Heaven. If these Screamers could enter Heaven wherever they wanted to, I wanted to know the structure of the buildings if we were forced to fight in them.

Although if these Screamers can force people to log out, I doubt there's much we can do to fight them in an enclosed area anyway.

Chloe and I walked into what looked like a museum. The place was interactive with moving mannequins and janitor-looking machines with brooms that jumped out at us.

"This museum's a Basetier dungeon?" Chloe asked as she raised her guns and began firing. It only took two of her bullets for the janitors to flop forward on their broomsticks and then vanish from our path.

"Seems so. Should we move to the next building, or are you interested in exploring this place as well?"

Chloe shrugged. "It's less boring than the other buildings we've been through. Come on."

I followed her through the museum. Things continued to jump out at us. Sometimes they were robotic security guards in steampunk attire with batons, and other times they were just interactive aspects of the museum, such as a winch we had to spin to open the gate to move to the next area.

By how quickly Chloe took out the monsters, I could tell she was fighting to let off some stress. I was actually more interested in the pictures displaying the musket wars on the walls and in the diorama displays, telling a story of the horrible world below that the floating city was trying to escape.

One side of the war seemed to be led by someone who looked like Windsor, and I could have sworn I recognized the man with a mustache leading the other side.

A voiceover started calling, "And so the founders followed the Creator into the sky to escape the hell below for a new heaven. It's here that our found …"

The voice trailed off as Chloe stalked around a corner where other displays waited. A gunfight with several steampunk robots broke out as they shot at us from the adjacent hallway intermittently. I used Ice Coffin to freeze them and let Chloe's bullets shatter them to let her take more of the Skill Points.

"Have you thought about what's going to happen when those gates open?" Chloe asked as we finally came to an empty corridor.

"What do you mean?" After seeing that there were no lights ahead at the end of the hallway, I found myself paying less attention to what she was saying. "Isn't that the point of a grand opening?"

She whirled on me. "Anyone will able to get through, including Siena… and Keri."

I nodded as what she was getting at dawned on me. "Siena will want to fight me to get her Ruby Edge back."

"That could be a problem if they show up at the exact same time as the Screamers, don't you think?"

"That is a worst-case scenario." I squinted into the darkness ahead of us, feeling we might be walking into some kind of trap. "It's going to be pretty busy. The odds we'll run into them is going to be small and—"

A line of lights suddenly appeared at the bottom of the wall ahead of us, showing that the corridor finished at the dead end. Then I heard the whirring of gears and the sound of artificial laughter.

"Chloe, get beside me. Now!"

She ran to my side and I rubbed the air in front of me with the palm of my hand, casting Ice Wall just as the wall at the end of the corridor rolled up like a curtain, revealing three eyeless robots with mini-guns. With a loud whine, the bullets tore up the walls, ceiling, and floor in their wave of attack. I wanted to say that they hit everything but us, but the attack was powerful enough to break through the ice and we got the back end of the shots.

These things are tough for a Basetier dungeon! But then, it is balanced against the difficulty of the rest of this cakewalk of a dungeon.

There was some more laughter from the clicking robots as another belt of bullets was connected. I saw that there was no cover in the corridor and as Chloe began firing at them, the bullets had little effect on the robots.

"Damn, for Basetier bosses these things are tough!" she called, as though reading my mind. "Any ideas?"

"Only one."

I knew I had been relying on my Color Blades a bit too much recently, but the satisfaction I got from bounding into the display and carving up the robots with a few wide slashes of the glowing weapons would have convinced anyone to try and keep hold of them. Sparks flew everywhere as I tore through the machines.

I knew I would have to give the weapons up eventually, so I considered each time I used them as a parting gift, despite how unhappy it made Chloe.

"Those swords are too OP!" Chloe called as I stood tall in the wreckage of the three robots. "They're like the answer to every question in this game. They almost take the fun out of solving the problems the world brings up."

I shrugged. "With Siena after me, I thought I should make the most of them considering I won't have them long."

"Still," Chloe pouted. "You keep stealing my SP."

"You're Hero rank, Chloe. Skill Points are only good for learning abilities after your stats are maxed. From then on, it's all about how you use it, skill on skill." I jumped down from the display window. "Besides, we don't have the time to spend here when we're supposed to be checking out as many buildings as we can anyway."

She sighed. "I guess. Let's go."

I nodded and went to walk out with her but then stopped when my contact window popped up in my vision.

Windsor Wona: "Come to my office immediately."

I smiled. "It's a good thing I finished this quickly. Windsor just asked me to go see him. Can you handle the rest of the search yourself?"

Chloe put her hands on her hips. "Okay sure, just leave me here, why don't you."

I put my hands up innocently. "Hey, come on. I'm working here. I'll see you later."

She turned from me. "Whatever. You don't want to be late."

I used the 'Wake-Up' option and felt myself jolted awake, the museum surrounding me darkening and then disappearing. One reality was swapped for another as my eyes eased open to see the logout text while the recliner I was sleeping on raised me into a sitting position. I took off the helmet, rubbed my face, and stood to make my way out of the GC. Chloe's legs were still on her bed, as she hadn't logged out when I had. Dice, too, was still in the Dream State, scanning other areas of Heaven for the openings.

As I stood, I noticed that the cold metallic layout and seeing their feet sticking out from the wall made the place look like a morgue. The door hissed open and I made my way through the corridors toward the elevator.

Windsor's office was on the twelfth floor of the facility. As the elevator stopped and I walked out onto his floor, I was relieved that my cloudy head had abated, which I had found was key when talking to someone like the president of the largest VR games developer in the world. It was the third time I had visited this floor in the four days I had been working here, and every time I passed through I saw the people behind the glass walls going about their jobs. They were all individuals and yet in their suits and pencil skirts, they only seemed like more wallpaper to me.

If they would stop looking at their computers for a second, how would I look to them? Some undernourished basement dweller, probably.

Eventually, I came to the large office to find Windsor staring at his laptop. I again observed how uncharacteristic the room was except for that one photograph standing up on his desk. It depicted him and another man who looked a little like the enemy leader in the musket war portrayed in Heaven's museum. The two looked to be celebrating, and on the frame of the photo, the title read: Wona & Mirth.

"Oh him? He's dead now," Windsor said, breaking me out of my reverie.

"Huh?"

Without looking up from his laptop, he gestured to the picture. "The man in the photo. He died."

"Oh, I'm sorry to hear that." I frowned but then shook my head. "What did you want to talk to me about?"

Windsor looked up from his monitor. "Samuel's trial is set to begin in two weeks' time. Are you okay with that?"

I nodded. "So long as he stays in his cell until then. Is that really all you wanted to ask?"

Windsor crossed his hands in front of his face and smiled. "The Wona Company is really going to need you in the coming weeks, Noah. I need to know that once Samuel is in jail you aren't just going to pack up and run off."

"You don't have to worry about that. I've got other reasons for wanting to stick around."

Windsor nodded. "Very well, then. Tomorrow's the big day. I'm relying on you to make sure that everything goes smoothly, and if not …"

I recalled what Dice had said before we began scouting the area. "If not, you would want me to identify one of the Screamers, right?"

"Correct. As far as I'm concerned, these Screamers are a mystery that will never be solved unless we can find out who they are. So far, every encounter reported—usually from some Range avatar—has come with corrupted video evidence. Whatever they're doing, it's only in the testing phase. Like us, they're beta testing each sabotage for one main event."

Windsor stood from his desk and made his way around it toward me. He put his hand on my shoulder and gave me his wry smile.

"If things go wrong, we need to be able to turn it to our advantage. You should really employ more people under you. There's a lot leaning on this, and you can't do it all by yourself, you know."

I nodded, feeling the intensity behind his words. "I can handle it, trust me. If they show up, I'll be sure to get their user I.D. before I wake up, and I'll tell the others the same."

"Good. Now let me show you what I've been working on." He took his hand away and made to leave. "I've been dying to let this cat out of the bag. In fact, I wonder if you can help me with it. You see, I have this idea for an attack. It can do a lot of damage if it lands, but it's also really easy to dodge for quick opponents. The problem is getting your opponent to stand still long enough …"

He continued talking as he walked out, apparently expecting me to follow him. Instead, I turned back to the photo on his desk, seeing the picture of the young Windsor Wona and his Caucasian companion with a mustache and goatee. I felt like I recognized him, but I couldn't pin down where it was from.

Wona and Mirth… was that the original name of the company?

Frustrated because of my failed memory, I turned back and followed Windsor out of the office.

Chapter 5

OPENING DAY

Frank looked up as the massive gateway swung open and crowds of people around her began to enter. Celebratory horns played in the background and balloons filled the sky. Once the colorful orbs reached a certain height, they exploded, their popping making them sound like invisible fireworks.

"Finally!" Siena cried as they began to move. "I was beginning to think they would never open."

"You seem excited, Siena." Keri moved up beside her. "Can't wait to try out one of the new dungeons, huh?"

"Are you kidding?" She snorted. "I've been trying to get my hands on Noah ever since he stole my Color Blade, but he's been hiding behind these gates for the last week. Now I finally have a chance to snag the little prick."

Frank rolled her eyes. "She's only been raving on about it every minute of every day."

Keri scratched the back of her head and smiled light-heartedly. "I guess I drown it out."

"Hey, that's insulting to my ravings. Enough of this!" Siena shoved the avatar in front of her forward, but it was a tank and he wouldn't budge. "I mean could this line go any slower? What's the holdup?"

With the massive troll-like avatar blocking their view, Frank had no idea what was making everyone go so slowly.

"Step on this!" Siena yelled and then put a hand on the

shoulder of Frank's Dragon Armor. "I'm going on ahead, see you guys in there!"

She then flipped herself up onto the tank's broad helmeted head and began jumping from shoulder to shoulder over the crowd.

"Well, there she goes," Keri sighed.

The way Siena had jumped over the others' heads did give Frank an idea and she crouched down. "Keri, get on my shoulders and tell me what you see."

Keri nodded and climbed up. When Frank rose again, Keri squealed a little and clutched her helmet, but then she leaned in the direction of the gate.

"They've narrowed off the path so that everyone who enters is getting their user I.D. scanned. I wonder why."

Frank shrugged her massive shoulders and went to let her down.

Keri waved off her hand and grinned down at her. "A little longer. It's nice being this high up for a change."

It took another hour to get to the end of the line.

"Alright. Stand on the pad, say your username, and continue on to Heaven," said an elderly NPC sitting on a podium next to the entrance.

Frank let Keri down from her shoulders and stepped onto the pad. "FranktheTank."

"Next!" the old man called.

Keri walked through behind her, and then they were inside. Siena was nowhere to be seen. They moved forward until they arrived at the first platform and its connecting bridge. As they saw the vast drop to the water below them, Frank heard Keri gasp.

"Wow!" she called, putting her hands over her mouth.

"I know," Frank replied in awe. "According to the map, the whole city's in the sky. It's a pretty massive place as well."

Keri ran onto the first bridge as the island they were standing on bobbed up and down under the weight of the people that passed over it. "What should we do first?"

"I think we should start off by finding Siena. She would never let us live it down if we did a dungeon without her, besides." Frank spun, scanning the crowd through the slits in her visor. "She can't have gone too far."

They continued over the bridge, seeing players already trying to interact with the NPCs, who were all dressed in bright colors like it was some kind of festival. They eventually made it to a larger hovering island with a huge bronze statue surrounded by pathways and tall buildings. Airships and blimps passed overhead as the crowd lingered here, trying to choose what direction to go in their exploration of the grand new setting.

I feel like a tourist.

Suddenly a group of people moved from in front of the statue and Frank saw a small Range girl standing in front of her. She recognized the gnome-like girl and called out to her.

"Tessa!"

Tessa turned around and then looked down when she caught her eyes. She walked up to them, looking sheepish. "Hey, Frank... you know, I'm sorry about ..." She stopped and sighed. "They're not threatening me anymore. They just kind of stopped all of a sudden, like they no longer cared that you had the Transfer Orb."

Frank nodded. She knew perfectly well why they weren't after the orb anymore. "I had a feeling something like that was going on. I forgive you. Now, let me introduce you to Keri."

"Hi," Keri said with a wave.

Keri didn't know about Tessa's betrayal and Frank thought it would be better to keep it that way if she wanted them to be friends.

"Isn't she the girl who ratted you out to Catastrophe?" Siena asked as she appeared suddenly, sticking her nose up at Tessa.

Frank rolled her eyes. *So much for that.* "Yes, and she just apologized for it. Catastrophe was giving her IRL threats, so let it go!"

Siena narrowed her eyes but nodded. "Yeah, I guess they *do* do that. Okay, fine. Have you thought about what dungeon you girls want to try first?"

"I thought you were looking for Noah." Keri looked around.

"You didn't find him?"

Siena put her hands on her hips and shook her head. "I was using the item tracking software to try and find him. The map beacon must be faulty because I couldn't see him anywhere near where it was telling me he was."

"What about... Chloe?" Keri asked hesitantly. "Have you seen her?"

Siena shook her head again and Keri looked down solemnly.

"Tessa, are there any dungeons you want to try out here?"

Tessa smiled mischievously. "Well, we never did do that underwater dungeon we were planning to do on Jossi Island, but I've heard there's a portal to one out here. Maybe we should try—"

"Nah!" Siena interrupted. "I'm not up this high to do an underwater level. I'd rather try the airship one. I've been told that in one of the Secotier dungeons you get to be in an airship battle!"

Tessa ground her teeth. "I want to do an underwater dungeon."

"Airship battle!" Siena shouted back.

"Underwat—"

"Enough!" Frank snapped. "Siena, just show us to where the beacon pointed out the Ruby Edge, maybe we can see something that you can't."

"Alright, alright." Siena murmured and then led them across the bridge to their left.

Frank was surprised they wanted to do a dungeon before they had even explored the place. She was still in awe of the vast levels to the floating city and the many bridges that led to the different city districts. They came out into a wide-open setting that looked to be the city center. There, Hundreds of people looked to be waiting for party members to show up before heading to the Gateways. Dozens of them glowed on the many bridges coming off from the island.

In the center was a fountain similar to the one in New Calandor, but carved to look like a hawk in mid-flight, water shooting from each extended feather. Being as high up as they were, Frank wondered how the water could remain so still. She could already see parties making their way toward the Gateways to try out the many new dungeons that she assumed would echo the steampunk theme of the island.

"You see, according to the item tracker, he's supposed to be right here," Siena said, pointing to the fountain.

"Yeah, doesn't look like he is… unless he's in the statue," Keri suggested.

Siena grinned. "You're right!"

She jumped up onto the fountain's statue and began punching it. "Come on, you coward! You've left me waiting for too long already, get out here!"

Many of the waiting players looked up, some confused, others looking distraught at the scene Siena was making.

"Are your friends always this crazy?" Tessa asked with a smile on her face.

Frank was about to reply when her attention suddenly drifted to a group to the left of them. However, it wasn't really the group that caught her attention, just one of their members… it was like he had just appeared out of nowhere. Contrasting the moderately equipped party members, the player was of Spell Caster height but wore a full set of Silver Armor.

She felt even more confused as the group of six moved off, but the armored avatar didn't follow them. Instead, it slowly turned to face her, the gauntleted hands trembling, its armor rattling all around it.

Wait… why is he staring at me?

The armored figure then looked up and Frank followed his gaze. There, in the air above them, was a floating circular platform. A sudden scream arose from the armored player and every avatar within seven meters of him grabbed the sides of their heads from the high pitch of the sound.

Frank could hear the noise loudly even though the player was still at a distance to them. At first, she thought it was some form of a siren attack, but she didn't see any of the players' Hit Points lowering. In a wave of light around the armored form, avatars within a seven-meter radius of the player flashed out of existence.

This sudden disappearance was enough to catch even Siena off guard, for she jumped from the fountain statue and stood up next to them with a baffled look on her face. The wailing ceased as the armored player began to stagger forward.

"Is it just me, or is this place a little less crowded than it was before?" Siena asked.

Frank pointed to the armored form. "He did it? Oh, crap!"

As though simply pointing at him had drawn his attention, the player turned and jerkily began rushing through the crowd toward them. Frank gulped and Tessa pulled at her arm, trying to get around the fountain to put it between them.

"Frank, didn't your mother ever teach you that it's impolite to point at people?" Keri cried.

The air around them began to flutter with a swift breeze, and she looked up just in time to see a red-coated avatar come to land on the head of the fountain's statue.

Chapter 6
SCREAMERS

Being the leader of the group, I decided to place myself in the center of the area, with Chloe and Dice to my flanks. Chloe was handling the market and Synth Square districts while Dice was focusing on the area of empty bridges that led further out toward the majority of Heaven's dungeons. I knew if something was going to go down it would be in the center of the city and I wanted to keep Chloe nearby to back me up.

As I had expected, the first thing Siena had done upon entering Heaven was tracking me down using the item tracking software. I knew that if she found me she would make the job Wona had given me that much more difficult. Fortunately, I was able to convince Windsor to get one of the game designers to make me three platforms similar to those at the start of Cloudy Pathways that could hover around the city in order to go from place to place without the use of mounts.

Apparently, some of the designers had used them before when creating environments in-game and had simply called them 'Bird's Eyes.'

Standing on the circular stone above the city center's fountain, I watched as Siena moved to the fountain just below me, confirming that she was using the item tracking software. I let the Ruby Edge flash into my hand, resisting the urge to call out to her and taunt her to try and get up here to take it from me. She stalked around the fountain looking flustered before moving off again.

"Anything abnormal yet?" Chloe asked through my messenger patch, a piece of software that allowed me to talk to my teammates without the need to bring up a window.

"No, just saw some old friends. What about you, Dice? Anyone show up without having their user I.D. scanned?"

There was silence for a moment before Dice replied, "Eight hundred and ninety-six people have entered, eight hundred and ninety-six I.D. codes."

"Eight hundred and ninety-six?" I exclaimed. "I'm surprised this place can still float."

"It's a game, Noah," Chloe replied. "The physics don't have to make sense."

I looked over the edge of the crowd entering through the bridges, swamping what were once clear pathways. "I know that. Eight hundred and ninety-six is still a lot of people, though."

"It's over nine hundred now," Dice corrected. "It will most likely be in the tens of thousands by the end of the day."

"Wow."

I swept the area, looking for anything abnormal, but could barely see anything from this high up. "Not if something goes wrong. Chloe, get on the ground and make your way over to me. If these Screamers show up, I doubt they will appear in the market area."

"Are you sure about that?" Chloe asked. "It's pretty busy here. People want to know what they can get in these shops. It would be a good place for them to do a lot of damage."

"Just get over here. There's someone I need you to distract."

Chloe's voice became cold. "You don't mean …"

"Chloe, come on, I need you."

She sighed. "Alright, I'm coming."

I returned my focus to the area below, watching Siena return with Keri, Frank, and another girl I didn't recognize. Seeing Frank in her full Dragon Armor reminded me that she still had the Wakizashi I had to steal back from her. If only there was a way to lure her to a Tertiatier dungeon and …

Focus on the job at hand, Noah. You're not here for your own problems. You're being counted on for this.

After a short conversation, Siena began making a scene, climbing up onto the fountain statue and bashing it with her fists. Distracted from the crowd for just a moment, I almost missed the sudden appearance of another avatar in the crowd.

"Dice, read me the numbers now!" I hissed.

Dice's voice came back quickly. "Do you see one? Six players just showed up whose I.D. codes weren't picked up by our scanners. There's no way they could have gotten in here without being scanned!"

Wait... six? Isn't that the same number of beta testers that went missing?

"The president was right then." I peered down and gasped after I swore the armored avatar looked up directly at me. "I have one in my sights. How do I find out his I.D.?"

"You just have to get close enough that your sensors pick him up as an enemy or an ally," Dice replied. "Should be within seven meters."

"What should I do?" Chloe asked and then suddenly screamed. "Oh god, can you hear that?"

As soon as she said this, I heard a high-pitched wailing below and through Chloe's contact link. Wincing, I cut it off and scanned the city. Below me, and in three more areas within my vision, entire circles of players about seven meters in radius began to vanish from islands and bridges. They simply disappeared, leaving cavities in the crowd like holes in Swiss cheese.

That noise... this must be the Screamers!

Two things revealed themselves to me all at once. The first was that their screams could affect anyone within range of scanning them. The second was that this meant the only people who could fight them were Range fighters or people using weapons with range specialty.

I think I've got just the weapon.

As fast as my fingers would let me, I brought up my menu and equipped a weapon I had first acquired in New Calandor: my

Boomstick. I then jumped from the floating Bird's Eye platform and cast Cyclone below me to pad my fall. Air rushed up at me and I came to land on top of the hawk statue on one knee, Ruby Edge in one hand, Boomstick in the other. As soon as I landed, I pointed my Boomstick and fired a Wind Blast at the Screamer, causing him to stumble back from the fountain a few meters.

I couldn't tell if it was seven meters and so I blasted him back once more. The Screamer tumbled backward but then rolled to his feet, the people around suddenly confused by a fight taking place in a non-combat zone.

The benefits of being an admin. This guy can't even fight back. All he can do is …

He arched up as another cry ripped through the air, making those around the Screamer clutch their ears in pain and then vanish in a circle around him. By sending him into another crowd of people I had only given him more victims to force out of the game.

"Dice, how's it going?" I asked as the scream died down.

"I count only six of them," he replied. "I'm going to try and get close enough to get one of their I.D. codes."

"You'll have to sneak up on them. The radius of their scream's effect is as large as a player's scanning range."

"Seriously? What are you going to do?"

I grinned. "I need a distraction. Are you listening in Chloe?"

Chloe's panicked voice returned. "I'm almost there! Everyone's running to the dungeons and trying to escape these guys!"

I nodded. "Come from the west and try to shoot him in the head, if you distract him for long enough I might be able to get in range without him noticing."

"I'll try."

I rose to my feet on the statue and looked around at the fleeing masses, leaving the Screamer alone on the wide pathway of the city center. I had already confirmed one of its weaknesses with the relative ease when I had blown the Screamer back.

Windsor did mention that the weight of their armor didn't seem to affect their speed. It only makes sense that they would be lighter too.

He was advancing on the fountain again and I was about to jump down and blow him out of range once more when I heard a shout from behind me.

"Noah, get down here! That sword is mine!"

I glanced over my shoulder to see Siena leap up onto the hawk's wing, her Reaper's Scythe flashing into her hand.

Crap!

"I don't have time for this, Siena!"

Siena scowled. "I've been waiting for over a week, you'll make time!"

I pointed to the Screamer walking toward us. "See that guy? He can make anyone within scanning range log off just by screaming. You really want a challenge? There it is."

Siena scrutinized the armored figure and then rolled her eyes. "Fine then, but you're next."

She jumped down from the statue and raised her Reaper's Scythe at the approaching form. "Hey you, come and get some!"

"Siena, wait, I wasn't joking! He really can—"

The high-pitched wail began and I felt like I could almost count the steps before Siena came within his range. However, a sudden loud gunshot cut through the scream and the silver form staggered. Chloe emerged from the crowd, guns raised.

"You wanted a distraction?" Chloe gestured to the crouching Screamer. "Well, there it is."

I paused, not because of Chloe's sudden entrance but from the effect her bullet had on the Screamer. It had been a headshot, that was clear, but where it had hit made the armor flicker like the helmet was no more than an illusion spell that was losing its effect. It suddenly made sense why he had been blown back further by my Wind Blasts; he hadn't altered his stats to make himself lighter. The armor wasn't real.

As the Screamer rose, his helmet disappeared completely and he looked out from underneath his long dark hair at the one who had shot him. Chloe froze, her eyes suddenly widening and she looked like she was struggling to breathe. Hesitantly, she raised her hand and stepped forward into the Screamer's range.

"Chloe, no!" I called.

The only thing I heard before the Screamer released its piercing howl was Chloe utter a single name.

"Lucas?"

Chapter 7
THE ENGINE ROOM

As the scream broke the air, Chloe bent double, clutching her ears before she vanished from the flickering circle around the Screamer. I was still trying to comprehend what she had just said. The name she just uttered. Lucas Nix, Chloe's brother, and one of the beta players who went missing from Wona's asylum, had reappeared inside the Dream State. He was one of the Screamers.

Get it together! I have to get his I.D. code before he disappears!

Lucas had his back to me after he had forced Chloe from the game, but his wails still cut through everything around him. I knew that if I got any closer to him while he was doing this, I would end up in the same boat as Chloe. I had to get close enough to scan him as soon as he stopped. Yet before he ceased his wailing, the Screamer whirled around and took off running.

I want to say that he ran into the crowd, but from the way everyone who came into contact with him or even came near him flashed out of existence, it was more like he was cutting a path right through them. The bright side to this was that it made him incredibly easy to follow. I sprinted through the center city in his wake, tailing him toward the bridge where several players disappeared before he cut off his screams so that he could more easily lose himself in the masses.

"Dice, he's heading your way." I paused in the rush to organize my thoughts. "Toward the dungeon Gateways."

Dice's voice sounded like he was out of breath too. "Why is he running? Couldn't he just teleport out of here?"

I ground my teeth. "I don't know, just try to cut him off!"

"Alright."

Behind me, I heard Siena call, "What are you doing, Noah? Get back here!"

I looked over my shoulder to see that she was chasing me.

"Did you not see what just happened?" I shouted back. "This is more important than your boasting, Siena!"

As I shoved my way through the crowd, I heard Siena yell, "You're underestimating the power of my boasting!"

Coming to the end of a bridge, I rounded a corner and stopped. No one was staggering like they had been shoved out of the way; they all looked the same. I couldn't see where he had gone, at least not from this height. In a panic, I brought up my menu and selected the Key Trigger 'Bird's Eye' which summoned my floating platform.

I leaped up onto it and triggered it to ascend just before Siena reached me. She jumped, desperately trying to grab hold of its edge, and only just missed. Cursing in frustration as I rose up into the sky, high above the buildings, she glanced around as though looking for something to climb.

From this height, I could see the subtle movements of the crowd below as Lucas' armored form elbowed his way through them. As I had suspected, he was making his way to the docks bridging off from the islands where most of the dungeon Gateways were located. I leaned on the platform in his direction and the circular stone took off over the city.

The wooden bridges that led out over an open space were in the same place that Chloe and I had left to go on the Cloudy Pathways dungeon. The longer and narrower the bridges were, the higher the tier of the dungeon. Some of the bridges leading out even had gaps you had to jump over to get to the Gateways, like the old Crash Bandicoot style 3D platformers that would give gamers nightmares of jumping out into space.

I watched from overhead as Lucas leaped over these gaps

with precise movements that even I found impressive. However, I had to remember that only the most advanced gamers had been allowed to become beta-testers for Wona. My admiration stopped as soon as I saw the rope hanging down from the end of the bridge and the red Gateway below it that the player had to swing into to access.

Oh no, that's The Engine Room. He's trying to get into a Tertiatier dungeon!

With a deft handling of his avatar, Lucas jumped the last bridge, grabbed hold of the rope, and swung feet first over the drop and into the Gateway.

"Son of a—"

I crouched on the platform, causing the Bird's Eye to drop toward the fiery Gateway and then stood when I reached it. Looking at the red Gateway, I realized I only knew this dungeon by reputation from talking to the other Hero rank players. It was called The Engine Room, a maze of gears, crushing levers and a blazing furnace that supposedly made the giant balloons beneath the islands of Heaven work.

"Noah, I lost him," I heard Dice say.

I nodded. "I know. He's gone into The Engine Room."

"But that's one of the hardest dungeons in Heaven!"

"I know. Try and get the I.D. codes of one of the others." I clenched my jaw, thinking of what Windsor had said to me yesterday. "I can handle this one."

"Okay, good luck."

Taking a two-step run-up, I jumped from the platform. When I was within range, the option appeared in my Key Triggers and I selected 'The Engine Room.'

As soon as my leather boots hit the corrugated iron floor and I heard the hissing gears and felt the heat of the furnace all around, I knew this was a bad idea. I scanned the area, the narrow passages leading through the dungeon making it look like Freddy Krueger's boiler room. The thing that really surprised me was how warm the place was. The heat was almost comparable to the Onjira Desert.

I walked down the corridors, ducking the flying pistons

and rushing hydraulics threatening to knock into me. Merely avoiding the environmental hazards was difficult enough and I knew that only the most dedicated players would have been able to both dodge the flying metal and fight monsters or other players simultaneously.

Two steam monsters arose like grinning ghosts from the pipes. I used a Wind Blast to clear them away but it did little against them. However, after using my wind magic so much in the Cloudy Pathways dungeon, I shouldn't have been surprised when a message announced:

—— WIND UPGRADE 'VACUUM' ——

At the same time that a window appeared showing the full arm rotation needed to cast the spell, several more of the steam monsters appeared like grinning poltergeists from the red-hot walls.

Well, no time like the present to try this new spell out then.

"Out of my way!" I shouted as I rotated my arm and the immense force of the level three wind spell cut down the hall.

The torrent of air rushed through the tunnels like a river, and although it only killed the steam monsters I had hit already, the force was enough to blow the others out of my way so I could run between them. It also cut my Mana in half.

I can only hope that saved me some time.

I spun at the sound of running footsteps rushing down the metal floor in a corridor off from the one I was in.

On instinct, rather than feeling it would actually help, I equipped my Ruby Edge with a flash. I looked around the corner and saw no one there—not Lucas or a new monster. Figuring it to be one of the rattling machines around me, I continued on. Ahead of me was the end of the corridor that led down to a wider space. I knew that if I was going to face the Screamer I was going to need as much room as I could get.

"Careful, Noah," a familiar voice said in my head. *"He's close."*

A dark speck seemed to appear just out of my vision, but as I turned to see it, I saw nothing. "Dice, is that you?" I ask over my comms.

Dice quickly returned. "What? I didn't say anything."

"Really?" I rubbed the sweat from my face. "Augh, never mind then."

Below the platform was a massive rotating gear leading down into the new area like a descending escalator. I stepped on the jutting cog, and it carried me to the lower floor. When I jumped down, I jolted back with a start. The armored form of the Screamer was right behind me, facing the wall at the back corner of the room. Although he had stopped running, his hands were still shaking, causing his gauntlets to rattle. He looked mentally disturbed, but after what Chloe had told me of him, this wasn't a surprise.

"Lucas?" I called. "Are you Lucas Nix?"

"I'm not disappearing," he whined. "He said I would disappear. Why am I not disappearing?"

I furrowed my brow in confusion.

"Who said that, Lucas?" I walked closer, trying to keep his mind off of screaming so I could scan his I.D. code. "Who said you would disappear?"

"Maou, come, please," Lucas replied, beginning to shake all over. "Maou said that Maou would come, why won't he?"

"Maou?" The name meant nothing to me, but it was something to go on at least. "Is that the name of the person who told you to go to Heaven?"

He nodded and then looked over his shoulder, his wide eyes shooting to my Ruby Edge. "You... you're not Maou."

I suddenly realized I was still holding up the Ruby Edge as I approached.

"You're not Maou!"

I was so close to being in range, all I had to do was... The wailing began and I threw myself toward him. As I fell within range, I saw the scanner pick him up, the border of his visible stats outlined in red to show he was an enemy. I saw him clutching his own head as he screamed. I felt myself being lifted, being pulled up into darkness and gasped, sitting upright on the recliner as the message 'NotThatNoah LOGGED OUT' appeared before me.

"Did I get it?" I asked, taking off the helmet.

Dice sounded relieved. "Barely. We're still missing the last three digits but it should be enough to identify his code type."

I sighed and lay back down, my bed raising me up into a sitting position. As I came up with it, I noticed Chloe was standing beside me, staring intensely at the monitor beside where my helmet had retracted. She was wringing her hands in front of her and shaking her head in disbelief.

"It's him. His hair is a little longer, but the Screamer's face looks just like Lucas." She shook her head. "He didn't even recognize me."

"He also has the starting numbers of a beta tester's I.D. code, along with the other two I identified," Dice said.

"I guess that confirms it then."

I stood up and moved beside her to watch the area of The Engine Room, the view of the camera showing a low angle from where I had just left. I gasped when I saw what was lying on The Engine Room floor. Two red objects lay before Lucas. No one had told me what would happen if players were forced to log off while in a Tertiatier dungeon and I grabbed my head as panic washed over me, seeing that the results were exactly the same as being defeated in one.

"Oh no, I should have used a Kamikaze Orb!" I grabbed my head in frustration. "Ah, she's going to kill me!"

Both my red Captain's Coat and Siena's Ruby Edge lay on the corrugated iron floor. Lucas stared down at them, eyes vacant as if he didn't know what to do with them. He then walked forward, expression baffled.

"Why won't I disappear?" He was breathing heavily now. "Maou, come, help me disappear."

There was the sound of boots hitting the iron floor and then a familiar voice said, "I can help with that."

I turned to Dice. "Who's that talking? Can you zoom out to see?"

The view of the room, which was from a downward angle of where I had fallen, became an upward angle like that of a security camera. From off-screen, a hooded form ran in, and before Lucas could start wailing again, the avatar slashed out twice with a familiar, glowing green blade.

The Jade Edge… but that means…

As the Screamer's cries were cut off, Lucas' avatar vanished from the dungeon with a flash. The form turned slightly and began collecting the items I had left behind. When he bent down to pick up the Ruby Edge, I saw the pointy protrusions coming out from his hood, the things I had originally mistaken for horns but were actually his elven ears. There was no doubt: it was Sirswift.

I turned to glare at Dice who looked just as confused as me. "Why the heck is *he* still in the Dream State?"

Chapter 8

INVESTIGATION

By the way everything died down after such a chaotic turn of events, I should have figured this was what would happen. It turned out that President Wona chose the worst possible time to go on a nerd vacation.

I entered his massive office in a huff of rage, ready to confront him about Sirswift, but his lean secretary in her pencil skirt told me that the stress of working on the opening had made Windsor shut himself away in his private GC with little to no contact with the outside world.

I guess I can't really blame him. He must be desperate to locate the glitch that allowed the Screamers to get in, or maybe even find out who they are. Still, it feels like he's running away. I wonder if he did this after what happened to the beta testers, leaving his lawyers to deal with everything IRL.

Seeing the tired look in his secretary's eyes, I assumed this to be the case. I turned to leave. Even if I succeeded in getting one of their I.D. codes and Dice managed to get two others, I still felt like I'd failed. In games with open worlds like the Dream State, bugs on an opening day could mean the difference between having sustainable customers and losing half of the fans.

After what happened, I wonder how many hundreds of players will try it again. First impressions can be a big deal for some people. Grand re-openings don't usually have as big a turnout as their openings. Was it really worth it just to lure in the Screamers to find out who they are?

I recalled the crowds spread out below me as I came through the office corridor, the way they had packed the bridges in their colorful avatars as balloons flew above them like it was some kind of carnival. It was the perfect situation to sabotage, and where the Screamers could do the most damage.

But Lucas didn't seem in his right mind. Someone was directing him.

Ever since finding out that Chloe's brother was a Screamer, I'd had my suspicions about the other Screamers as well. However, after what Dice had told me, the connections between the beta testers and Screamers were gaining weight. I listed them to myself as I entered the elevator and punched in the number of Chloe's floor.

Firstly, there was the same amount of beta-testers missing from the Wona-owned asylum as there were players who invaded Heaven without being scanned. Second, the few player codes that had been picked up by players before being involuntarily logged out had the same first four digits in their I.D. codes as those beta-testers. Lastly, and probably the most obvious of the connections, was Lucas Nix himself, one of the six missing beta-testers and my only direct link to them.

And then there's this Maou that Lucas mentioned. Is he their leader? I might have to talk to Data about this. He might know who he is.

The elevator chimed as it arrived at Chloe's floor. I entered the hallway and made my way to her room. When I came to her door, I was about to knock when it swung open. Chloe poked her head out and looked down one end of the hall and then the other. She then grabbed me by my shirt collar and pulled me inside. I stepped back from her when she pushed me aside and slammed the door shut.

"Hey, are you okay?" I asked.

It was merely a rhetorical question as I took a look around her lush apartment complex. It was as large as my own, although Chloe had gone to the effort of making it her own with a few soft toys on the bed and a Dream State wall scroll she had put up to give the room some color.

"Do you think I'm okay?" She shook her head, looking flustered. "Until just the other day I thought my brother was more likely dead than alive, then he just shows up in the Dream State and screams me out of it like he didn't even recognize me."

I nodded and made my way to the couch so I could sit down. The drapes were pulled, but it was a bright day and warm light came in through them. She moved to sit down beside me, but then remained standing, as if expecting Lucas to come through her door any second.

"Mysteries are everywhere, Chloe. Sirswift still being in the game despite being in prison, your brother's reappearance as a Screamer—heck, the Screamers in general… and then there's this Maou."

Chloe raised her hand to her face. "Would there be any way we could track Lucas' user I.D. code to find where he's getting into the Dream State from?"

I looked down. "I don't think so. Dice says they're using something to stop us from tracking them, probably the same software Brock uses. Do you still have access to Wona's records?"

She nodded. "But a few of the names of their old employees were blacked out. How am I supposed to—"

I put a hand up to stop her. "We need to find an earlier copy of their employee list and compare it to the new one to find out who's been blacked out. I know of three people from back then who might have a copy. I'll be able to find them quicker over the game."

"What about Windsor? Couldn't we just speak to him?"

"He's shut himself off after the incident. I couldn't get into his GC either."

Chloe nodded. "Okay, let's go then."

"I should go alone."

She gave me a sour look. "Then what do I do?"

"Keep digging. See if you can find out anything about this Maou or his connection to the Screamers, or how they can force people to wake up from the game. If Windsor doesn't know, it must be something other than the Dream Engine's game mechanics."

Chloe crossed her arms. "Why are you making me do all the hard work?"

I grinned and stood up to leave. "Because I'm lazy… and feel I'll have a better chance of getting the info I need if I can talk to these people on my own."

I moved to the door to leave, but before I could reach for the door handle a revelation seemed to hit Chloe and she rushed over to me. She grabbed me by the other hand, moved in, and kissed me on the lips.

I stared at her in confusion. *What is it with this girl and stealing kisses from me?*

"Is that your goodbye?" I asked as she pulled away.

"No." She looked down. "I was just reminding myself that there's more to life than the game."

A shiver went up my spine. I quickly opened the door and backed into the hallway. "I hope it helped."

She stepped forward, frowning. "What's wrong? You seem distant."

"Nothing… I'll see you later."

I walked out and swiftly made my way down the hallway. Hearing those words from Chloe had made me feel uncomfortable. Although not word for word, they were almost exactly in line with what Sue had told me whenever I joined Brock and David in the computer rooms to play games during high school lunch hours.

I feel stupid. Our first kiss in the real world and all I can think about is my dead ex-girlfriend.

I returned to my suite and sat down on the soft bed. On the bedside table was a cellscreen, and I decided it was long past time that I contact my mother. It had been over two weeks since we had spoken last, and it would be good to let her know I was okay. The last time I had seen her she had looked ragged; the news of me being alright must have been a relief, for even the gray rings that were usually under her eyes had vanished.

I updated her on the move and used the retractable screen

camera to show her my new room. It was fortunate that the last time she had seen me I could barely keep up a conversation, putting responsibility for my disappearance solely on Wona. In fact, she seemed more concerned with my location than how I was being treated.

"Just look it up online," I said over the screen after I failed to explain where the facility was verbally. "Surely you know how to use a GPS."

"No, no, it's quite alright, dear. I can hear that you must be feeling better. The next time I come see you, we can go visit Sue's grave. You didn't appear to be very awake during the funeral."

Thanks to the drug I had been on, I only vaguely remembered the crowd of people dressed in black that had surrounded the wheelchair I was forced to sit in. I assumed that looking like a cripple was the only reason Sue's parents didn't blame me for being the one behind the wheel during the accident that took their daughter.

I shook my head. "That whole month was a blur to me. It's a good idea, though. I just need to sort out everything here and then we can go together."

There was nothing I wanted less, but I knew it was something I would have to do. Memories of Sue still pulled at me, even when I knew I should be focusing on finding Chloe's brother.

Maybe that's why I pulled away from her. Her situation with Lucas is so similar to my own struggle to find Sue.

"Take your time, dear. The grieving process shouldn't be rushed."

I nodded, coming back to the conversation. "You're right. Okay, give me until next week and I'm sure I'll be fine. I'm being treated really well here and should be fully recovered in no time."

"Well, that's good to hear. And make sure to ring me if you change facilities again. You can't imagine how stressful it was when I couldn't get in touch with you."

I almost laughed, thinking of how I had spent most of the week on Brock's couch. "I will. Love you, Mom."

"I love you, too. Bye."

I put the screen down and sighed. *Right, back to it then.*

I sat up, exited my room, and made for the elevator, determined to get answers. I had three leads on people who might have had knowledge of the Wona employees from back before the first beta test: Data, Brock, and Samuel. I didn't know who I wanted to talk to least: Samuel or Brock. Therefore, Datalent was my obvious first choice.

Finding my old teacher and protector wasn't too difficult. He still worked for Wona after all, now as an in-game overseer. He had told me his new job was simple: make sure everything was in place and worked the way it was supposed to. It didn't sound simple to me. Like Windsor, Data and his team had their own GC that could be opened by people of his rank. Seeing this first hand, I realized that the best way to contact him would be just to message him while in-game.

I entered my own team's GC, took a dose of DSD with some water, and logged in. Returning to the game, I realized my best option for defense now that my Captain's Coat was gone was to wear my Night Down Robes. I was definitely no longer the badass Red Mage I saw myself as a week ago.

It may have high magic protection, but still, I really need to buy some new ones.

It wasn't until I received a complete map that I found out that New Calandor was in fact at the dead center of the Dream State. Learning this had amused me, as before I had reached New Calandor I could have sworn that the Barrens was the northernmost point, completely ignorant of how massive the Dream State really was.

I chose it as my first destination, acting as the hub as Galrinth once had. Once I appeared in the Victorian city, I messaged Data to ask the time and place we might be able to meet.

"I'll be busy until after lunch," he had replied, but quickly followed with, "But there is something I would like to show you. Meet me at the summit of Claw Plateaus at one o'clock."

I had heard of the Plateaus before, but like many areas between New Calandor and Land's End, I had yet to explore it in-depth. Considering I had a few hours to spend here before we were supposed to meet, I went about remedying this fact.

I retrieved my summoning stone and called forth Peragon. My half-Pegasus, half-dragon flew down from the sky and I jumped on its back. There were three settlements from here to Claw Plateaus, including a navy militarized coast, a set of underground mines, and a way station all connected by a railway that trains rattled over daily.

I thought an hour to see each place would be enough. I was mistaken.

Chapter 9

DEVIL

I barely heard Data's call over my comms two hours later. "Noah, where the heck are you?"

I was attempting an event called 'The Great Train Robbery.' After hearing Data's voice, I ducked behind the train cart as bullets flew at me from the Bandits on horseback following it, and then looked at my clock. It was 1:10 pm.

Son of a… I poked my Boomstick into the air over the rim of the cart and cast my Perfect Storm spell. It was the first time I had used it, but considering I was about to leave anyway, I thought I might as well see what it did.

A sudden darkness covered everything and a dozen bolts of lightning rained down from the sky. Having already loosened a few of the Bandits up with a couple Fire Balls, the lightning spell was more than enough to finish off whoever it hit. However, the forks of light seemed to hit at random, missing a few Bandits who continued to shoot at me. I ducked behind the cart and pulled out my summoning stone again.

"Yeah, yeah, I'll be there in a second!"

I jumped out of the rail car as Peragon flashed under me and took off into the sky, watching the train chug on ahead without me as the horsemen pursued it. I guess that abandoning the mission meant a fail for me, but I wasn't the only one on the train and doubted the other players would give up as easily.

Wind rushed in my face as I leaned forward to increase my

speed. At the pace I rode my mount, it took me less than five minutes to get to the Claw Plateaus. From the way it looked, the reason for the name of the place seemed obvious.

Five giant black spikes of earth jutted high into the darkening sky on the eastern coast of New Calandor. The middle three were larger than the outer two, and the center pillar was even larger still. They loomed over the grassland, the sun behind making their shadows stretch all the way to the ocean far behind them.

I rode Peragon between them and up to the summit of the middle 'finger.' Data was there, standing on a circular platform at its peak. It wasn't until I drew closer that I realized it was another Bird's Eye. I summoned my own Bird's Eye and jumped down from Peragon, dismissing it into the summoning stone as my boots clapped on the glowing stone.

"You get to use one of those too, huh?" I asked as I raised it to be on level with him.

Data nodded. "Tsh, I'm an overseer, Noah. Without one I wouldn't be able to do my job properly."

"I still don't get how you do *your* job. I mean, there have to be millions of variables in this game. How could you watch even half of them?"

Data grinned but did not meet my eyes. "Let me show you."

He stretched his neck and looked up as his Bird's Eye suddenly began to ascend further into the air. I did the same and followed him up. We continued climbing, up into the thin clouds overhead and then past them. I paused for a moment to look down and gasped to see how much the Dream State had shrunk below us. I could see all the way south from the snow-covered plains of Lucineer up to the Galrinth Fields, through the thick forests and into the Onjira Desert and Barrens. The land stretched further into the New Calandor frontier below us all the way to the cape at Land's End.

It almost makes the Dream State look small.

"Keep going," Data said, as he stopped above me. "Just a little higher."

I nodded and looked up again, ascending into the blue sky

that was slowly becoming darker, like we were going to reach the Dream State's equivalent of space. However, when I focused on that blackness above I saw that the darkness appeared to separate into hundreds of little black cubes and that the only reason I could see them before was that there were even more of these cubes above them.

Data stopped his Bird's Eye and I tried to stop when level with him but overshot by a few meters and had to descend again.

"What are they, stars?" I asked.

Data shook his head. "This is the first layer of rigs and test data."

"Rigs?"

"These cubes are used for the animated movement of different surface elements in the game. Most of them are automated, but some have to be done manually. That's where overseers come in." Data pointed to the area I had just come from. "See that one over there that's moving further away? That's what moves the train you were just riding."

I looked up at the million more cubes above us and pointed. "What about all of them?"

"Everything in the game. The higher up you get the lower they are in the game's layers. Every single monster, NPC, and item that appears has its own little cube with its data inside it like those."

It's like the world is a pincushion and these are just the heads of the pins.

"What about the Chaos Engines?"

Data shook his head. "For the clouds themselves there are, but the Chaos Engines are a little different. The monsters from them have their own separate area linked to one of the debug rooms. That allows for random number generators to produce any monster they see fit depending on the tier of dungeon."

I knew from talking to Windsor that a debug room was a separate area of the game where objects or mechanics could be tested before being applied to the game world itself.

"So... the Chaos Engines are like portals to these debug

rooms?" I asked. "Like the one Windsor always goes into when trying out new stuff."

"That's right." Data spread his arms to the world spread out below us. "This is what I wanted to show you, Noah, to give you some perspective. This game, this world, is the result of thousands of game designers and technicians working god knows how many man-hours, just to produce this for its fans."

I nodded. "And it's all built on a cover-up."

Data's eyes met mine. "Is that why you wanted to see me?"

"Something like that." I looked north to where the floating city was still barely visible over the curve of the land. "One of the beta testers that went missing from Wona's asylum showed up again in Heaven as a Screamer to sabotage its grand opening."

Data turned back to the view. "I've heard of them. Or it might be more accurate to say that I was warned about them, that they appear wherever they want, that they can force any player they want out of the game and that their identities are still a secret. I assume your theory is that if one of them was a harmed beta tester, then they all might be."

I nodded. "The one we cornered also mentioned someone called Maou. I've been trying to find out if he might be someone who used to work for the company as well. We found an old list of employees who used to work for Wona back then, but some of the names have been blacked out."

"Sounds like quite a mystery you have on your hands, Noah," Data said, his tone showing that he was humoring me. "Good luck with it."

"I was wondering if you might have a list of people who worked for Wona back then, before the beta tester accident."

"Tsh, I'm not a record keeper, Noah. I wouldn't have that kind of information. Besides, I was employed only in the later stages of the testing, after they had ironed out all the kinks. Brock, Sam, and I were only on the same team for about a month before Brock left and Sam joined Catastrophe."

I ground my teeth in frustration. "So, I'm more likely to get a list from one of them. Two people I really didn't want to have to talk to."

"Your best bet would be to get it from Brock. He kept a blog recording all of the people he worked with and everyone affected badly by the drug before Wona took it down. He's probably your best bet... at the moment." Data shook his head. "Although he hasn't been in-game for a long time, and I've heard it's near impossible to find him in the real world. Wona can attest to that."

I assumed Brock would stop moving around so much now that Wona was no longer hunting him. It had been a while since I had spoken to either him or David, and I wondered how they were doing after what happened in Apollo's Lookout. I was hesitant. Brock and I hadn't parted on the best terms. Thinking of how I betrayed him, killing him and stealing his Color Blade, I might even go so far as to say that they were the worst terms.

No, the Color Blade was Data's before he handed it over to Brock.

"You tried to stop me from joining Wona by giving Brock your Sapphire Edge, didn't you?"

Data raised his palms in a shrug. "It didn't do much good. I underestimated you."

With a flash, I equipped Data's Sapphire Edge. "You want this back?"

Data appeared to consider it but then shook his head. "Tsh, no point. You can keep it for now. I'm too busy to play games in this world anymore."

I smiled and gestured to the world below us. "Looks like you're above all that now."

Data inclined his head and smiled. "You could put it that way."

I stepped to the edge of the Bird's Eye. "One more thing before I go: have you ever heard of the name Maou being mentioned before?"

"*You* mentioned that name before." Data shrugged again. "Before that, though, can't say it rings a bell."

"Pity. I guess I'll see you later then."

"Don't make it too soon," Data sighed. "I'm going to be busy in the coming weeks with these glitches needing to be smoothed out."

I waved him a goodbye. Instead of using the Bird's Eye to lower me back down to land, I decided the thrill of skydiving might take my mind off what I knew needed to be done next. I stepped over the edge of the platform and dropped from the darkness... and felt nothing.

From this height—a height I figured even mounts couldn't reach—there wasn't even any wind resistance to blow up at me. When I hit the stratosphere of the Dream State, the feel of the cold air hit me like a punch to the face. Even this uncomfortable feeling was a welcome experience after realizing what I would have to do next.

If Brock couldn't be found in the Dream State, and the likelihood of finding him IRL was just as unlikely, there was only one person who might have a roster of the old employees. I might be wrong, but if Sirswift was somewhere in the game, I could use the item tracker software to find him by locating the Ruby Edge he took.

I watched the New Calandor Frontier expand and become more detailed as I dropped. By the time I reached the peaks of Claw Plateaus, I knew I could call Peragon, but I continued to drop anyway. I would have to get the item tracking software before I could begin my hunt, so instead of selecting my summoning stone, I chose the 'Wake-Up' option as soon as I was about to hit the grass.

Despite how the ground had been rushing up at me when things went black, I awoke calmly. Being able to pull out of the game mid-fall had given me the feeling that I had slipped right through the ground and could simply plummet forever. The recliner brought me into a sitting position and I stood. I saw that Dice was in-game himself, so I pressed the red button beside the door.

"Dice, I need the item tracking software installed on my Dream Engine. Any chance you could do that for me?"

"Yes," he replied over the speaker in his cold tone. "I'll be out in a moment."

It looked like not helping him in his fight against Siena had made our relationship clear. We were not friends, we were colleagues, and it seemed he would act accordingly now that he knew I had the power to make him lose his job.

A professional relationship… I guess I can't ask for more from a person who was trying put me in a coma when I first met him.

Dice's recliner whirred and he pulled the Dream Engine off. Without a word, he tugged a cord from the wall and plugged it into the helmet I had been using before pressing a few buttons on the touchscreen panel on the GC's wall.

"It's installing. You should be able to use it the next time you go under."

"Thanks."

Dice frowned, appearing troubled by something. "I've learned something since we last spoke… and in the spirit of us working together and all, I suppose I should tell you."

I inclined my head. "Depends on what it is."

"I actually learned it by accident. As you've probably guessed by now, I'm of Japanese descent." He said this as though his real name, Daisuke, wasn't already a dead giveaway. "Anyway, I was born and raised here. I know a little bit of my native language, enough to recognize a word my parents used when I was growing up."

"Eh?" I said, still confused about what he was talking about.

"My mother used to always call me Sukoshi Maou whenever I was bad." He frowned and looked down, brow furrowed. "I asked my mother last night when I got home what it meant. Sukoshi means little."

"And Maou?"

Dice's eyes caught mine. "Maou means Devil."

Chapter 10
PURSUIT

Finding out who the robed avatar really was in-game by tracking the Ruby Edge would hit two birds with one stone. The most obvious bird to hit was finding if Samuel Wona was still in the Dream State despite being kept behind bars, but being able to reclaim the Ruby Edge for Siena was motive enough for me to find him.

As soon as I returned to the Dream State, I used my Transfer Orb to teleport myself to Heaven. I made my way over the bridges to the long floating island that had most of the material stores. I ended up in a warm shop with a fireplace next to where I had confronted Data before first entering Apollo's Lookout. The place had high-quality, steampunk-themed coats in display cases on the wall and even more on clothes hangers that went all around the walls.

There was an old woman with pins in her hair behind the counter. Going through her inventory, I drew upon my infinite Moola to purchase a cloak with superior stats to my Night Down Robes. It was boiled, dark green leather and had a higher weight stat, which would slow me down a little, but it was worth it considering the boost it gave to my overall defense. It was nothing fancy, but it would suffice.

I equipped the cloak with a flourish and left the store. Pulling out my Transfer Orb, I chose to go to New Calandor next. With a flash, I appeared on the cobbled streets of the Victorian era city.

"Alright, Dice, walk me through using this thing."

"Alright, pull up your menu," Dice's voice instructed and I did so. "Now that the software has been installed there should be an option in your configuration that you can activate. It's called ITS."

I didn't have to guess what the acronym meant. When I turned it on, a semi-transparent map appeared in the corner of my vision, blocking one side of New Calandor's thoroughfare. There was a white space in the top left-hand corner of the map with the words "Enter Item Code" in gray lettering inside of it.

I recalled Siena using the item code to track down Dice after he had stolen the Color Blade from her. Having just learned how useful item codes were for finding the Transfer Orb, I had made sure to write it down after I gained possession of it.

I said, "S612E8N5A," and the numbers and digits filled the blank space above the map.

Automatically, lines of light began to run over the map as a stream of digits and codes flickered at the bottom of my vision like a password cracker. Three of the lines appeared from the sides and top of the map and intersected at a single point near the lower middle, just west of Galrinth. Another image appeared of a floating landmass above Penance Peaks. I remembered the place; it was called Sky Island.

I had memories of Data taking me there to get Peragon with Sirswift and then later teleporting there to escape Catastrophe while it was under his command, just after Bitcon revealed himself to be Sirswift. It was fitting that the first place I had managed to defeat the murderer was the same place I would find him again.

As I thought this, however, another scanning line of light went over the profile of the island. Looking at the place vertically made it look like the side of an iceberg floating in the sky, the majority of its earth under the clouds, rather than the tall hills at its peak. When the line stopped, it did so right in the center of it.

Seeing the dot of red light appear within the earth baffled me. *Why does it say he's right in the middle of the island?*

"Dice, are there tunnels inside of Sky Island?"

"Yeah, a whole dungeon full of them. It's called The Catacomb. I'm surprised you don't know about them considering you must have been there to get your mount."

I inclined my head in resignation. "I was so eager to ride Peragon and check out all the sights that I forgot to even explore the place. I'm guessing it's a Secotier dungeon."

Secotier was my first guess considering that was the same tier of dungeon you needed to complete before you were given access to the area.

"No, Tertiatier," Dice replied and I facepalmed. "But it's probably the one with the easiest difficulty. It's usually the first Tertiatier area people go to considering the number of Skill Points you have to accumulate just to get there."

"Seriously?" I groaned. "Okay, looks like I'm going to Sky Island then."

Always Tertiatier. Just once I wish I could enter a dungeon and not be afraid of having everything I've had equipped stolen. On the bright side, this does give me the opportunity to defeat Sirswift and get the Ruby Edge back.

I turned off the ITS, went to my items and got out a Transfer Orb. As soon as I activated it, I scrolled down the location list and selected Sky Island. With a flash of light, I appeared on the high bridges of the area's Synth Square. I looked around the pristine landscape with its green hills filled with monsters that one could defeat and turn into summoning stones. Even now, players were summoning mounts from them and flying off or coming in to land on their monsters of various sizes and species.

There was a giant waterfall coming down from the hills that seemed to lead off into nowhere and—that which I was recently ignorant of—a collection of caves beneath my feet.

"Alright, so where do I go to get into these tunnels?"

"You have to get between the hills," Dice replied, ready on hand as my guide. "He looks like he's heading in your direction. Must have just defeated the boss."

Or enough monsters to get the Resource Items he needs.

"Okay, thanks."

Why he was even here was a mystery to me, but not one I could solve by waiting outside for him. For all I knew, he would teleport away with a Transfer Orb as soon as he reached the outside. I strode from the Synth Square and up the track leading into the hills. Trees and thick bushes covered most of the area, but there seemed to be a hiking track that made its way between them. I knew from when I had found Peragon in this place that mounts could hide in the woods or be out in plain sight depending on how difficult they were to beat. The easier ones were harder to find, encouraging newer players to explore the area rather than risk being killed countless times.

I eventually arrived at a gap between the two larger hills on the island, and sure enough, right between them was an entrance to the tunnel leading down to The Catacombs. Before I was about to enter, a message appeared in my vision.

Siena_the_Blade: "I've got you now."

My brow furrowed in confusion.

"Noah!" Dice called. "The guy you're tracking is being attacked by two other players."

"What?" I asked, but then looked back to Siena's message.

"Actually only one of them is attacking, the other one just seems to be standing there. You might want to hurry it up."

It just came to me that Siena hadn't seen me lose the Ruby Edge in The Engine Room. She was obviously tracking the weapon as well, thinking it to be me, and if Siena found him before I could, I would be far too late to ask any questions.

"Crap!"

I entered my config menu again and pulled up the item tracking map to guide the way through. Summoning my Color Blade, I let its sapphire glow light my way as I ran headlong into the dark tunnels. My only hope was that he didn't die before I arrived, but it was Siena he was fighting and I knew that the longer I waited, the worse my odds became that he would survive long enough for me to question him.

Chapter 11
THE CATACOMBS

Come with me to Sky Island, she said. We'll get you a great mount that can support a Heavy, she said. You should have enough Moola for one by now, she said.

Frank sighed as Siena waved her into the tunnel leading down into The Catacombs. Of course it had to be a Tertiatier dungeon. What else would satisfy Siena_the_Blade? It should be okay, Frank told herself, as long as she unequipped her Dragon Armor and made sure not to take her Amethyst Edge out of her inventory before they started fighting. She had nothing to worry about, right?

Optimism? Frank, you know better than that.

"Come on, we can get you a mount later; the monsters aren't going anywhere!" Siena called and then strode deeper into the darkness. "Noah, on the other hand, could leave this dungeon any second!"

Frank followed her into the opening, hearing Siena's voice echo along the iron-enforced walls. If that didn't ruin their element of surprise on Noah, her own clanking footfalls would.

"Are you sure it's even him?"

"It's about time he stepped out of his safe zone and into an *actual* dungeon. Good thing, too. I didn't want to have to drag him into one by force." They came to a Y-junction and stopped. "Now, if the item tracker is right, he should be coming up into this area down here. The Catacomb's interlaced with the rock—

lots of levels to fight on. Should be fun."

"For you maybe. I can't jump around like you, and these guys are way out of my league."

Frank followed her as she dashed down the left pathway, leading to a stairwell with steep steps that were so small Frank could barely fit the back half of her red, armored boots on them.

"You lured me up here with the promise of getting a mount. Why do you even need me to fight him?" she asked.

Siena grinned back at her. "You owe me fo—"

Frank rolled her eyes. "Yeah, yeah, you helped me get my armor. I really need to get a new suit so you'll shut up about that."

They continued their descent until they arrived at the bottom of the stairwell. It led out onto a wide-open cavern with gaps in the floor, revealing a maze of platforms below. Siena strode out onto the floor, checking the wide gaps at their feet and then the map, shaking her head and then moving on to the next.

Frank moved along them with her and unequipped her Dragon Armor in favor of her default Heavy gear so she could more easily clear the openings without the need of a run-up. When she had first started playing in the Dream State, she had dedicated her Skill Points to lowering her weight as much as possible but still keeping her defense. Because of this, she was lighter and quicker than most Heavies, but this also took away some of her strength and stability against more powerful attacks.

Down several of the crevasses, she could see other players navigating their way through or fighting whatever monsters spawned down there. They looked like some form of cave bat or mole but they were too far out of her scanning range to tell. It wasn't until Siena found one of the emptier openings on the floor that she stopped and a grin lit up her face again.

"He's down there," she whispered. "The one at the bottom."

Frank gestured her down. "Then go get him."

"One more thing." Siena looked up at her, grin turning evil. "Pass me your Amethyst Edge."

Frank's eyes widened and she looked around. "Oh no. How did you—"

She hadn't told anyone she had found it and she was sure she hadn't used it around Siena before. Siena just rolled her eyes and raised her hand out like a beggar, but without the pleading.

"Oh, come on, Efty. I'll give it back right after I'm done, I swear."

Efty was the nickname Siena had given her, short for FranktheTank, which she still hadn't gotten used to. Sighing resignedly, she entered her items menu, accessing by far the rarest item she had ever possessed, to give away her Amethyst Edge. She didn't really expect it back. It wasn't because Siena would lose it—she doubted anyone could beat her in a fair fight—but knowing her, she would do some mental flip-flop to try and keep it for herself.

Yeah, like having me carrying it around for her... Wait, is that what this is all about? I'm her blimmin' sword bearer? Oh, man! Well, at least being her squire I'll get to see some interesting fights.

She passed the rare blade to Siena, and her friend grinned, holding the glowing purple sword aloft with glee in her eyes.

"Yes! Oh, and one more thing: you can watch, but don't interfere. I want to see the look in Noah's eyes after I defeat him single-handedly." She appeared to pull her comms up and annotated, *"I've got you now."*

Without waiting for a response, Siena leaped down into the three-dimensional maze below. Frank groaned as she watched her slide down the walls, as graceful as a special ops commando out of a helicopter. Making her own way down, she was forced to grip the narrow walls hand over foot, the exercise making her look like an obese monkey learning to climb.

They passed several floors before reaching the bottom. She dropped down onto the floor with a thud and looked up to see not Noah, but a man with elven features in a three-point hooded cloak staring back at them.

Wait, is that ... ?

Siena ground her teeth. "Oh, come on. Do you mean to tell me that Noah lost my Ruby Edge to you? What are you even doing here?"

The man raised his hand and Siena's glowing Ruby Edge flashed into it, as though in challenge. Frank thought the man looked somewhat familiar, resembling one of the people that had chased her in the Broken Clock Tower. Still, there was something different about him, a hesitancy that the man who had chased her hadn't possessed.

Besides, wasn't Sirswift locked away after Noah signed up with Wona? If this isn't him, then who is it?

Siena shook her head and let her shoulders drop in apparent disappointment before raising her own Color Blade, the red and purple radiating from them lighting the darkness of the passage. "Hmmph. Fine then, I guess you'll just have to do."

She dashed in and struck out. The hooded avatar ducked the first strike and then spun, just barely avoiding the second. Siena continued her barrage, but the man swiftly raised the Ruby Edge to parry her following blows before leaping backward, casually lifting it once again in challenge.

Siena blew out a raspberry and then wiped her face, as though spittle had escaped her grinning mouth in her excitement. "Is defense all you've got?"

Rising to her challenge, the hooded man charged in himself and began swinging his blade with deft precision. This seemed to take Siena by surprise, for he nearly landed a blow. Frank thought that if she wasn't so quick, he might have been able to hit her. Then he did hit her. In one of her more daring moves, Siena parried one of his blows and then leaped over him, striking at him from above. The man's own blade caught her sword, bashing it away and then slashing at her arm on the backswing.

Frank gasped. It was the first time she had seen Siena lose that much health. Siena landed, grabbing her arm from the remnants of the pain the slash would have given her. Frank suddenly felt wary, that maybe her confidence in Siena might have jinxed her. Despite being hit, Siena's smile only widened.

"Hoho, not bad! I'm almost glad that it's you who has my blade and not Noah. This fight would have been over far too quickly otherwise."

She ran in and clashed with him again, the color of their swords seeming to tremble in the darkness with each connection. She managed to slash away one of his cuts, but before she could get in a counterattack, a sudden gust of wind caught their hair and clothing. They raised their arms and backed off from one another.

As soon as the wind faded, a third figure dropped between them, landing on one knee, the blue glow of his sapphire blade joining that of the red and purple.

"You know, I heard that last remark, Siena," Noah said as he rose to his feet. "Keep talking like that and you're going to hurt my feelings."

Chapter 12
OPPORTUNITY

Siena gave me a pitiful glare. "Good. I hope you get your feelings hurt. First you steal my Ruby Edge, and then you lose it to someone like him!"

From the difference in their health bars, I was tempted to say that someone like *him* was winning against her in a one-on-one match. As soon as I had heard Siena talking while fighting him, my suspicion that maybe this wasn't Sirswift had piqued. Sirswift was a talker, a gloater. It was one of his main weaknesses, and unless he had made it so his avatar couldn't talk, this guy wasn't really him.

"I may have lost the Ruby Edge, but *he* didn't steal it from me." I ground my teeth at the false accusation. "One of those Screamers logged me out involuntarily while I was in a Tertiatier dungeon. This guy merely looted it after I left. He never killed me. Now, if you wouldn't mind, I'm going to get it back."

"But I would mind!" she growled. "Wait your turn!"

"You've had your chance, and it doesn't even look like you did very well, either."

Siena whirled on me. "I'm not done!"

For the first time, the pretender spoke up.

"How about this ..." With a dramatic pause, he gestured out an open hand and the Jade Edge flashed into it, its green glow being added to the red, blue, and purple. "I've got two of these and you each have one, and I'm very eager to see how far I can push myself in this world. So, what do you say?"

"You want to go two on one... against me *and* him?" Siena's eyebrows knitted together in confusion, but then she grinned excitedly and nodded several times. "Oh, heck yeah! Let's see if you can back up those words, Legolas. How about it, Noah?"

I still couldn't figure this stranger out. Whether he was Sirswift or not, he was now challenging both of us simultaneously. If it had been me and a newbie, it might have made sense, but not Siena. He was either incredibly skilled or incredibly stupid—most likely the latter.

This isn't why you're here, Noah.

"I have questions first."

The man lowered his blades and shrugged. "Alright."

My comms window popped up with his contact details. As it had said right after I'd left Apollo's Lookout, the name of his contact appeared, calling him *Sirswift.*

What on earth's going on?

"If you can beat me, together or alone, not only will I give this weapon back, but I'll throw in the Jade Edge and any answers you might want for free. Sound like a deal?"

What's he playing at? I have to think about this.

"Deal!"

Siena didn't wait for my answer. She ran in and struck down on him, but the stranger parried. Before I could even register what was happening, the hooded man leaped back from another of Siena's blows while swinging his arms. He then jumped up, casting a powerful wind spell below him that shot him up onto the floor above us.

I gasped and looked up. "What the... how did he—"

"Noah!" Siena glared at me from under the gap and then gestured to the hole. "Some help!"

"What do you—"

"Do what he did... to us!"

Alright, fine. I guess we're fighting him, then.

From the strength of the wind spell he cast, I could only assume he had used Vacuum, as no other spell would have been able to lift a player up like that. I didn't think the spell would be able to lift a chain mail-clad Warrior like Siena without me creating some form of seal around us. I circled my upward-facing palm above my head to cast Ice Wall on the wall above us.

"Get on!"

We jumped onto the plate of ice as I cast another wall on top of it to complete the seal. I then swung my arm and cast Vacuum at our feet. Like a cork from a wine bottle, we shot up onto the next floor. Not wearing any armor, I managed to land easily. Siena on the other hand, barely managed to catch the edge of the platform before pulling herself up and running after the dual wielder.

It seemed she didn't care about coordinating our attacks, for she charged straight at him, and caught in the rush of combat, I followed suit. As soon as she reached him, the man leaned back to avoid her first slash, reversing the grip of his blade, and then spun as Siena's second cut hit nothing but air. Her third blow landed right on his defending Jade Edge just as his Ruby Edge lashed out to catch my own attack, as though he had predicted my every move. He then cut out, catching me on the ankle and taking a quarter of my health.

This guy's incredible! It's like he's not even trying.

Siena wasn't at all deterred. She dashed in and slid low, her greaves sparking against the stone floor and her blade slashing low in turn. The hooded man jumped, flipping over the attack, and then he spun, both blades striking in sequence as Siena somersaulted and continued slashing at him down the passageway. I ground my teeth and charged after them, but once again my attacks were caught on his Color Blade, green for defense while the red one struck out at Siena. Finally, my Mana bar had regenerated.

"That's it!" I shouted and flicked my hand out.

Wildfire filled the passage, engulfing both Siena and the hooded stranger in orange flame. However, instead of just accepting the blaze willingly, I could only watch as the man leaped up, stabbed one Color Blade into the dirt wall, and then swung himself up from it onto the next floor above. Then, using an ability I had never seen before, his blade dislodged from the wall and flew up to meet him.

Was that a Range Niche ability? I shook my head, aghast. *This guy's insane. He's on a completely different level to us. I don't think we can win.*

"Noah, he's getting away!" Siena shouted, breaking me out of my daze.

I ground my teeth. "I don't have enough Mana for us both to follow him!"

"Why didn't you say so?" Siena spun back and threw a blue bottle my way. The item vanished as soon as it hit me, making my Mana shoot up. "Now, send me up! I can handle him by myself if I need to!"

By yourself? Then that would leave Frank …

I nodded and did exactly as she asked. I caught up with her, then cast an Ice Wall behind and below us before using one last Vacuum to send us up. As soon as she reached the edge of the third floor, Siena flipped herself onto the ledge and sprinted after the hooded man in her lust for battle. As she met with the hooded figure, she struck and he defended in turn before slashing back, their cuts and parries lightning fast.

"Enjoy yourself," I whispered to her and turned.

Rather than follow her, I ran to the next gap in the floor, and with a quick glance to see that she wasn't looking, jumped down it.

Knowing Siena, she would be far too preoccupied fighting the stranger to think of what I might do if left alone with Frank. I couldn't have asked for a more perfect distraction to get her to myself.

If I'm not going to get any answers from this guy, then at least I'm not going to leave here empty-handed.

Rolling my hands, I cast Cyclone to pad my fall, landing with a thump on the floor that the fight had first started on. And there, just where we had left her, FranktheTank was staring up through the gap as if she could still see the fight taking place. She turned and gasped upon seeing me, taking a step back as I stood.

"Now… I think you'd agree, after what happened at the top of the lookout …" I raised my brow at her. "We have unfinished business. You have something that belongs to me."

Frank shook her head. "I-I don't."

I quickly pulled up the ITS, entering the item code from the Wakizashi from memory. After all the effort I had gone through to put the video evidence on the short sword, I wasn't going to forget something like that so easily.

When the tracking was done, showing that the item was located directly in front of me, I smiled. "You're lying. You still have the Wakizashi with the video evidence in your inventory. Give it to me."

"How do you …?" her eyes widened and she pointed behind me. "Siena, look out!"

I looked over my shoulder but the passage was empty. I quickly spun back to see Frank's plodding form running to one of the side exits to The Catacomb.

I ground my teeth and ran after her. "Oh, no you don't!"

When I reached the junction she had turned down, I stopped, seeing the steep slope leading even further down into the dungeon. From the way she was sliding down it, it was obvious that she had chosen her direction blindly and fallen. I shook my head and ran down the metal slope, the narrowness of it reminding me of the chute people would use for laundry in old hotels.

"She's getting away, Noah!" a voice called tauntingly, but no comms window popped up in my vision.

"Who are you?" I shouted but then pulled my hands up instinctively.

A cloud of bats rushed up at me from another connecting chute, but before I could cast a spell to kill them, they passed me by and I continued running, and then sliding, and then falling.

"Argh!"

The slide had become so steep that I couldn't keep my feet and I could hear Frank scream as it became vertical beneath us. I went to cast Cyclone again but dropped through onto a stone floor beneath before I could. Cold wind whipped at me and I glanced about, seeing that we were at the very bottom of the iceberg-shaped Sky Island. The rock platform we were standing on was open to the elements.

Frank had rolled out of the way as I'd landed and then ran to the edge before seeing that her mad dash had led her to a dead end.

"Give me the Wakizashi, Frank!" I shouted, wind screaming in my ears.

Frank shook her head, braided hair whipping around her wide face. "No way!"

"Why? You don't even know what it is!" I shouted over the screaming wind. "You don't even know what's on there!"

"I won't give it up!" she screamed, even as I advanced on her.

Suddenly there was a loud crash against the side of the island near us. I looked around but couldn't see what had caused it. Out of the corner of my vision, I saw what I thought was the flapping edges of pointed, white wings. Then there was the sound of footsteps running on the platform. I could barely register what had happened before a force collided with my face and I was sent sprawling to the floor.

"That felt good," I heard over the wind. "She might not know what's on there …"

As though being pulled out from a blanket made of thin air, an arm appeared that reached up to take something off a head that wasn't there. Like the invisibility cloak from Harry Potter, the avatar of a Range niche wearing familiar brown leathers revealed itself when the cap-like object vanished from his head.

"But I do."

I pulled my head up from the platform to see Brock was now standing between Frank and me. I had always wondered how Brock had evaded Wona's tracking system. Whatever it was, I hadn't expected it to look like something out of a children's story.

"Pitiful," Brock muttered at me under his breath.

Rising to my feet, I stood to face the person I had wanted to meet with next, but also the least. "I'm pitiful?" I rolled my eyes. "Yeah, yeah, big hero. Why don't you go back to avoiding the police and leave me to do my job."

"Bah, your *job*. You're just a sellout." Brock gave me a smirk. "Stealing and lying to your friends just to make sure you get the job you want. You're as bad as Sirswift."

Anger tugged at me like a hook. "What did you say?"

"You heard me!"

I bared my teeth. "Actually the wind made it difficult to hear. Come a little closer, would you?"

Brock ignored me and turned to Frank. "You want Noah to leave you alone, don't you?"

Frank breathed out heavily, sounding exasperated.

"I can help with that."

"What, by giving you the Wakizashi instead?" Frank shook her head. "Listen up, I'm on neither of your *sides*. I'm not giving this thing to either of you. For Pete's sake, you two have been fighting over this thing for over a week now! You're supposed to be friends! How is this that important? How pathetic are you two? Why don't you both just—" She raised a hand. "—give it up?"

Silence covered the platform as we glared at each other. The sudden tension between us seemed to slip away with Frank's forthright words. One second I was ready to start a fight with my old friend, the next I was wondering what I was even doing here.

I didn't really need the Wakizashi. I just had to make sure Frank kept it to herself. Heck, I didn't even come here to fight the fake Sirswift and take back the Ruby Edge. I came to see if I could get the old roster of Wona employees.

And the one person most likely to have that information is right in front of me. Here I was about to try and get rid of him. What am I, a moron?

It felt like a bucket of cold water had just been thrown over me and I rose from the fighting stance I hadn't even realized I had lowered myself into.

"Man... she's right, we really are pathetic."

Brock frowned at me. "*We?*"

"That's right, *we!*" I looked down in my shame. "Because we both have information we need to reach our goals, but this grudge of ours is getting us nowhere!"

"That's because you gave in to Wona!" Brock shouted.

"And what you wanted would have prevented Sue from getting justice, but that's not the point!" I sighed and stared into his eyes. "You want to get revenge for your friends who died and went insane, right? Well, Chloe and I almost have enough information to find out who was actually behind it. All we need is the roster of old Wona employees before the beta tests happened."

Brock's brow furrowed. "Old roster? What the heck are you talking about?"

"Six avatars, Brock." I raised the equivalent number of fingers. "Six have shown up in the Dream State with the ability to forcefully wake people up from a DSD trance. During the sabotage of Heaven's grand opening, we managed to corner one and find out his name as well as the user I.D. of two others. The I.D. codes were the same as the second round of beta testers who went missing from the asylum, and the one we cornered was identified by his own sister as being one of these beta testers. It was Chloe's brother, Lucas Nix."

I let silence take over while this sank in. I could see Brock's gaze drift as the realization dawned on him. However, it was Frank who spoke up first.

"Holy crap, that's heavy."

Brock shook his head, fighting to retain his anger. "But how does that lead you to who caused the overdoses?"

"We don't even know if they were overdoses yet!" I looked around, suddenly realizing that talking in a place where we needed to yell just to be heard wasn't the best place to discuss this. "Give me twenty minutes to explain this to you in person. I'll have Chloe come and bring you all the research she's done."

Brock's eyes drifted to the floor. "But how do I know that I can trust you?"

Frank grabbed her helmet in frustration. "Meet somewhere neutral. Do I have to spell out everything for you two? Gah! *Boys!*"

Brock nodded reluctantly. "How about David's place?"

We both knew David well enough that he would warn either

of us if things looked fishy. Besides, I hadn't seen David in a while. Considering he was friends with both of us, I felt he deserved to be present when we hashed this all out.

I nodded. "We'll meet there tomorrow evening. That will give Chloe and I the time we need to organize all the information we've gathered. You bring the—"

"The employee roster yeah. Yeah, I got it. I'll see you there."

Brock ran to the edge of the platform and jumped out over the drop, summoning his Ice Dragon and soaring over Penance Peaks. When he was gone, I turned back to Frank, who almost flinched back from my gaze.

"Until we've sorted this all out, I need you to promise me you'll keep the Wakizashi safe and to yourself."

Frank rolled her eyes, but then nodded. "I've been doing it for this long, haven't I?"

I grinned at this and pulled out my summoning stone to call Peragon to follow Brock's leave. It appeared in a flash and I climbed up onto it. There was a lot I had to have prepared before heading to David's tomorrow and I could only hope that Chloe had found more information while digging through Wona's files.

And I still have to find out the identity of this Sirswift imposter. Did Samuel give his avatar with its valuable stats and rare Color Blade to someone else before he was hauled off to jail, or did someone steal it?

Riding Peragon into the fields, I decided to give Windsor one more try before I returned to talk with Chloe.

Chapter 13
THE SPECIALIST

As I walked down the seventh-floor corridor, I heard laughter from the office and pushed my way through the double doors. The two laughing were Windsor Wona and his new specialist, Vega.

"What are you two finding so funny?" I demanded, outraged that Windsor wouldn't have told me when he returned from his VR retreat.

"And here he is!" Vega called, sitting on Windsor's desk. "The man who truly knows his priorities. I can see why you hired him, Win."

Win? Is that a nickname?

They both laughed again at the confused expression I made, only now starting to come around to the fact that they were laughing at my expense.

I made my voice cold. "Tell me."

Windsor wiped an invisible tear from his eye and calmed himself. "Come now, Noah. You of all people should know a tryout when you see one."

"Tryout?"

My brow furrowed as Vega stood up from his desk and flicked a hand out like he was holding a sword. "So, *I-really-am-that-Noah*, did I pass?"

Seeing the way he gestured out his open hand like he had before our fight, it suddenly clicked. "You're the one using

Sirswift's avatar."

"Bingo!"

I turned to Windsor in annoyance. "I asked you why Sirswift was still in the game. Why didn't you tell me you gave his avatar to someone else?"

Windsor's face went troubled. "Noah, I don't recall you asking me about Sirswift."

"I—"

He raised a finger. "But I do recall you asking about my nephew, Samuel, and I freely answered that question by showing you where he is. Sirswift, as you might have already guessed, is right in front of you."

I balled my fist at the purposeful misdirection. "Why would you trick me?"

"I thought fighting him yourself would show you how good he is." Windsor stood from his chair and walked around to stand between us. "You see, Noah, Vega is a video gaming *prodigy* in the purest respect of the word. Games it would normally take people years to master, he can master in a week or so. The hardest difficulty is the only difficulty level he plays! I had to pay him a very high rate just to get him to consider working for us. Think about it. He told you himself he's only been playing in the Dream State for a week and you saw how he good he is."

Vega gave Windsor a suspicious look. "Why, Mr. President, are you trying to seduce me?"

Hearing their laughter, it was finally beginning to sink in. The fact that he had taken on Siena, even with Sirswift's avatar, showed how quick of a learner he was. I had thought he was on another level to us, and I was right—I just didn't consider to what extent. However, recalling the fight brought up another question.

"You say this was a tryout. Well, did you win? Did you manage to beat Siena and get her Color Blade?"

Vega sighed and shook his head. "Afraid not. Granted, it was my first PvP. It seems I still have a lot to learn about the Dream State's various items."

"But you had both of us on the ropes!" I asked incredulously.

"How could she have possibly managed—"

"A Kamikaze Orb," Vega interrupted. "She lured me into a dead end and let one off before escaping down one of the holes. She said something about it being better to run away than to lose. Fortunately, I refused to fight her one-on-one with both of my Color Blades. Otherwise, she would've gotten the Jade Edge off me as well."

I shook my head. "That bloody girl …"

"She is something, I'll give her that." Vega nodded. "Not many humans can give me a run for my money."

I paused but then asked, "Humans?"

Vega rolled his wrist. "Bots are another story, but enough about that."

Windsor was smiling between us now and he raised his hands like a conductor. "So, how about it, Noah? Would you say he passed? Will you accept him into Catastrophe?"

I nodded, still slightly speechless. "I guess so."

"Fantastic! I will break out the champagne!"

Not a personal joke then, just a job tryout that happened to end rather humorously. Lucky I left when I did. There's a good chance I would've been blown up otherwise.

"You two go ahead. I'd feel guilty leaving out our other new teammates. I'll go and collect Chloe."

"Good idea. I'll call for Dice," Windsor called as his pencil-skirted secretary walked through with a tray containing the bottle and some wine glasses. "You'll have to play catch up when you come back. We've already had a couple."

I can tell.

I made my way back through the doors to the elevator. I had to make sure that everything was organized with Chloe. She needed to know what was happening. The elevator stopped at her floor and I moved to her suite. I knocked, but she took a moment to come to the door. She opened it slowly and I noticed all of the paper sprawled out across her floor.

"Oh, you're back," she said, letting me in.

I looked around as I walked past her, seeing the stacks of

mixed up documents. Chloe moved in and sat down in a space of the floor not covered by the various white sheets.

"For a computer game company, there was a surprising amount of physical reports they allowed me to go through."

"I can see that. Did you find anything?"

Chloe nodded and brought out a piece of paper. It looked to be a printout of an email. "According to this, someone on the original crew pushed forward the DSD trial before it was ready. And according to this—" She lifted another piece of paper. "—they weren't actually overdoses, more like premature human trials that didn't have enough resistance prep. It seems the older solutions of DSD were volatile but they had decided to push them forward in order to weed out these problems."

I shook my head. "If I'd known that when I talked to Brock I might have persuaded him to meet with us more easily."

Chloe spun about, nearly knocking over a stack of papers. "You talked to Brock? When?"

"About thirty minutes ago, in the Dream State. He said he's willing to meet and give us the names of the ex-Wona employees. If you were to see a list of them, would you be able to identify the ones that were blacked out?"

Chloe nodded. "If I had both of the lists and had the time to make a comparison with all this, sure."

"Good. We're meeting with him tomorrow. Do you think you could have it all ready to display to him by then?"

She grinned at me and pointed to a stack of paper on her bed. "What do you think I've been doing all day? I've made a pile of everything relevant to the failed beta tests. I've got a list of I.D. codes of the original testers, a bunch of emails showing that the drugs were tested way before they should have been, and even a list of all the asylum patients that went missing. I can have them all scanned into a simulation by tomorrow. All we need is that employee list to fill in the blacked out names."

Not worrying about the mess around us, I strode over and pulled her back to her feet. I then smiled and took her in my arms. "I could never have done this without you. You know that, right?"

She looked down in embarrassment. "Well, we both have our reasons to figure this all out. I'm glad you and Brock managed to look past your grudges and decided to meet up like this."

I looked away, biting my lip. "It's not that simple."

She shrugged into my arms with a contented sigh. "Better than nothing."

I frowned and she looked up at me in confusion. "What's wrong?"

"I don't know. I guess you looking for Lucas has brought back all the memories of the time I was looking for Sue in the game. I care about you, and don't want you to have to go through the same hell that I did."

Chloe smiled, looking astonished by something. "You actually care, don't you?"

I scoffed. "Of course I do!"

She caught my eyes again, tilting her head slightly, her lips begging to be kissed. I obliged, and the passion and warmth behind it expressed better than words how much it meant to her. We kissed for a while, but before it could get too heated, she pulled away.

"Now you're just distracting me." She blushed and her eyes drifted to the floor. "Come on, let me show you what I've found."

Chapter 14
DRAWING BOARD

We arrived at David's place the next evening after sharing a quick dinner of spaghetti Bolognese at the facility's food court. Before my accident and muscle atrophy, I wouldn't have batted an eye at walking there, but with the generous salary we were receiving from Wona, it wasn't too much to get a taxi from the facility to David's apartment in the suburbs.

We must have arrived too early, for as soon as we exited the taxi, we found his door on the first floor of the building locked, with no one inside.

Chloe raised an eyebrow at me. "Not the warmest welcome. What do we do now?"

I shrugged. "I guess we wait for Brock to show up."

We sat down on the veranda covered with dead leaves and waited for a good twenty minutes before Brock finally arrived in his truck. As drugged up as I had been at the time, I recalled it was the same one that he and David had used to break me out of the Wona asylum a month back.

He opened the door and stepped out, running to the edge of the driveway and looking around before sighing in relief. Unlike his Range Niche in the game, Brock was tall and lean with big arms that would have more believably belonged to a bowman, rather than his archer avatar. He then turned back to us, as though confused by our baffled expressions.

"Thought someone was tailing me, had to go around the

block a few times to make sure."

"Still so paranoid." Chloe frowned. "I thought Wona was no longer after you now that Noah made it so you hadn't broken your contract?"

Brock rolled his eyes. "That's what they want you to think."

I shook my head. We didn't have time to deal with his paranoid delusions. After all, we had our own paranoias to discuss.

"I knocked on the door but no one's home." I followed him up to the door and Brock pulled a spare key out from under the doormat. "Do you know where David is?"

"He'd still be at his new job. Should be back soon."

Chloe raised her brow. "Davey has a job now? What does he do?"

"His roommate got him a job at another hospital as an orderly. Apparently pretending to be one for a day convinced him it wouldn't be so bad." Brock grinned. "Usually does night shifts so he can just play old computer games in the office, but he did the day shift today so he could do this with us."

We entered the apartment and I shook my head. "I can't imagine David actually working a proper job."

Like the other times we had been there, the place was a mess; the curtains weren't even open, and a dusty, damp smell filled the living room. I walked over and opened the window to get some airflow but eventually realized I'd just have to get used to it. There were three tattered couches and we sat down on two of them, facing each other.

I put down the backpack I had been carrying and pulled out two Dream Engines.

"I was expecting you to have stuff in there that you could show me," Brock said, his jovial tone absent. "Not a game."

Chloe shook her head and pulled out a USB device from her pocket. "There's a program on the Dream Engine called Drawing Board. It's like an office suite that will allow me to show you all the data I've collected. I've got hard copies you can have, but I think we should wait till David gets here."

"Speak of the devil," I said as I saw David swerve into the

driveway on his bike.

After seeing the truck parked outside, he rushed into the house and took off his helmet, eyes wide.

"All together again." He turned to Chloe in confusion, clearly wondering who the girl with me was. "Wait… holy crap."

Chloe had the same reaction to David's skinny form. "Yeah… you're not like that in the game at all."

David laughed and grabbed his scrawny arms. "Yeah, I tried weight lifting once, didn't have the genes for it. Besides, why spend days working out when you can just go and be a tank in-game, am I right?"

She turned away and he took one of the other seats. "So, what's the plan?"

Brock gestured to Chloe. "She has a device to use on the Dream Engine that will apparently show us what *they* think will convince me Wona isn't to blame for the beta tester overdoses."

David caught my gaze. "Hold on, hold on. I thought I told you I didn't want to get involved in this thing between you two."

I shrugged. "You were the only one on neutral ground that we could both really rely on. To be honest, I think you'll be glad we did after we're done here."

He raised his eyebrow and then turned to Brock. "Did you bring your helmet?"

Brock pointed a thumb over his shoulder. "In the truck."

"Better go get it, then."

Brock stood. "Yeah, best make this quick."

He went outside as David went into his room to grab his own Dream Engine. Being the hospitable one, when they returned David supplied us all with a drink of water to take the soluble drug and then offered to take the floor. Chloe, Brock, and I lay down on the ratty couches as the DSD quickly took effect.

"Alright," Chloe's voice said as soon as we were under. "I'm going to send you all a file. It should show up as an option under the Dream State login once it's loaded."

It showed up in my vision as soon as she finished talking, and I selected it. When an empty room materialized around me, I saw that the others had appeared as well.

David laughed. "That was close—nearly chose the Dream State out of habit."

"When did you learn to use this program?" I asked Chloe, as further details of the virtual seminar room appeared around us in lines of blue light.

Wow, why don't more people use this? It could give the illusion that people from all around the world are in the same room. Businesses would love it.

As she had explained, it was an interactive office with a Drawing Board on one wall and the files of her evidence located in a separate box at the bottom of our vision.

"Dice showed me. He's really good at the technical stuff if you give him a chance." I nodded grudgingly and she turned to the board. "I went through several years' worth of records and here's all the stuff I've found."

She spread out every file she had scanned. The important parts of the documents zoomed in too quickly to pick up, as though in fast-forward. This first show was obviously used to impress us with the number of files rather than displaying what they actually contained, for she returned them to the box and began putting them on the Drawing Board one by one. I couldn't blame her; she had spent nearly two days working on this presentation. She deserved to show off a little.

"Here's the list of Wona employees back before the beta tests began." She ran through the list of one group. "From top to bottom, here are the beta testers themselves." She brought up a long list of names, some of which were bolded, and an even smaller group that were highlighted. "The ones in bold are the ones that were either killed or were affected negatively by the first solution of DSD. The highlighted ones are those who disappeared from Wona's asylum."

She zoomed in on these names. They read: Lucas Nix, Paris Flaugh, Ray Cranel, Kristie Tein, Michael Joslin, and Malic Milano.

Chloe bit her lip, but then pulled out another list. "Here are the executives of the Wona Company. Of course, there's Wona himself; Glen Budowski, who ran finance and marketing; Kylie Bower, Executive Chief and head of communications; Erik Milano, who led the design team; and, as you can see, the last one is blacked out."

"Why?" David's digital avatar looked confused. "I mean these are Wona's records. Why would they black them out?"

"She's getting to that." I gestured for Chloe to continue.

She nodded. "There were names blacked out in the chemistry file as well, and even names in some of the emails I've found, but the contents of the emails themselves were not blacked out." She brought up one that looked to be a warning notice.

It was from Kylie Bower to Windsor Wona and it read:

> Concerns on the DSD
> 25 November 2059
> Dear Windsor,
>
> After doing a thorough investigation into the compounds involved, it is obvious that the solution is not ready for human trials. I suggest we delay the test until we have more results in from animal testing.
>
> Kind regards,
> Bower
> Executive Chief

Brock shook his head. "They couldn't have done any more experiments on chimpanzees. Animal rights groups had already shut down their labs by that time. But if they weren't ready by that point …"

Chloe scrolled down the email. Below the letter was a reply from Windsor Wona.

> Re: Concerns on the DSD
> 26 November 2059

Kylie,

You have my word. No beta testing will be done with this solution, despite what my colleague might insist. We will only go through with the beta testing when we know it's ready for human trials.

Sincerely,
Windsor Wona
CEO

"This is dated a day before the first rounds of beta tests happened," Chloe continued, appearing to take the date right from her memory.

"Then Wona lied!" Brock shouted. "He was obviously trying to bide his time until he could get the results and move forward with more human trials."

Chloe shook her head. "I don't think so. I mean, read this one. He sent it the day after."

She brought up another letter on the board. Like with the list of executives, the name that the email was sent to was blacked out. It read:

Malfeasance
27 November 2059
Dear █████████,

I hope you know that after what you have done there is no turning back. After everything we have worked for, your recklessness has cost us the lives of several of our game designers! I will not tolerate this. Because of the friendship we once had, I wanted to tell you this face to face, but I see that is impossible now. I've reported this to the police, and you will be charged with malfeasance.

```
Windsor Wona
CEO
```

"That's a little too convenient, don't you think?" Brock muttered. "You really believe that will convince me?"

"Even if this email doesn't speak for itself, which I think it does, once you know the time this email was sent, it will. The second round of testing happened the very next day," Chloe said, voice cold and directed squarely at Brock. "Whoever Windsor emailed that day, they didn't reply to him until a day after. Read this."

She pulled up another email on the Drawing Board. It read:

```
Re: Malfeasance
28 November 2059
My dear friend Win,
```

I know what this means, and I know that you sold me out. This may be the end of me, but the echoes of my soul will continue to resonate through the Dream State to hurt you and all you hold dear at every turn. You will know my work when you see it, and when you do, you'll wish you kept my sins closer to your chest.

```
Your friend,
████████
```

Chloe stared at Brock. "When I found these emails I asked Windsor in person. He can confirm that he gave no order to execute either of these tests. They were done without his knowledge. I also contacted the executives who no longer work for him and they backed him up."

"So what? They probably signed confidentiality agreements like me. Besides, if he's not responsible, then who is?" Brock countered.

Silence befell the boardroom.

David put his hand up to give a suggestion—maybe to point out that the executives of such a company wouldn't have had to sign such forms—but then he lowered it again, as if remembering that he wasn't supposed to take sides. I spoke up instead.

"Maou."

They all looked to me so I decided to take the lead, Brock's eyes widening ever so slightly from the name. I stepped forward, and although I knew how it would affect Chloe, I pulled up Lucas' profile.

"Listen, I can't vouch for the rest of this. But what I do know is that I talked to this guy." I pointed to the young man's picture. "He and several of the other brain damaged beta testers were recorded sabotaging Heaven's grand opening. I was there, and when I asked him who told them to do this, he said it was someone called Maou."

I dragged the last letter Chloe had shown us back to the board and pointed to the black marks over the name of the sender.

"Hurt you and all you hold dear at every turn? You will know my work when you see it? You'll wish you kept my sins closer to your chest?" I circled the missing name with my finger, causing the Drawing Board to highlight the other blacked out names and connect them with glowing red lines. "These acts of vengeance match our mystery man's words. I think *this* is Maou."

Chloe nodded and turned back to Brock. "But we need the list of old Wona employees to find out who he really is. That's where you come in."

It wasn't until I looked to him that I saw Brock was smiling now. Not just smiling, he was laughing. David smiled nervously, as though thinking his friend had suddenly lost his mind.

"Ah, Brock?" he asked.

Brock waved at him as it to say 'It's nothing!' but then continued to laugh. "We don't need the list… to know who sent that!" He took a few quick breaths and shook his head. "Oh man. Maou? I thought you were pushing it when you were blaming it on a single Wona team. But now you're trying to tell me that you're blaming the failed beta tests on a dead man?"

"Well, excuse me for not wanting to judge every single individual in a company and trying to find who's really at fault!" I shook my head and went to continue, but Chloe stopped me.

"So, you know who it is?" she asked, sounding hopeful.

Brock raised his hand to his face, still grinning. "Seriously though, Maou?" He rotated his wrist, as though it were obvious. "Not Maou, Mal... Malcolm!"

Through Brock's laughter, several things hit me at once. The first was the memory of what Lucas had said in The Engine Room. He repeated: *"Maou, come, help me disappear."*

Not "Maou, come,"... Malcolm.

The second thing to hit me was how Brock had said that the blacked out executive was a dead man. It brought back the memory of what Windsor had told me when he saw me looking at the picture on his desk. *"Oh him? He's dead now."*

Wona & Mirth.

I then realized that I knew the man's name, that I had known it for a while, ever since I had read a post on Brock's blog before it had been taken down.

"Malcolm Mirth," I said. Brock nodded. "Maou is Malcolm Mirth, the head chemist of Wona and the DSD project."

I turned back to Chloe, who looked utterly confused. "But if he's dead, how on earth is he still affecting the game?"

"I... I don't know, but we seriously need to confront Windsor about this." I looked at Brock, who was staring back at me, taken aback at my grave expression. "And you have to come with us."

David grinned. "You're pretty much inviting him into the belly of the beast here, Noah."

"It's necessary." I inclined my head, searching my brain for an apt analogy. "Sometimes you have to swallow some medicine to take out a virus."

"Noah, do you *really* think a ghost is behind everything?" Brock narrowed his eyes at me, but then he sighed. "Heck, I've been running from these bastards for too long anyway. Time to see what I've been running from, I guess."

I felt my shoulders relax. "Thank you."

Chapter 15
WONA AND MIRTH

When we arrived back at the facility in a cab, Brock was twitching and looking around like he was walking through the Black Gate of Mordor with the One Ring. I'm pretty sure none of the people here even knew what Brock looked like, let alone cared who he was. David accompanied us for—as he claimed—moral support.

He looked around the facility as the gates closed behind us, leaving us in the shadow of the tower. "As I said, man, the belly of the beast."

"Shut up, Davey," Chloe said. "Besides, it's more like walking into a Tertiatier dungeon."

Brock shook his head. "Except I have more to lose than just my items."

"And more to gain," Chloe replied.

I couldn't help but smile. "I've missed this."

We came into the main entrance like returning conquerors, making our way to the elevator. Whether it was coincidence or just misfortune, Vega was waiting for us when the elevator opened.

"You guys look like you're on a mission," he said, one eyebrow raised at our determined expressions.

I inclined my head. "To save the Dream State."

His other eyebrow rose to meet it as the doors closed behind us. "Sounds fun; mind if I tag along?"

Chloe and I shrugged but David asked, "Wait, who is this?"

"Everyone, this is Vega," I introduced, similar to how Windsor had introduced me to Vega. "Vega, everyone."

When the doors opened again on Windsor's floor, the five of us strode out and down the corridor to his office. Knowing my luck, the only person there would be his secretary, waiting to tell us that he'd returned to the debug room. However, it seemed that my luck had changed, for Windsor was sitting in his swivel chair looking out his back window. He saw us coming in the reflection.

"Noah! Ah, you brought some friends, I see."

I stalked forward, seeing that the framed picture on his desk had been turned down. "I thought we'd need some help if we're going to stop the Screamers from sabotaging the re-opening of Heaven."

"Well, I did say you should hire more people for your team."

He spun on his chair to look at us, smiling with recognition when seeing Brock's face, who looked more than a little uncomfortable around the person who he thought had been trying to hunt him down for the better part of a year.

"And what can I do to help you fine young people?" Windsor asked.

I stopped in front of his wide desk, picked the photo up by its frame and pointed to Malcolm's smiling, goateed face. "First off, you can tell us everything you know about what happened to him after he left your company, how he died, and why he's now commanding a group of insane gamers that are destroying the Dream State."

Not until now did I fully recognize the man I was pointing to. I first thought I recognized him because he resembled the mustached leader of the opposition in Heaven Museum's mural, but now I knew I had seen him even before then. He had been the man demonstrating the Dream Engine in the first security video Windsor had shown me. The man had been with Wona from the very beginning.

Windsor's usually jovial expression darkened. "Do you know what you are asking of me, Noah? I once considered this man a good friend, and you want me to just talk about how he died like it was a fond memory."

I gestured to Brock behind me. "It's taken a lot of courage for him to come in here. I think for that he at least deserves to know about the person who killed several of his good friends, don't you?"

Windsor narrowed his eyes at me for a moment but then leaned back in his chair. "Very well… Vanessa!"

His secretary walked in. "Yes?"

"Get these two guests key cards for the facility. We're going to need to use our devices if I'm going to give them an answer that might satisfy them."

"Full GC clearance?"

Windsor nodded and Vanessa went back into the side room.

"I don't get it." I gestured to the photo again. "If the guy behind everything was one of your old executives, why did you tell me he was dead?"

"Because he *is* dead."

"Figuratively?" Chloe asked, her tone rising in pitch. "As in, he's *dead* to you?"

"No, he is literally dead." Windsor stopped himself and shook his head. "You'll just have to see for yourself."

Vanessa returned with key cards on lanyards that she handed to Brock and David. They took them, and without answering, Windsor led us out of his office. We followed him down to a GC on one of the lower floors. From the blinking lights above the door, I could see why Wona had given them security passes.

The six of us took up half of the recliners. Chloe showed David how to use one and I showed Brock.

"You really think something will come of this?" Brock asked as I pulled down the Dream Engine for him.

I passed him a DSD vial from the cabinet on the wall. "I honestly don't know. I'm just trying to keep an open mind."

"Humph, hopefully not so open that your brain falls out."

"Ha-ha," I said sarcastically.

I sat down on the recliner beside him as Windsor pulled down his helmet. "I'm about to show you one of Wona's darkest secrets.

I'm not going to make you sign waivers, because I imagine one of you is rather suspicious of them by now." Brock narrowed his eyes, but Windsor just continued. "That being said, after you've seen this, I doubt anyone would believe you if you told them anyway."

David laughed. "I dunno, Mr. President. After spending so many hours in your world, you would be surprised with what we might believe."

We all put on our helmets and let the recliners drop us into horizontal positions. Less than a minute later, an empty loading screen lit up in our minds.

We found ourselves sitting on soft chairs in Windsor Wona's special theater room—the same room where he had shown me the evidence relating to my accident and revealed Brock's lie about not signing the confidentiality agreement. However, the narrow room seemed to have been purposefully widened so we could all have a front row seat.

"This isn't another slideshow, is it?" Brock whined.

"Let's start at the beginning," Windsor announced.

The screen became black with the date and location written in white: "2038, Wona & Mirth Laboratories, Jaco Island, East Timor." It then showed a close-up of a face that, from its dark mustache and goatee, I recognized to be the same person from the picture on Windsor's desk. Malcolm Mirth. He made some final adjustments to the camera and looked over his shoulder to see the feed on a computer monitor beside him. Smiling, he pulled back further to show rows of glass cages containing chimpanzees wearing what looked to be prototype Dream Engines. They were mere skeletons of what the helmet would become, and we could see through them to the top of each chimpanzee's head. The tops of their skulls had been removed, and electrodes had been drilled into their brains.

Chloe cringed away. "Oh, those poor animals!"

"I know. It's not pretty, but it was all a part of his project," Windsor said, sounding like he had been compliant with such experiments. "At least they weren't human."

"Not yet," Brock retorted.

The screen suddenly changed to show Malcolm drag a chair between the glass boxes of animals. The helmets all seemed to be linked through some rigging in the ceiling. Malcolm drank something from a vial and sat down. He then put on his own version of the Dream Engine, altered from the ones that were on the apes, and connected to the others by thick cables.

"What's he doing?" I asked.

"He is loading his dreams into the software." Windsor raised a remote and clicked a button several times. Each time he did, it showed a different date with Malcolm sitting on the seat and loading his dreams and memories into the helmet. "He did this every day ..." He continued clicking the remote as the setting changed from the East Timor Wona Laboratories to the American Wona laboratories, the very building we were sitting in. "Even when he came home, he continued his experiments."

Brock's eyes widened. "Was that after the animal rights groups shut him down? I remember they reported that the chimpanzees suffered from body dissociation, acting like they were human."

Windsor nodded. "I think he was trying to upload a part of himself into the game, compiling a copy of himself into it by harnessing other conscious minds, memory boosters, hypnotics, and psychedelics. I don't know all the details, but I've confirmed from these videos that he did this every day in one way or another for just short of twenty years."

Chloe leaned forward in her chair. "My god. And all the while he was perfecting the effects of the drug… on himself?"

"It seemed that because it worked on him, he was confident it would work on others to get them into the game." Windsor shook his head with sadness in his eyes. "But he underestimated how much his body had already adapted to drugs over the years and didn't compensate for that when testing it on the betas."

Brock gripped the arms of his chair. "Why didn't you try to stop him?"

Windsor whirled on him. "Don't you think I would have if I knew? I had no idea that Malcolm had brought the dates forward!

I didn't even know that the tests were taking place!"

He brought up multiple smaller videos next, showing all of the beta-testers dying or struggling with the drug at once. Brock's grip tightened on his chair as he watched each of his friends dying, despite having seen the videos so many times already.

"I was too busy working on the game mechanics and design to pay attention to what our chemistry division was doing!" Windsor continued, his voice trembling. "These are the victims of my negligence."

"Then it was your fault!" Brock accused.

"If fault can be determined by a person's ignorance and inaction, then yes, but not by design. For that, you have Malcolm to blame."

Vega spoke up for the first time. "But how did *he* die?"

Windsor pressed another button on the remote and the screen showed yet another security feed from a Wona laboratory. However, unlike the first one, the rows of cages were replaced with rows of empty recliners.

"As soon as I found out what he'd done, I called the police to come and arrest Malcolm. Thanks to a hefty payout to the Ministry of Justice, we managed to keep the details of the deaths and their cause silent."

Similar to the first video, it showed Malcolm Mirth drag a chair down the rows into the center of the room. However, unlike the other videos, he seemed to be rushing, his hands shaking with panic as he took the drug. Even in the grainy security footage, shifting red and blue lights could be seen through the laboratory windows: the lights of police cars.

"I think I drove him to do something desperate. For nearly twenty years, he had free range to do his experiments thanks to my funding. But he no longer had that safety net and ..." Windsor gestured to the screen.

The footage continued as Malcolm took multiple pills and slammed on the Dream Engine helmet.

Vega's brow rose with an obvious, sudden interest. "What's he doing? Did he want to record his death on the Dream Engine like his dreams?"

Windsor watched as the person he had considered his friend started to twitch and convulse on the recliner chair. "I think… he thought that, after the amount of himself he put into the game, he could transfer his mind into it as well. It had been months since we had talked in person when he did this, so I have no idea what was going through his head."

"And he was dead when the police showed up?" Brock asked.

Windsor nodded. "Escaping into the game was his desperate final act."

I shook my head. "Then who's commanding the Screamers?"

"Some sort of manifesto he left in the game?" Chloe suggested, but then continued. "But why did you black out his name on all of the records?"

"Trying to cover your ass?" Brock's jabs had lost some of their power by this point. I think even he knew they were beginning to sound cruel.

"I'm pretty sure that was Glen. He said that if anyone found out what he had done, it would be the end of our company." Windsor raised his palms. "To be perfectly honest, the other chemists learned more from Malcolm's death than any of the beta testers. The next beta test that you were in was the thing that stopped us from pulling the plug on the project entirely. In that way, Malcolm's sacrifice is what saved the game."

I sighed. "And now his spirit has risen from the grave in an attempt to destroy it… metaphorically speaking. But where does this lead us with the Screamers? Do we even know how their screams can force people out of the game?"

Windsor cupped his chin. "Whatever it is, it's nothing to do with the Dream Engine helmet. It's shown to be still going even after the player has woken up."

"So, it's something to do with the DSD then."

"I'm not a chemist." Windsor shrugged. "I'm more interested in how they appear in places they shouldn't be able to. I've actually been thinking about this since the very first report. There's a code related to the Transfer Orbs that would allow a player to do this, but not when that function was turned off in an area, as it was during Heaven's grand opening. There's only one other way they could appear in places like that."

A memory of my conversation with Data suddenly came to mind. He had told me that the monsters from the Chaos Engines came from the debug room, the clouds acting as portals to take them from one place to another. It only made sense that, with some tweaking, some of the portals could work in reverse. But if that was the case, then Windsor would have noticed them going in and out of it.

Unless ...

"Chaos Engines can appear in any dungeon, right?" I asked.

Windsor's brow furrowed and he turned toward me. "Anywhere the game designers coded it into the system. What are you getting at, Noah?"

"Data told me that, besides your personal GC, the only way to get in and out of a debug room is through the Chaos Engines. What if the one commanding the Screamers is reprogramming the Chaos Engines to allow them to get in and out?"

"No, I would have seen it in my own—" He paused as if suddenly seeing where I was going with this. "Unless there was a second debug room... one made in secret during the game's production, one that's separate from my own. One that could transport anyone they wanted *anywhere* they wanted through the Chaos Engines."

"And if the waking really has something to do with the DSD ..." Chloe continued.

Brock nodded. "We'll find the answers if we get into the debug room."

"Hah, sounds like a good hunt!" Vega grinned, eyebrows waggling in a way that reminded me of Siena. "But how do we know what Chaos Engines lead to Wona's debug room and what Chaos Engines lead to the Screamers? There are thousands of them! Should we go to the designers and ask them who designed each one?"

"Good luck," Windsor said sarcastically, shaking his head.

"Some of the designers who made them don't even work with Wona anymore. Are you really going to contact each one?"

"So …" I rubbed the back of my head in exasperation. "I guess our only option is in-game trial and error."

"Dungeon crawling?" Chloe eyed me. "We're going to need help."

I nodded. "Brock, you wouldn't be willing to tell our other friends that we're all good now and that we need their help, would you?"

Brock raised a brow at me. "Are we all good now?"

"Jeez, Brock!" David waved at him. "How can you not be? You saw it. The person who's responsible for killing your friends is still affecting players in this world. How could you turn a blind eye to that?"

"I don't know, maybe because he's dead?!"

I grinned. "Is he, though? Checking out these Chaos Engines and finding the debug room might be the only way we can find out."

David turned. "We can at least tell the others and let them decide for themselves."

Brock sighed. "Sure, whatever."

With that noncommittal response, Brock pulled himself out of the simulation. David went next, and Chloe and Vega exited last. That left just me and Windsor.

"Stubborn, your friend is," he said in a Yoda impression.

I was not amused. "For over a year, he thought Wona was out to get him. I don't know, but maybe that's a part of it. From what you've told me, you're not the all-seeing eyes of this company that you led me to believe. Can you really blame him for not wanting to work with you, let alone trust you?"

"I may be Wona, but I'm not *Wona.* In the end, it's up to him." Windsor shrugged. "Who knows, maybe he'll loosen up if I give him back that blog I had shut down."

I raised an eyebrow at him and shook my head in exasperation. "And you wonder why he's being stubborn."

Chapter 16

REUNION

Instead of organizing to get everyone together myself, I decided to spring this on them intervention style. After finally being brought into the fold, David was more than willing to act as the guinea pig. Being a neutral party, he managed to convince Siena, Frank, and Keri to meet up with us. My only contribution was to involve Data and Dice, who had designated our beautiful rendezvous point and transportation to it.

"There's a reason the Yarburn shore is the most popular place in the Dream State," Data said when he met me on the beach, watching the turquoise water wash against the sand. "Some of the islands are unexplorable but I've given one the open access status to the I.D. codes of everyone in the group. That way we won't be interrupted."

I nodded, standing on the shore beside him. "I bet the details would get a bit rough around the edges though."

Data grinned. "Tsh, you'd be surprised."

I figured I didn't have to imagine it considering I was about to be shown. Off from the cavern was an island where we were all going to meet up. The dense stone stuck out above the trees, and the gorges allowed us all to look out over the wide rocky shore. Avatars walked along the beach below, either trying out the water itself or locating the many Gateways down on the shore that led to dungeons where support abilities could be learned.

They arrived one by one, floating over on the circular platforms.

I stood with Chloe; David was shuffling nervously between Brock and I, knowing he would have to be our intermediary. When Siena, Frank, and Tessa came over, Siena stalked up to me, one eyebrow raised.

"What's this all about, Noah?" she asked, sounding unimpressed with being called all the way out here.

"Better wait till everyone's arrived. I know how much you hate hearing people repeat themselves."

She gave me a slight grin at this. "You're right about that."

As we waited for Keri, Tessa wandered around the rocky terrain. Upon crossing Dice's path, she suddenly halted and pointed a hateful finger at him.

"You!" she shouted. "Not threatening players anymore, huh?"

Dice sighed and shook his head. "Tessa, I only told you the name of the dungeon to send Frank and what we'd pay for the orb. Colban was the one who threatened you."

"But he was on *your* team!"

"And now he's not." He poked a thumb over his shoulder at me. "We're under new management now. Besides, guilt by association is never a good way of accusing people of things they didn't do."

"If it makes you feel any better," I cut in, "both Samuel and Colban are being held in prison and are awaiting trial for murder."

Tessa crossed her arms in a pout and returned to Frank's side. "Yeah, well, it's a start, I suppose."

Finally, Keri flew in and jumped down from Data's Bird's Eye platform. Being the last to arrive, she immediately glared at Chloe and me and purposefully stood as far away from us as possible with Frank and Tessa. I couldn't help but feel a little guilty about how things had turned out between us. *I* knew what I had done was right, but not being able to convince her—along with the way she had reacted to my decision to recruit Chloe and join Wona—still made me feel bad.

Brock glanced at Data uncertainly across the circle. That was an improvement at least. Brock wasn't scowling at him like he usually did when in his presence. I guessed it was because Data had given him his Sapphire Edge to help stop me. In a strange turn of events, it appeared I was more on Brock's bad side than Data was now.

The tension in the group was almost palpable. The eleven of us stood awkwardly in clear groups, battle lines drawn.

And I'm trying to get all these people to help me? I better pick the teams carefully.

"Alright, alright, we're all here, including the bastard who stole my sword before I utterly wasted him," Siena began, sounding frustrated just being in Dice's presence. "Heck, even Frank's little friend is here for some reason."

"I came with you!" Tessa shrugged. "Heck, it's not like you're some secret club. Besides, you guys look like you needed another girl to balance this party out anyway."

Vega, sitting on the rock's edge, pulled back his pointed hood and grinned. "I guess I can be added to that list of people you've wasted too, eh Siena_the_Blade?"

Siena did a double take, as though just realizing he was with us. "So, you're the new Sirswift." She shifted up to him and batted her eyes. "Tell you what, I can waste you anytime you want."

It appears he actually managed to impress her.

I shook my head. "I know this is going to be hard, Siena, but if you could have both lips touching for the next ten minutes, it would help a lot."

Unsurprisingly, doing this didn't stop her from blowing raspberries mid-sentence while I was telling everyone what we had uncovered. Brock, Chloe, and I took turns telling the story, eventually explaining everything we wanted to say. After we told everyone about Malcolm, Siena's additions were reduced to a single whistle.

"Wow, you guys have been busy." Siena grinned at Brock and put her hands on her hips. "No wonder you two have teamed up again. So, you guys are trying to track down not just a chemist, but a *ghost-chemist.*"

As serious as the situation was, Siena framing the situation like that was enough to make even me scoff.

"That's better, Noah!" she exclaimed. "I thought you guys had forgotten we were even in a game with the lack of fun you were having. Now that you're trying to act like a great leader, you seem to be lacking the one thing that drew people to you in the first place. Seriously, when was the last time you did a dungeon for a reason other than your job?"

Chloe shrugged. "Two days ago."

Brock shook his head, still not fully onboard. "I want to get this out of the way quickly. You all know what we have to do, right?"

Siena nodded. "That's why I'm glad you left me out of this domestic dispute until now. Taking sides, party politics, team scraps—it's all a waste of my time. But searching dungeons for a Chaos Engine that leads to a secret debug room?" She spread her arms with a proud look on her face. "I'm your girl."

Frank nodded. "I'm in; let's do this."

"Tsh, I'm too busy to get involved." Data was giving us a suspicious grin. He then sighed. "You guys are just lucky that looking for glitches in this game is my job anyway."

It was a relief. Everyone seemed game—everyone except for Keri. As silence came over us, I noticed she was looking down at the rock before her eyes rose to meet Chloe's.

"Is this how it is? You tell us some story about a ghost in the game and you just think we're going to forget what happened and follow you?"

Chloe gripped Keri's arm, her eyes wide and her voice shrill as she cried, "Would I lie about something like this? About my own brother?"

"How do you know the Screamer is even Lucas?" Keri shouted back. Then she looked down. "For all we know, it could just be an avatar that looked like him."

"He has the exact same I.D. code as back when he was a beta tester!" Chloe shouted. "Are you saying that's just a coincid—?"

I put a hand up, knowing that Chloe and Keri screaming at each other wouldn't get us anywhere. "It's okay, Keri, but you heard it from Brock's own mouth. The person who killed his friends, who you were so eager to bring to justice, is still affecting this game. We're not asking you to join Wona. Just search a few dungeons for Chaos Engines to see if they go anywhere. Are you willing to do that?"

She turned her back on us. "As long as I don't have to be in a team with Chloe or you. I'll go with Siena, Frank, and Tessa."

Chloe bit her lip and looked away.

"That's fine." I raised my hands. "We have several dungeons with undetailed Chaos Engines to choose from."

"Oh, oh! Is there an underwater one?" Tessa asked, sounding a little too excited.

Data grinned. "There is. It's in a dungeon on Jossi Island called Lantis."

"Let's do that."

Keri spun away, ready to walk off. "Alright, let's go, girls." However, before she left, she looked over her shoulder at Chloe. "How sure are you that this Screamer was Lucas?"

Chloe's eyes remained focused. "I'm sure."

Without replying, Keri turned and walked off. Siena shrugged, and Frank and Tessa followed her, unaware that they needed Data's Bird's Eye to get off the island.

He waited a moment to see if they would return but then sighed. "Making them swim won't help our cause. Don't worry about giving me a dungeon; I could probably go over three of the dungeons with fewer Chaos Engines in the same time it takes you guys to do one."

He headed down the hill after them, leaving the four of us to fight over the rest. The dungeon with the most Chaos Engines was Apollo's Lookout, and considering I desperately didn't want to do that dungeon again, I suggested, "David, you wanted to explore that dungeon you appeared in before I blew you up, right?"

David inclined his head. "Yeah."

"Great. Chloe, take David and give him the full tour."

Chloe rolled her eyes and grabbed his large shoulder. "Alright, come on, Davey."

David grinned as she led him down the hill. "Just like old

times, eh Chloe?"

"Yeah, yeah."

She led him off, leaving Brock, Vega, Dice, and me. I eyed Dice, who hadn't spoken up since we had entered, professional enough not to talk unless spoken to. Putting him with Siena would have driven her nuts... but Data on the other hand.

He already acts professionally in the game.

"Dice, you go help Data. I'll keep my comms open just in case I need to ask you anything."

Dice nodded, his expression remaining solemn. "It's about time," he said as he vanished into the bushes.

I'm either a great employer for him to treat my orders so seriously or a really bad teammate for sucking the fun out of his job. Then again, considering how much he seemed to enjoy working with Sirswift and his team, I wouldn't say that's a bad thing.

"And then there were three," Vega announced as he stood to face Brock and I. "Now, what dungeon should we do, fellas?"

"If the deciding factor for the dungeon is how many Chaos Engines it has, I recommend we go to The Hall of Doors." Brock's eyes went vacant in memory as he delved into the vast knowledge of the Dream State he had accumulated over the years. "It has more Chaos Engines than Apollo's Lookout and can be accessed quickly."

That dungeon sounds familiar. Didn't Windsor mention it once?

Vega shrugged. "You're the master here, eh Brockodile?"

Brock gave me a confused look. "Who even is this guy?"

"Would you believe me if I said he's the best player in the Dream State and he's only been playing it for a week?"

Brock smirked in good humor. "No."

"Then do I have a surprise for you." Vega put an arm around Brock's shoulders.

Brock didn't look comfortable being so close to him, even in the game. I assumed that Vega's gift came with a lack in other areas, such as not having a very good sense of social space.

I summoned my Bird's Eye and gestured for them to get on. Brock shook his head and pulled out a Transfer Orb.

"I've been there before. This will be quicker."

I nodded and we touched the green orb. I saw the area option pop-up in my Key Triggers: New Calandor - Hollow. Grinning, I selected the option. After having my train ride prematurely cut short by Data, I was eager to return to exploring the vast Frontier.

We appeared in an opening in the wide grassland. Before us was a slope leading down to a massive hollow in the earth, I hadn't seen it on my other passes due to the large ceiling of earth that covered it. Together, we made our way down to the maroon Gateway that lit the shadows of the basin. I had learned from doing so many dungeons that the redder the Gateway was, the harder it was supposed to be, which only made sense considering The Engine Room was pure red and was considered the hardest in the game.

"Tertiatier?" I asked.

Brock lifted a brow at me. "For a place that has the most Chaos Engines in this world, would you expect it to be anything less?"

I raised my palms. "I guess not. I was just hoping for a Prima or Secotier dungeon for once."

After reaching the glowing Gateway, we all selected The Hall of Doors and vanished into the portal. We reappeared in a massive hall—that I thought looked more like a mausoleum— that was filled with giant stone archways made of beautiful purple and green patterns like the inside of an abalone shell. Around the high walls were moss-covered carvings and massive stained glass windows. As we walked in, our footsteps echoed through the enormous length of the place. I hadn't been this impressed with a dungeon since I first entered the Druid's. I quickly became suspicious.

"You know this place," the same voice I heard before whispered in my head.

I looked around, feeling like something dark was following me, and opened my comms. "Dice, was that you?"

No response. Brock and Vega gave me odd looks, so I returned my eyes to the dungeon.

"The lore in this place ..." I decided to guess rather than ask. "I bet this is where the Druids move from place to place throughout the land."

Vega grinned as we started to make our way through the massive hallway. "I thought you didn't know about this dungeon."

"It's just a hunch."

Brock grinned. "The lore of the Dream State is pretty interconnected if you pay attention to that kind of thing."

"So you don't know, either?" Vega asked.

Brock shook his head.

I laughed. "Maybe I should have brought Data after all."

"I'll admit it," Brock said, raising his hands. "Data is more of a lore geek than I am. As stoic as he is, he has his uses."

From his admission, it was obvious that when Data gave Brock his Color Blade to stop me, a steady truce had grown between them. Vega didn't pay our banter any heed.

"So, should we try one of these?" He gestured to one of the large doors leading off from the hallway. "Screw it, let's try this one."

"Careful. Most of these doors act as the Chaos Engines," Brock warned. "Sometimes it's an empty room with an item; other times it could be one of the hardest monsters in the game."

Vega shrugged and stalked forward. "The point of this dungeon is that we don't know until we open them, right? That means there's no point in speculating, so we should just go ahead and—" He pulled the large doors open, showing a wide opening into a dark room. "—open them!"

At first, nothing appeared from the darkness, but then there was a cry like the screeching of tire wheels, and a large Air-rex flew out from the room's cloud and up into the high ceiling of the hall. Vega somersaulted back from it, and just as Brock was lining the pterodactyl-like monster up with a bow he had equipped, a specialty dagger Vega had thrown was spinning toward the creature. He landed, spun, and fired a Plasma Beam that caught the dagger. As soon as it hit the creature, both it and the weapon exploded, killing the monster with one hit.

Air-rexes were of medium strength as far as Dream State monsters went, but it seemed it was the speed with which Vega had killed it that made Brock pause speechlessly, watching the Skill Points all go to Vega.

"How long did you say he's been playing here again?" Brock asked me.

"It will be my second week tomorrow," Vega answered, sounding nonchalant.

Brock looked at me incredulously.

I raised my eyebrows. "Told you so."

It seemed Vega didn't want to waste any time, for he was already running to the next door across the hall. "And what's behind door number... two?"

He pulled the doors open, but his excited expression fell when he saw that the room didn't have another churning cloud of a Chaos Engine. Instead there was an item, a piece of armor that I recognized. It was the exact same silver helmet I had seen on Lucas during his invasion of Heaven.

Completely ignorant of what the Screamers had looked like, Brock said, "The point behind this dungeon is to get a full set of this armor. The idea is that each item works as a piece of the key to get you into the boss room."

I walked in and picked up the helmet. "Seriously? Then ..."

Do each of them have a whole set of these? I recalled the way the helmet had flickered after Chloe had shot him. If that's the goal of this dungeon, you must be able to get the rest of the set here as well. But why would a Screamer choose this armor in particular as an illusion?

"I don't get it," Brock started, obviously obsessing over another subject. "The Dream State is one of the biggest game worlds there is and the only big MMO accessible by the Dream Engine. If you're such a good gamer, why hadn't you tried it out sooner?"

Vega winked at him. "If you're the best at something, never do it for free. I'm the best gamer, or at least one of the best, so I knew Wona would approach me eventually. Besides, I don't like playing one game for too long a period. It pins down the mind and traps you within its limitations. I knew that if I played this before, it wouldn't be as fun or as freeing as if I tried it without presumptions."

"And when Sirswift was arrested, it was the perfect timing to bring you in." I finished for him, already knowing the end of his story. "With his mixed Niche avatar, you would be given exactly the freedom you needed. I've read prodigy gamers are ridiculously good at pattern recognition, reaction times, and are extremely fast learners. Of course, all it would take was a week to get used to this world when you already had the most powerful avatar there is."

"I'm not sure if you're trying to flatter me or psychoanalyze me." Vega raised his slender elven palms and started toward the next door. "In either case, I'm on a limited time contract. Why wouldn't Wona let me into the party guns blazing?"

"Besides having to prove yourself first?" I shrugged, thinking of what I had to go through before I'd proven myself.

Brock grinned. "Jealous that you're not Windsor's golden boy anymore?"

"Are you looking for an argument?" I asked. "Do you really think I care about something like that?"

Brock shook his head. "Whatever."

Over the next few hours, we tried out over a hundred more doors, fighting a large Mountain Lion, a Swooping Bird from Onjira, and even a painted zombie from a dungeon I hadn't tried yet. We also found more items of the same Silver Armor the Screamers wore. Brock and I managed to get a few kills but I assumed it was only because Vega let us. He even had the nerve to give us tips as we fought, as if his knowledge of strategy was already more extensive than our own.

"You're wasting your Mana," he said after I had used my Perfect Storm spell to take out a cluster of Flying Fish—a prey class monster from one of the Chaos Engines. "You saw what I did with the Air-rex, didn't you? Brock, if you had just fired an arrow into each fish before he cast his spell, he could have killed every single one of them without needing a second attack."

"Well excuse me if Noah didn't wait for my lead," Brock countered.

"You were trying to kill off the fish one at a time!" I called back. "Besides, I could have used a water spell first if I wanted to."

"You see!" Vega exclaimed. "I let you guys fight on your own to see how you work as a team, and you end up arguing. Talk to each other during a fight. We're not lone-wolfing this dungeon, you know."

"Speak for yourself, Mr. One-Hit-Kill," Brock retorted.

Vega inclined his head and walked to the next set of doors. "I only do that when I know I can."

He swung the next two open. This time, however, his eyes widened and he leaped halfway across the hall in shock. Brock and I followed suit as we heard a rattling sound from the shadows. From them, a medium-sized avatar emerged, Silver Armor shaking unsteadily into sight.

"A Screamer!" I called. "Stay seven meters away from him or he'll knock you out of the Dream State!"

"Oh, come on!" Brock called. "What are the chances one shows up in the one dungeon we decide to look at?"

"Considering we went to the place that had the most Chaos Engines?" Vega answered as we continued to back off. "Pretty high. I don't know about you guys, but I think we're on to something."

"Keep him at a distance!" I reminded them as the Screamer advanced on us.

Chapter 17

LANTIS

A s they arrived in the Lantis dungeon, Frank was glad she'd remembered to take Keri to the Mermaids on Jossi Island to get the Aqua Lungs ability before heading there. Luckily, Jossi Island was a stone's throw away from the Yarburn coast, and the dungeon Tessa wanted to try was located just in from the shore.

Despite going out of their way to make sure she could come with them, Frank noticed that Keri had been strangely quiet since their meeting with Chloe and Noah. She figured that after Chloe had taken Noah's side she might've been a little sour around her, but after seeing her reaction to hearing about Chloe's brother, there seemed to be something deeper with their past. Frank had no desire to touch on that.

Although not entirely underwater, the dungeon known as Lantis had the most underwater areas available to satisfy Tessa's desires, as she could still only do Secotier dungeons. Frank looked around at the wide, echoing tunnels they had entered. Her eyes scanned the many pools that connected further into the cavern.

The monsters in them resembled either shark or octopi but weren't very strong—at least not by Siena's standards. If it weren't for the water they were fighting in, Frank doubted they would have even stopped her from ranting as she cut them down.

"Whaburbleyou-ink?" Siena said under the water, the weight of her chainmail allowing her to walk easily over the floor of the pool, talking even as they rose up into a bubble of open air within the cove. "Vega still technically lost, right? I mean, I wasn't the one who died during the fight."

"Why don't you just challenge him to a fair fight next time and see for yourself?" Tessa asked.

"Bah! A fair fight? You have no idea what this game is all about." Siena tried to continue when another water area of the dungeon began. "Okay fine, I'll stop using Kamikaze Orbs against—."

Frank ducked under the water, picking up the shell Resource Items on the tunnel floor, hoping she could get enough to synth new armor. She figured that if she earned a new set she might be able to get Siena to shut up about the Dragon Armor she'd helped her get from the Dragon's Nest. She hadn't been able to do a dungeon by herself that had the items to synth armor as good as the set she was already wearing.

I guess I should be thankful, but I'm not thankful enough to be reminded of it every day.

"How many Chaos Engines does this dungeon have anyway?" Frank asked as they emerged from the water once more. "I mean isn't that the reason we're here?"

Siena shook the water from her hair. "Those pools we passed had a few. There are more inland, but I think I recall them telling us that they can create Chaos Engines anywhere they want, so I don't think it matters."

"Then why are we even here?" Keri asked.

"I don't need an excuse to do dungeons, but if it helps my friends, it's win-win."

They came out into a wide cavern surrounded by glowing turquoise pools. Although the entire dungeon was technically underwater, there were many places in the dungeon that took place in air bubbles trapped within the wide caves. The water reflected off the limestone and Frank's armor as they moved between the pools. With loud splashes, several large Flying Fish jumped out of them.

"Time to get wet," Siena said, pulling out her recovered Ruby

Edge.

Tessa started firing her crossbow. "You're already wet! Give us a chance for once!"

Frank splashed into the pool with her Amethyst Edge drawn, illuminating the water with purple light. She slashed through the giant fish while Tessa took out the others in the cavern. They were only prey class monsters—the weakest kind. She moved on to the next pool to find more and discovered why this place was considered a Secotier Dungeon. Below the surface of the pool was an enormous underwater sea snake with a blade-pointed face and fins. When a scroll unveiled and said: Leviathan, she knew it was the boss.

She quickly kicked to the surface, burbling as she tried to stay afloat. "Boss! Hey, the boss is down here!"

"Bout time," Siena called. She ran and dived into the underwater battleground.

Siena unequipped her chainmail so she could swim instead of walk along the bottom of the pool. Swimming allowed her more speed, much more than Frank's plodding as she attempted to run under water. Even Keri swimming in her robes showed how futile walking was other than for collecting items at the bottom.

Keri cast a draining spell on the Leviathan, adding to the epic amount of damage that their Color Blades did while its razor blade fins lashed at them. Keri's healing stopped their Hit Points from getting too low, and while Tessa was still reloading, Siena finished off the monster with slow sweeping slashes, the red glow streaking in a line through the dark water. The Leviathan exploded in a flurry of bubbles.

Maybe we should've chosen a harder dungeon. This was almost too easy with our Color Blades.

After the Leviathan had vanished, the hole in the floor of the pool became unplugged, sucking Siena, Tessa, and Keri through the hole. Still wearing her armor, Frank was slower to be sucked down and saw that the Leviathan had left a Resource Item—no, several of them. As she was sucked past it, she managed to catch the shining, blade-like objects.

—— ACQUIRED 'SHARP SCALES X10' ——

Like Dragon Scales? Could I make new armor out of this?

Before she could look at the item's properties, Frank was sucked into the whirlpool behind her other teammates. It drew her down a dark tunnel, pulling her through it like some kind of hydro slide right up into the lagoon of the waterfall from which they had entered the dungeon.

—— DUNGEON COMPLETE ——

Despite being able to breathe underwater, she felt the urge to splutter from the sheer feeling of being drenched. She sat up in the small pool and looked around. In front of her she saw her teammates already waiting for her on the bank, and behind her was the steaming aqua-blue Gateway that hovered over the water's surface.

"What took you so long?" Tessa asked.

Frank slapped her shell-covered arm. "Armor."

Keri nodded and Siena moved in to help her up. She then stopped and her eyes widened at something behind her. Tessa looked up over her shoulder to see what it was and Frank turned. Standing on the high rock above the waterfall was an armored form. It was the same silver avatar she had seen during Heaven's grand opening.

"Ah, I'm pretty sure that's him, right?" Siena asked. "The one Noah was talking about?"

Keri was suddenly in the water, calling, "Lucas! Lucas, is that you?"

The Screamer's head twitched upon hearing that name and then walked forward from the rock, dropping with a splash into the pool below. The avatar emerged slowly behind the Gateway, water streaming from it.

"Keri, get back!" Siena called.

Keri's glare was intense. "No!" She stared intensely at the armored form. "If you are Lucas, where have you been all this time?"

Frank felt suddenly frazzled. She didn't expect to actually run into one of the Screamers. With the number of dungeons there were, the odds of one showing up were low enough to make her suspicious.

"Get back, Keri!" Siena warned. "You know what they can do."

"I have to know!" Keri yelled.

Before she could get any closer, Tessa fired an arrow from her crossbow. It hit the visor and stuck out of the player's face for a moment before disappearing. As Chloe's bullet had done to the last Screamer, the helmet began to flicker. However, unlike last time, when the Screamer's helmet vanished, the face under it wasn't swathed with long dark hair, but with blonde hair—and it didn't belong to a male avatar, but a female one.

"Girl wearing full armor." Siena pointed in amusement and looked at Frank. "She's doing a *you*, Efty... wait."

Frank wanted to say there was more to her avatar than just the armor she wore, but thought better of it. She didn't want to give the Screamer a target to run toward like last time.

Keri stopped and stared at the girl. "Wh-who are you?"

"I think I know her," Siena said, frowning. "That's—"

A sudden panic filled the blonde girl's face and a tremor ran through her armor, rippling the water at her feet. Lifting her head, the Screamer started to perform her namesake. The wail filled the lagoon, echoing off the rocks and seeming to shake the pool as she staggered toward them.

Siena acted immediately. She grabbed Keri, picked her up, and passed her to Frank. She then yelled, "Turn around! Tessa, run!"

Frank spun as Tessa fled into the bushes. Just as she claimed to have done against Vega, Siena pulled out a Kamikaze Orb, ran in, and ignited it. The explosion ripped through the air, seeming to struggle against the noise before engulfing the Screamer.

How many of those things does she have?

Frank staggered forward onto the rocks, her body blocking

Keri. The heat lasted for less than a minute before her eyes widened. She felt shocked—not that the Screamer was gone, but that she had survived the blast herself. The blast of a Kamikaze Orb was as strong as a single-hitting level three spell, and yet it had only taken her Hit Points into the red.

It wasn't until Tessa had returned from the bushes and Siena returned soon after with that big smile on her face that Frank rolled her eyes and understood why she could withstand such an explosion. "Please... don't say it."

Siena ignored her. "I knew that armor would come in handy. Dragon Armor has the strongest defense against heat magic. I bet you're glad I helped you to get it now!"

Frank bared her teeth. She knew Siena was right. The thing had saved her life. "I thought you said you were going to avoid using Kamikaze Orbs from now on?"

Siena shrugged. "My mother always told me that running away is better than losing."

Tessa raised an eyebrow at her. "Funny, I always thought running away was the same as losing."

The Ruby Edge flashed into her hand. "Running away helped me get this back, didn't it?"

Keri stood, shaking, her eyes intense. "That wasn't Lucas!"

"No." Siena looked to the rocks she had just blackened with her blast, as though waiting for the area to regenerate like the Dream State usually did after a skirmish. "But I'm pretty sure it was one of the beta testers. For a second there, I thought I actually recognized her."

"Did you see her I.D. code?" Keri asked. Siena nodded. "Try and remember it; Chloe might be able to identify her for you."

"I swear I knew her face ..." Siena looked up, trying to reclaim the memory. "Kristy! No, Kristina ...?" She shrugged. "In any case, she came out of nowhere."

Frank suddenly remembered why they had been there in the first place. "Is there a Chaos Engine around here? Maybe we can find out which one she used to get here."

Tessa nodded. "Further into the mountains, I'd say."

Chapter 18

RESOLVE

It was fortunate we all had some form of range fighting capability—me with my Boomstick, Vega with his spells, and Brock being a Range Niche. Granted, Vega's range spells didn't reach as far as my own without a specialty weapon, but as far Brock and I were concerned, being 'one of the best gamers' should make up for that.

After what I've seen him do, I wouldn't be surprised if he could stick himself to the ceiling and drop bombshells on people from above.

"Seven meters back, boys," I said as we backed off from the Screamer.

The armored avatar looked from me to Brock to Vega and then back to me as he advanced in staggering steps.

"And how are we supposed to measure seven meters, Noah?" Brock retorted. "You don't happen to have a ruler on you, do you?"

"Let's just say if you're close enough that your scanners can pick him up, you're too close."

We were also fortunate that The Hall of Doors had such a wide floor space to move about on. Although he hadn't started screaming yet, we spread out around him with a good distance between us. For reasons that went above me, Vega had pulled out his Jade Edge and was waving it around. I knew from my previous fight with a Screamer that this was not a good idea.

"I would put that away if I were you, man," I called. "If they take you out in a Tertiatier dungeon, it's the same as if they kill you. You'll lose whatever items are in your Key Triggers, that thing included if you have it equipped."

Vega grinned. "That's the point."

"What?"

Brock frowned. "Am I missing something here?"

I shook my head, watching as Vega waved the glowing green blade in front of the Screamer as if trying to get its attention. It was working. The Screamer was watching the Jade Edge swaying back and forth, mesmerized by it like a charmed snake. I shook my head but decided to remain focused on the Screamer's back, ready to launch a spell if needed.

Before I did, Vega called, "Do you remember the rooms we found the last piece of armor in?"

I nodded. "A few."

"You two might want to head back there as soon as I'm gone. I'm going to do something Siena taught me."

My bafflement piqued as the Screamer began its high-pitched banshee cry. Still, holding his Jade Edge before him, Vega walked into its scanning radius, but before he started cringing from the noise, he tossed the Color Blade toward it. The sword disappeared into his inventory, almost like the Screamer had accepted it on reflex, as soon as Sirswift's avatar vanished from the dungeon.

As satisfying as it was to see the image of one of my enemies be wiped out before me, it was quickly replaced with alarm when I saw the red Kamikaze Orb he had dropped. Brock and I bolted for cover in the nearest empty room: the door that had led to the silver breastplate. Even behind the door, we could feel the heat of the explosion; the booming surge of fire from the orb was enough to take out even the most powerful players if they weren't prepared for it.

"What the heck was he thinking?" Brock cried. "So much for being the best player in the game."

At first, I didn't get it either, but after a moment to think about it, Vega's ingenious plan dawned on me. I recalled how we had used the ITS to track items in the past using their individual codes. If my assumption was right, Vega had just sacrificed his Color Blade so we could track not the weapon, but the person carrying it.

"Now that's smart," I whispered to myself as the sound of the explosion died down.

"What are you talking about?" Brock shook his head as I opened the door to the hall.

"Let's go."

Before Brock could ask me anything more, I pulled out a Transfer Orb and teleported us to the entry of the hollow on the Frontier. It took less than a minute for Vega to return to the top of the grass slope.

"You just lost one of the rarest weapons in the game! Why on earth would you do that?" Brock called as he walked toward us.

"Because tracking that item is going to lead us straight to whatever Chaos Engine that Screamer comes out of as soon as he returns to the Dream State." Vega brushed his hands, as though done with a day's work. "If we get to it in time, we get inside the debug room and find out who's behind all this." He clapped his hands together. "Bada-bing bada-boom."

"But you could have used any item to do that!" Brock continued. "Why did you use the Color Blade?"

Vega shrugged. "I guess I figured that even someone with a mental illness would accept such a pretty sword."

I shook my head in amusement. "And you know its code?"

Vega almost looked hurt. "Noah, you really have to ask me that? You need to have a photographic memory to be as good as I am."

I raised my brow, deciding to keep my skepticism to myself. "In any case, we should log out and tell Chloe and David what we've found. Maybe Dice and Data noticed something in the data rig while we were under."

Brock eyed me suspiciously. "Weird how you always mention Chloe first these days. Are you two a thing now or something?"

"It's a bit more complicated than being on or off. With her

brother on the loose, we haven't really had time to seriously talk about it." I shrugged. "Let's just say she's staked a claim on me for now."

Brock shook his head in amusement. "Your villainess."

I wanted to argue, but after the way we had changed sides together, I couldn't really do it. One can have the best motivations in the world and still be judged on how they're executed.

"You're going to have to let that go," I said.

Brock shook his head and turned away. "Maybe when I know for sure that you're not pulling my leg about all of this."

"Why would I lie?" I yelled back.

"Boys, boys," Vega pleaded. "Let's see what the others have to say first, yeah?"

Brock looked away. "Whatever."

He vanished first, and then Vega and I selected the Wake-Up option quickly after. The whirring of gears pulled us back to waking. We looked up to see Chloe and David still sitting in their seats. Dice was leaning against the wall, looking unimpressed by how long they'd had to wait for us.

"Did you find anything?" I asked, addressing Chloe first.

Both Chloe and David shook their heads. "We didn't even make it through the dungeon. Damn Chaos Engine pumped out one too many powerful monsters for us to fight."

I grinned, knowing exactly how she felt. "I can't blame you. It took me three tries to beat that blasted place."

Chloe smirked. "Well, the first time you *were* up against your friends. What about you? Did you find any Screamers?"

I grinned. "Better than that. Vega managed to get one to steal his Color Blade."

David blanched with terror. "How is that a good thing?"

"We can track the Screamer by using the Item Tracking Software. It's our best chance to find out where they're coming from."

"What are you really hoping to find in this debug room?" Brock asked, as though he was still waiting for the point of my plan. "Even if they are there, they're just going to start screaming to take us out and find a new hiding place, and all of our hard work would have been for nothing."

"Weren't you the one who suggested that they might be using some kind of manifesto or code left over in the game by Malcolm?" I asked. "That's still *his* will playing out, and manipulating your old friends to do it."

Brock breathed out heavily and looked down. I could tell that every time I brought it up, he realized that getting justice for his friends was going to be more complicated than he had hoped.

No wonder he just wanted to blame Wona and get the Dream State shut down. People always want what's easy, and it would've been a lot easier than finding the actual person responsible. We don't even know who that really is yet. It can't be Malcolm.

"There are still things we don't know," I said, putting words to what I'd been thinking for a while, hoping to reach him. "You know, I read your blog when it was still up. I think Sue and I were some of the few who actually did."

"Easy, Noah," David said, seeming to sense Brock's anger broiling.

I raised a hand and continued. "I think it was the memory of what you said in those posts that made me seriously consider joining Wona when I was offered a job. What you said about Malcolm not answering your questions concerning how the drugs would let each player connect to the same dream, right? I knew that if I was on the inside I could get more information than just playing the blame game." I smiled at Chloe, who smiled back. "I admit I was lost in the fantasy for a while. That's until Chloe told me about her brother and the reason she decided to join with me. Now I know what we have to do, and Wona has given us the tools we need to do it. But we can't do it alone. Will you help us rescue Chloe's brother?"

"Yeah ..." David shook his head. "I'm still wrapping my head around that."

"Honestly, me too." Chloe closed her eyes. "Until recently, I thought he was dead."

"You see?" I gestured to Chloe. "Life isn't simple, Brock, but thanks to Vega, we have a direct path to the information we need to find out what's really happening to your friends and who's to blame. Don't believe Wona if you don't want to. Don't believe me. Believe your own eyes when we reach the debug room and find out who's controlling these guys."

Brock raised his head. His eyes were red, but he slowly nodded. He gave me an echo of the cheesy grin he used to always wear. "Jeez Noah, even when you make sense you still come off like a prick."

Seeing that look on Brock's face, I knew that he had finally come around, if only a little. Friendships took moments to destroy but ages to mend; at least we had made a start. I could see he understood now where I was coming from, and understanding was the best foundation for forgiveness.

"I'll work on that."

"Great!" David sat back in his recliner. "So, what's the next step?"

"I thought you didn't want to be involved."

Brock and I looked at him and he shrugged.

"Hey, I only didn't want to be involved before because you two were at each other's throats. If you're both on the same side again, you can sure as heck count me in, too."

There was a moment of silence and we all smiled dumbly at each other in the moment it took us to realize that the three musketeers were back together again. Then Dice interrupted us with his own report.

"If you three are done with this make-up session, this is what Data and I found." We all looked up at him, the only one in the room whose expression had remained solemn during our heart-to-heart. He pulled a screen from the wall to show a full map of the Dream State—six circles pulsing around six different areas. "There have been six other appearances of the Screamers around the Dream State during your little mission. Several parties vanished near Chaos Engines and reported the glitch. Only one party survived intact."

"Siena?" I asked.

Dice nodded and I grinned.

"Figures."

"It's almost like they knew we were searching for them," Chloe said, cupping her chin. "But how?"

We all looked around in thought before Vega stood from his chair and spread his arms excitedly. "We should be happy, you guys! Don't you get what this means? We're making them nervous, and that means we're on the right track. That means—"

I nodded. "We're getting closer. Alright Vega, can you give all the players working for Wona the code of the Jade Edge? Tell them to warn us if they see it reappear in the Dream State so we can find out how he's getting in from the debug room. Let's flush these Screamers out and see who or what's behind all of this."

"Oh yeah!" David cheered, putting a hand out as though expecting an on-three moment.

I felt bad for leaving him hanging, I really did.

Chapter 19

RETRACE

"So, when are we going to reach this Chaos Engine?" Frank asked.

The four of them moved between the green flax bushes and frond hanging trees leading up the Jossi Hills.

"*Engines*," Siena corrected. "There are a few around here. Like in Yarburn, they're mostly around the openings to caves leading to dungeons or—"

"Then how do we find out which one the Screamer came from?" Keri sighed, sounding agitated. "Why are we even doing this?"

"Because Chloe's brother was missing and is now one of them?" Frank suggested.

"His name is Lucas, and the guy left me for no reason, without even a word, over a year ago."

Siena scoffed. "No reason? Like being in a group of gamers dedicated to logging people out. Doesn't really seem convincing to me… if what we've been told is anything to go by."

Keri caught up with her, brow furrowed. "What are you talking about?"

"I should have just kept quiet." Siena shook her head, then stared down at Keri. "Listen, not all of the beta testers died, you know. Some of them suffered a far worse fate and ended up losing their mental faculties. Did you not see the girl before I blew her to kingdom come? She was unresponsive, she was shaking, and her face looked utterly vacant even when our archer here—"

"Tessa!" Tessa said, sounding angry that Siena didn't remember her name.

"*Tessa* shot her in the face! Now, don't you think that Lucas could've suffered a similar fate and is now being led by the nose as well? Chloe seems to think so. Why else would she be trying so hard to find these people? She's worried about her brother!"

Keri stopped and her eyes widened. There were no tears, but if the game had allowed it, Frank was sure that they would have been streaming down her face. Instead of responding, Keri ducked her head and began running back down the hill.

Frank went to follow her, but Siena held her back. "Leave her be. The girl's just having a hissy fit."

She spun with a huff and continued up the hill. Frank thought she could see a small crack in Siena's facade and had an idea why. Ever since Frank had met her, she knew that Siena's main goal in the Dream State was to have fun, but lately she had become nearly cartoonish in her attempts to draw out the excitement from everyone. It was almost like, with everything serious going on with the Screamers, she was attempting to overcompensate by acting ridiculous.

But she can't escape the fact this is actually affecting her friends. She's trying everything to keep up the levity, but all this drama must be getting to her as well.

Frank sighed and followed her toward the first cave that she claimed had a Chaos Engine. To her logic, it made sense that the Screamer came from the nearest one.

They arrived less than a minute later.

"Alright. See how there's a smaller cave above the main entrance?" Siena said, pointing to the boulders sticking out from the hillside. "I'm pretty sure that's where the Chaos Engine is hiding."

Frank nodded, following to where Siena was pointing. The entire hill in the surrounding area of the forest was made up of rock that appeared to be puzzled together with clay to form the opening to a cave, which was surrounded by bushes. In the lush forest, it was a beautiful setup, and Frank could see how the smaller cave above the first one would be barely noticeable under the low branches.

Siena stopped, and Frank and Tessa halted behind her. "Okay, so the idea is that we want to get into the Chaos Engine before it disappears. Tessa, you're the fastest. You should be able to get in there, so while Frank and I fight whatever monster comes out of that thing, you go straight for the cloud. I'll go first and Tessa can use me as a boost to get in."

Tessa nodded. Frank figured that with her tiny elven avatar, she was the only one who could fit in there anyway.

"Okay, let's do this."

Siena's Ruby Edge flashed into her hand and she rushed out into the opening in front of the cave. Tessa dashed behind her, and Frank lumbered behind them. Before anything could emerge, Siena slid on her knees, spun to link her hands together, and yelled, "Now!"

Tessa leaped onto Siena's linked arms, using her as a springboard to jump higher than the roof of the first entrance.

As soon as her small form came within scanning distance of the Chaos Engine above the cave, the darkness inside began to accumulate into the form of the monster that was emerging. Just as the Lupine beast appeared, Tessa was beside it, flying through the smaller cave as the growling monster landed.

Frank's Amethyst Edge flashed into her hand, and she utilized the weight of her armor into a downward blow on the giant wolf. It was quick, and she barely nicked the thing before it jumped up onto her back. Instead of trying to get it off her, Frank fell back onto it. The Lupine yelped as her armor drove it into the ground. Then she spun and stabbed down with her sword to finish it off.

Siena stood back, and as Frank rose, she saw she was sticking out her bottom lip, looking begrudgingly impressed. "You're getting better, Efty."

Frank nodded. "What about Tessa?"

Tessa emerged from the smaller cave, rubbing her head.

"Nothing's back there!"

Frank groaned and looked to Siena.

"What? You were expecting to get lucky with the first one?" She spun back to continue up the hill. "From the way you whine all the time, Efty, I wouldn't have taken you for an optimist."

Do I really complain that much?

Tessa jumped down from the upper cave and they continued on up the hill. They repeated this two more times, fighting a poison lizard and an armored knight from a dungeon wholly different to the setting they were in. But that was the nature of Chaos Engines, after all.

Where Tessa took out the lizard, Siena let Frank take the knight, claiming that in her armor, she would make for a more interesting fight. This would have been true if not for the fact that her Color Blade allowed her to easily cut through its armor.

"Now, I don't know exactly where the last Chaos Engine in this place is," Siena said as they finally came to the top of the hill. "All I've heard is that it's up high and in some kind of hole." She stopped and looked back at Frank.

Frank was staring in wonder at the view they had from this high up. Not only could she see nearly all around the outer shore of Jossi Island, but they had an even better view of the Yarburn peninsula west of them.

"Speaking of a hole ..." Siena started again, obviously trying to gain her attention. "Frank, you have to admit that Vega had an unfair advantage in The Catacombs with his magic, right? If we were out in the open or in some sort of ring where magic couldn't be used, surely I would have beaten him."

"Sounds like you're having trouble getting over this guy," Tessa commented.

"Get over him?" Siena said in outrage. "I don't want to get over him! I want to find a way to beat him. Until I do, I won't be able to get him off my mind!"

Tessa scoffed. "Sounds like someone's in love."

"Yeah, in love with being the best," Frank returned. "I'm sure there'd be some kind of Colosseum in the Dream State where you two could fight."

"Or fool around," Tessa cut in.

"Too bad there's no way you can do that in-game." Siena paused and turned to their skeptical gazes. "What? Am I really the only one here who's tried?"

"With who?" Frank asked. "Data?"

Frank and Tessa stopped and laughed.

"No wonder that guy's wrapped around your little finger!" Frank burst out.

"Why else but my feminine wiles?" Siena threw her hands up in exasperation when she saw that they were still giggling and turned back. "Bah, children."

Frank was about to ask how old Siena was in real life when her boot fell through the ground with the sound of snapping wood. They both spun back as the weight of her fall drove her down through the ground, hitting her helmet on the side of the hole. She gasped and reached out to grab the edge. Her gauntleted hand missed despite her wide reach, and she continued falling …

And falling …

And falling …

The last thing she heard was Siena say, "Oh, that's right, the Chaos Engine was in a well!" before her voice was cut off and Frank landed on a hard metal floor with a loud *clang!*

She winced and pulled off her helmet, rubbing away what felt like a bruise on her bottom, when she saw where she was. The place was unlike anywhere in the Dream State she had seen. Brightly colored lights filled an unnaturally dark and cool hallway.

Or does it only feel cool because I've just been in a place with the heat of the Bahamas?

However, as she looked around some more, she had to really consider what she was seeing. Artificial lights, buttons, metal grated floor, pipes, and a glowing ramp leading up to what looked like a sci-fi warp ring from Stargate.

A future era dungeon? No, wait. This might be the opening to the debug room!

She smiled. "You guys, I found it!" she called up. Then she

realized there was a ceiling above her, meaning they wouldn't have been able to hear her no matter loudly she shouted.

She started to panic, but then remembered there was more than one way to talk to them. She pulled up her comms and went to annotate what she had just said when—

—— PROGRAM ERROR ——

What the? She tried to message them again, but after getting the same program error window, she stood up and looked around. *Well, I'm here now. Guess I should explore the place.*

She walked down the glowing corridor toward the ramp. She didn't know if Siena and Tessa could follow her, but she didn't plan on waiting around to find out. Stepping up into the rings, she put her helmet back on and waited for the device to descend and take her to next area of the debug room. Nothing happened.

"Oh, come on!" Frank called. "After spending hours searching for this place, this thing isn't even going to work?"

The sound of Siena and Tessa hitting the floor behind her stopped her from cursing the roof down in frustration.

"Found it!" Siena called, as though she were the first one to arrive.

"This place is amazing!" Tessa called, her voice echoing off the walls.

Frank whirled on them. "Amazing my foot! This thing won't even work!"

Siena ran up onto the platform, and after a second with no effect, she began jumping up and down, almost like she was punishing it for disobeying her will. She looked from Keri to Tessa and back to the floor, cupping her chin.

"We must be missing something that makes it work."

Frank shrugged. "Maybe one of the others will know."

Siena whined like a child in her disappointment. "Oh man! But I wanted to be the first one to enter the place!" She huffed, brushed her ponytail to one side, and spun about. "Alright fine, let's go find the others."

Frank grinned, thinking of the items she had received after they had defeated the Leviathan.

And let's get me some new armor.

Chapter 20

THE VISIT

I was sitting in the living room of Chloe's apartment when I heard a knock at the door. Chloe was taking a shower, so I decided to go see who it was. When I opened the door, seeing Keri was more than a little surprising. It was my first time seeing her in real life, but like Chloe, she was of a similar size to her avatar. She also had the same round face, blue eyes, and blonde hair. Unlike Chloe—who was a little taller than her avatar—Keri was of a comparable height with her Spellcaster Niche.

She looked confused by my appearance. "N-Noah? The receptionist told me this is Chloe's room. Did she send me to the wrong place?"

"No, no. She's in the shower. Come in; she'll be out any minute."

Keri seemed hesitant, but then nodded and walked inside.

"So, this is how the other half lives," she said as she glanced around the large apartment in awe.

"Not bad, eh?"

"So this is what you sold—" She stopped and shook her head. "You know, never mind."

We sat down on the couch and waited for Chloe to get out of the shower.

"How was the dungeon with Siena, Frank, and Tessa?" I asked.

"Alright, but we didn't find anything wrong with the Chaos Engines. Siena went with Frank and Tessa to find more over the island after we ran into a Screamer." Keri looked down and grinned. "Siena blew it up with a Kamikaze Orb."

I nodded. "I heard you guys got away somehow. There were six attacks that happened at once. You guys were the only party that survived. Did you find the Chaos Engine he came out of?"

"The Screamer was actually a *she* this time." Keri looked down. "But that's not why I'm here."

The bathroom door opened and Chloe walked out wearing only a towel. "Noah, you can have one too, if you wa—"

She stopped and went red in the face. Keri seemed surprised by this, but after seeing Chloe's reaction, she began to giggle.

Chloe smiled awkwardly back. "Ah, I'm going to get changed."

Keri nodded. "I think that would be best."

She entered her room hurriedly.

"So, was Lantis fun?"

Keri nodded. "It was."

"Find the Chaos Engine?"

Keri shook her head.

"And may I ask what encouraged this visit?" I asked.

"Siena told me something I should have worked out for myself a long time ago."

"Which is?"

Keri shook her head. "There's no point talking about it until Chloe's out here."

On cue, Chloe exited her room and sat down with us. "What are you doing here?"

Keri's eyes drifted to the table between us. "I came to apologize. When you told me that Lucas was back, I thought it was just some kind of ploy to get us together again. But after seeing the Screamers myself, I'm starting to understand why you decided to join Wona."

"Keri, I didn't know about the Screamers until recently. I just thought that joining the company connected to Lucas' disappearance might have more information on what happened." This time Chloe looked down guiltily. "I should have told you everything that happened to him a long time ago. I... I just didn't want it to hurt you, you know? You were so torn up when Lucas abandoned you for his project and …"

Keri looked up to see the tears in Chloe's eyes. She stepped right over the table and the two embraced. It was my turn to look guilty. Being there to witness such an emotional moment between two friends made me feel out of place. I stood up to leave, but Keri pulled me back.

"Noah, wait."

I turned back to see tears in her eyes too, but unlike Chloe who was a blubbering mess, she looked determined.

"Siena managed to get the I.D. code of the Screamer before she blew it up. Maybe you should get it off her so you can find out which beta tester she was."

I lifted an eyebrow. "So you believe me now?"

Keri nodded. "Siena said she recognized her."

I nodded. "I'll log in and go talk to her."

I left the girls in Chloe's room to make up and headed to the elevator. I was glad Keri had come around. She wasn't as stubborn as Brock when it came to her friends. The lift took me down to the underground GC where Dice appeared to be waiting for me.

"Data said he's located the Jade Edge's item code in the game," he said.

I nodded and sat down on the recliner. "Let me guess: The Hall of Doors?"

Dice frowned. "How did you know? He says it appears there every hour or so."

I nodded. "I think they're using the Chaos Engines there to go from one setting to another without the need of Transfer Orbs. That's why we haven't been able to track them. There are too many Chaos Engines there."

I took a vial of DSD and lowered the Dream Engine helmet onto my head. "Tell Data to keep tracking. There's one more thing I have to do before we go after them."

Dice gave me the thumbs up, his face unchanging, as the recliner lowered me down into the darkness and I fell asleep. The next time my eyes opened, I saw the Dream State menu. I logged in and appeared in the last place I had been: The Calandor Frontier.

The first thing I noticed after I arrived on the wide field of grass was that I had messages waiting for me. I brought up my comms window and read them. One was from Siena, saying, "Ha-ha, we found the debug room before you! We're going on ahead!"

The next was from Frank, saying, "Siena's lying, we can't get past the main entrance. There's a Gateway, but for some reason, it won't teleport us inside."

I nodded, glad that Siena couldn't give away our whole plan without knowing how to get in.

"Dice, where are Siena and Frank now?" I asked.

"Both of them are on the Yarburn Coast."

I nodded, pulled out my Transfer Orb and selected: Yarburn - Coast. I appeared there with a flash and looked down the beach, trying to find them. I first noticed Frank's large armored form walking up from the shoreline. Siena and Tessa walked ahead of her. I ran to catch up with them.

"Alright you three, what did you see? Spill it."

Siena grinned. "Make me."

Frank rolled her eyes. "Come with me and I'll tell you, but I have to do something first. I've had enough of lugging this bloody armor around."

I nodded as she trudged onto the stone paths of Yarburn, making her way to the Synth Square. I followed with the others, making our way past palm trees and shops smelling of fish. Siena looked confused by Frank's sudden determination.

I strode to keep up with Frank. "So?"

"I fell into a Chaos Engine in a well on Jossi Island by mistake," Frank said as we came to the bridges of a dock that led out over the water, with each bridge leading to a different store. "It transported us to a sci-fi, futurey-looking hallway that led up to a platform and rings like a Gateway from Stargate. But no matter what we did, we couldn't get the blasted thing to activate and take us into the debug room."

"And we were searching for hours, too!" Tessa said to emphasize her annoyance.

I looked down in thought. "And you had your full armor on when you tried it?"

Frank nodded and Siena raised an eyebrow.

So the key is not wearing full armor.

"You see, your damnable armor didn't do anything that time!" Frank said to her, then walked into the synth store that looked to be an armory.

I gave Siena a confused looked as if to say 'What's with her?' and Siena shrugged in a 'Beats me' kind of way. Frank returned a few minutes later, but instead of wearing her red shell-like Dragon Armor, she was wearing a spiky, blue set that seemed to be made from scales and razor-sharp fins.

Frank looked around at us. "There. This is much lighter and has a much higher damage impact if I fall on top of things."

"Oh, good," Siena said. "That's the second set of armor I helped you get!"

"What? No!" Frank shouted, shaking her head and sighing. "Argh! You can't take all the credit. Keri and Tessa helped too!"

With all this talk of armor, an idea hit me.

The Screamers all have the same armor. Didn't Brock say that the point of The Hall of Doors was to collect the entire suit of armor to access the boss room? What if the portal they're talking about uses the same code? That type of armor as an illusion might be the right combination to allow us access.

"It won't work …" I said, the thought escaping me in my revelation before I stopped myself. I still didn't know if I wanted Siena's impulsiveness involved with what I had planned.

"What would it matter?" Siena asked.

I frowned as a theory began to coalesce in my mind. "Never mind. You got the Screamer's I.D. code, I take it?"

Siena grinned. "You bet I did, but I'm not going to give it to you until you tell me what you were thinking just then. You've just realized something, so now you spill it!"

I ground out a sigh. She had me, and I knew she would sense if I lied.

"The dungeon Brock, Vega, and—"

"Vega!" Siena interrupted suddenly as though shocked, but then calmed herself and rolled her wrist. "Sorry, continue."

"The dungeon we did was a hallway of doors, and behind each door was either a Chaos Engine or a piece of armor. It was the exact same armor that all of the Screamers caught on video just happen to be wearing."

Frank nodded. "And you think this dungeon has something to do with gaining entrance into the debug room? Like some kind of access criteria for completing the dungeon is the same code they use for the portal?"

Tessa shrugged. "It could just be the armor?"

I shook my head. "The armor they're wearing isn't real. It's just an illusion spell that's been manipulated to look …"

I trailed off as a sudden memory came over me. Since my time in the Dream State, I had only known one other person who had used the illusion spell in such a way. During my mission to save Sue in Rubik's Castle, Sirswift had cast the coded spell to trick me into thinking Sue in the room with us.

Wona told me that Sirswift was never very good at the technical side of the game. Maybe it was one of his friends who showed him how to do it… or maybe it was someone else, someone with more knowledge of the game's workings.

I gasped as all of the information seemed to come together at once like a giant jigsaw puzzle revealing a complete image. I had never really understood Samuel's motives before, why he would jeopardize his uncle's company by trying to have someone killed, or why he would try to cover it up without telling him about it. None of it made sense *if* he was working alone, but now I was starting to see the full picture. I was beginning to think that might not have been the case.

Malcolm's final wish was to harm Wona through the game, to sabotage the company that he was removed from before his experiments were complete. Why would Samuel go out of his way to disobey Windsor unless he was following Malcolm's orders instead?

Was Samuel getting his orders directly from Malcolm?

"Ah, Noah?" Siena asked.

I looked up at the three of them, eyes wide. "I-I have to go."

L ess than an hour later, I was in a cab headed toward the jail where Samuel was being held before his trial. As much as I didn't want to see Sue's murderer, I had already faced the buildup of seeing Sirswift in-game when confronting Vega, and I knew I would have to see him in court anyway. I was also too determined to see if my suspicion was correct, and that overtook any discomfort I might feel.

The taxi pulled over on the side of the road outside the police station. I paid the driver with a swipe of my card and got out. It seemed the Dream State wasn't the only place I had infinite Moola now. My first week's wages were more than enough to cover any expenses. Knowing that the longer I dragged it out, the harder it would be, I strode toward the station and walked into the reception room.

There was a kindly old lady in uniform sitting behind the desk who gave me a smile as I entered. "Hello dear, how can I help you?"

"Hello, I've been given permission by a family member to visit one of your detainees in the holding cells before he goes to trial."

"Okay." The woman shook her mouse and peered at the monitor in front of her. "Which inmate would you like to see?"

"Samuel Wona."

She looked at me and then back to her computer, typing in a few keys. "And you have been given permission, you say. By whom?"

"His uncle, Windsor Wona."

She typed in some keys again and sighed. "Jack, could you take this young man to holding cell B?"

A portly African-American man holding a cup of coffee

appeared from a back room. "Sure thing."

"Just don't be too long," the woman said. "I might need you in a moment."

Jack nodded and led me to a thick metal door. He swiped an I.D. card and I followed him into the corridor.

"Are you a friend of the inmate?" Jack asked.

I shook my head. "Not particularly. I just need to ask him something."

The policeman snorted and said, "Okay, detective," as if he found someone my age acting so serious amusing.

He led me through two more doors, both of them barred, before taking me to a small white room with a chair on either side of a metal table.

"This is the interview room. I'll bring Samuel in, so just hold tight for a moment."

Jack left the room, and I sat on one side of the table. My heart quickened as I waited, nerves and anger filling my mind. Five minutes later, Jack reappeared escorting a young Asian-American man in handcuffs. He looked confused for a moment, but then seemed to recognize my face.

"Ah, NotThatNoah," he said as he sat down in the metal chair opposite me. "Come to see me in my misery, eh? To gloat over your successful partnership with my rat of an uncle, hmm?"

The man before me had lured me to Rubik's Castle with his team by convincing me Sue was there. It was all just an attempt to take my Transfer Orb and put me in a coma to keep me quiet. While trying to reclaim the orb from him in the Broken Clock Tower, I realized how futile it was to fight him with his Instant Respawn ability. It was then that I knew that getting the power that Wona had in the real world was the only way I could truly beat him and bring him to justice, no matter what it cost. And I had.

I clenched my jaw, recalling why I was here.

"As satisfying as it is to see you in chains after what you did to me, that's not why I'm here. There's something I want to know."

"Loose ends, Noah? *You* were just a loose end I couldn't seem to tie up, that's all. But sure, I'll bite." He grinned. Every aspect of his avatar was different, from his height to his skin tone, but that grin was the same. "What do you want to know?"

"Your uncle showed me the email telling you just to scare Sue and me, but not to harm us. You might be a little overambitious, but you don't strike me as a killer. I don't think it was even your idea to crash into us that night, and I have a strange feeling I know who convinced you to do it."

Samuel's eyes narrowed. He looked around for a second before leaning in close and saying so only I could hear, "Are you hearing the whispers, too?"

I felt my blood freeze. "Whispers... you mean in the game?"

I had heard words occasionally while in the game, but I always thought it was just Vega or Dice talking over the comms feed—or maybe a glitch. With the hope that agreeing would keep him talking, I nodded.

He grinned and leaned back in his chair. "So, that's why you're here. You think you're the next one he chose! Hah, you're so full of it."

"What do you mean?" At first, I thought he was speaking of Windsor, but the way Samuel didn't say his name suggested otherwise.

"You think everything's about you, don't you? That he told me to run you off the road to kill *you*, that you're hearing him now because he wants *you* next." Samuel shook his head. "It has nothing to do with you; it all has to do with my traitor of an uncle. *He* knew that in the end, Windsor would turn me in, just like with him."

"You mean... Malcolm?" I asked, dread filling me.

"Their grudge goes way back and has lasted beyond death, it seems." Samuel shook his head and leaned forward again. "The whispers, they told me what my uncle did, and I'm pretty sure he knew. It was only when his dirty secrets were revealed that he snitched on Malcolm, too—his best friend!" He slammed his fists into the table. "Hah!"

"Easy," Jack warned, watching Samuel like a hawk. "One

more outburst and you're back to your cell."

"No, wait. Why did you listen to him?" I asked, trying to get all the information I could. "You should have known how trying to kill us all would turn out, so why?"

Samuel grinned. "Why do you think? *He's* living proof that immortality is possible in the Dream State. I thought that if I did what he said …"

I felt my stomach drop and forced myself to swallow. "That he would tell you how he did it… give you the secret to eternal life in the Dream State."

Sue's murderer nodded. "Bingo."

"But you were tricked," I continued. "It can't really be him, can it? He died over three years ago. Surely whatever is telling you and the Screamers to do this is just something he did to the software, some kind of code he left behind, right?"

"All I heard were the whispers." Samuel raised his hands, but his handcuffs prevented them from going very high. "I guess you could say he appealed to my ego, saying that immortality was waiting for me. It was worth a shot. I'm not even sure now. His words just felt so… human."

"Where did you first hear the whispers?" I asked.

"Never the same place twice. The only consistency was that I was always near a Chaos Engine when I heard them… and later… when I saw him."

I thought back to all of the times I had heard the voice in my own head. Apollo's Lookout, The Engine Room, The Catacombs, The Hall of Doors; each place had a Chaos Engine nearby.

Was I hearing Malcolm's voice all along? I had to pause as the second thing Samuel said finally registered. *Did he just say …?*

"Wait, you saw him in the game?"

Samuel leaned in. "It was just a flicker at first, something I mistook as being a glitch in a few dungeons. But then it started to take shape out of the corner of my eye, like he was gaining more of a foothold in the world the more I listened to him. What I felt from that darkness… well, I knew his influence would take over the whole of the Dream State sooner or later anyway."

My mind raced back to the times I had heard the whispers. I *had* seen dark flickers out of the corner of my eye as well. Nothing substantial enough to call a shadow, but they had been there.

Not just in the debug room then. If Malcolm is alive, he can enter the Dream State too, if only in a limited capacity.

"This doesn't make sense. He's been dead for years. Why would all this be starting now?" I asked, trying to find a reason not to believe him. "Surely he could have used the Screamers whenever he wanted if that was the case."

Samuel's shoulders rose. "Look at where we are, Noah. I failed, you failed, and heck, even Brockodile failed to take down my uncle's company. Even after all the hard work I did to soil its name, he still managed to find some way to weasel his way out of it. Don't you get it yet? This wasn't his first plan, or even his plan B. This is his *backup* plan."

My jaw clenched involuntarily as anger rose in me. *I'm being used to destroy Wona. And Brock too? But how is that even possible? Malcolm died before he even knew about Sue and me!*

"Giving you instructions made sense." I scowled. "But why is he now whispering to me? I have no reason to sabotage Windsor."

"Don't be so sure." Samuel sneered and raised an eyebrow at me. "You've changed sides before."

Breathing heavily, I got up. The guard seemed taken aback as my leg hit the chair and sent it skidding along the floor. He moved to let me through. I thanked him and left the station without looking back. Whether or not Malcolm was in the Dream State, or if the voices belonged to someone else, the only way to find out would be to enter the debug room and face the Screamers. I had to talk to them and find out just what in the heck was going on.

I need the armor from The Hall of Doors. Using it as an illusion might be able to get us inside. This had better work.

Chapter 21
THE PRINCIPLE DRUID

My first task was simple: get a complete set of the armor from The Hall of Doors. At least, it seemed simple when I started.

According to Dice, reprogramming an illusion spell needed either a collection of files or items that you could swap with the image of your garments in the spell's navigational code. I decided to leave the technical stuff to him and focus on collecting what was needed to get it done.

The last time I had entered the giant mausoleum of the Hall, my motivation was to check all of the Chaos Engines. Now that we knew of one that was a direct link to the debug room, I went straight to the doors that had the items. Unfortunately, they had been swapped around and I was forced to fight whatever monsters the Chaos Engines produced.

Being a Tertiatier dungeon, I was still pushing my luck, particularly in facing so many Chaos Engines alone. That's why, when Brock showed up in the hall with a flash of light and offered to help, I couldn't think of a reason to refuse.

In my mind, this was the kind of olive branch I had been waiting for him to extend since we had joined sides again.

"Siena told me about your theory of the Screamers' armor," he said.

I nodded. "I only need one copy of the armor to make the illusion on whoever I want. You don't need your own."

"First you'll have to get all of the armor pieces." He raised an eyebrow as if waiting for me to deny this. "I thought I might speed up the process by helping out."

"I won't say no to that, but what changed your mind?"

Brock grinned. "What can I say? You've made me curious."

Together we turned toward the next door and opened it. The cloud of a Chaos Engine converged into a large Basilisk.

"This is one of the tougher monsters from the Cobra's Den," Brock said. "It can stun you with its bite."

"Not a problem."

I jumped away from its first lunge, jaws snapping at me. Brock fired a metal arrow into its side. Remembering what Vega had done to the Air-rex, I cast a Plasma Beam in the direction of the arrow. Working as a conductor, the line of lightning caught the arrow and it exploded, cutting the giant snake's Hit Points in half. I then pulled out my Sapphire Edge, spun, and cut through it to finish it off. Although I didn't get bitten as it fell on me, the game couldn't seem to tell between a bite and getting scraped by the fang, because after the Basilisk had vanished I couldn't move.

Brock turned to the next door as I failed to rise.

"Wait a minute, it got me."

Brock raised his palms as he approached the next door. "It's alright. I'm not a noob, remember?"

Being stuck there, I couldn't help but hold my breath as he opened the next door.

"Alright, I have a right greave here," he said as he entered and returned with a piece of leg armor. "What does that leave?"

I sighed and felt the stunning effect wear off. "A backplate, a gauntlet, and the left shoulder armor."

"Okay then, let's get on with it."

I rose to my feet and we continued down the large hall, opening doors, fighting monsters, and collecting items. Every so often there was a room with a gag item, like a vase on a plinth that did nothing according to the information shown in our inventory.

The majority of the times it was a Chaos Engine. At one point in the dungeon, we fought the same Mother Spider I'd encountered in Widow's Forest. I cut it down with my Sapphire Edge as easily as Data had during our first encounter with it. A collection of Spirit Lanterns from the Penance Mines was behind the next door, and Brock took them out with some ice arrows. Behind the next was a broken-down robot that looked the same as the models from Heaven's Museum, and Brock used one of his lightning arrows to fry it.

We managed to collect every piece of armor before we came to the end of the long corridor. Our trudging footsteps echoed around the hall as we came upon the massive stained glass doors at the dead end. We selected the doors and a list of the items we received was shown to come together to look just like one of the Screamers.

Words then appeared in front of our vision:

—— **Inside awaits a true challenge. Are you prepared?** ——

—— **YES/NO** ——

Not only was this the first dungeon I had done in the Dream State where we had to collect a set of items to get to the final boss, but it was the first dungeon that had warned me of the boss before entering.

This must be a tough one. Is this the same code to use the Gateway to the debug room?

Brock said, "Yes," and the doors swung open with a boom.

"We've got the armor. If we lose here, this whole thing would have been a waste of time."

"Scared?" he asked. "Come on, Noah. It's only when we've got something to lose that this game is any fun anyway."

I smirked. "Data said something like that when I first met him."

"No, he didn't."

I nodded. "He totally did."

We walked through into a wide hall surrounded by shelves

of old books. The library appeared to be similar to the one from Druid's Keep, but more organized and with sunbeams shining down in different colors from the window above.

There were already more than enough connections between the Keep and this Hall that my suspicion of their resemblance only seemed to crystallize when a small, old man in familiar robes walked around the corner of one of the large shelves. A scroll unrolled to reveal the boss's title: Principle Druid.

"Looks like the Dark Warrior didn't get them all, after all," I said.

Brock raised a brow at me. "What's that supposed to mean?"

"The Principle Druid was originally the boss of a Secotier dungeon in Onjira." I gestured to the old druid in his broad robes. "The dungeon was updated a couple months back so that it was taken over by a character NPC called the Dark Warrior. He pushed the Druids at the top into the Cursed Pool and made them the insane monsters in the dungeon, but it appears the Principle Druid managed to get away."

"So this dungeon is like Druid's Keep two-point-oh?" Brock asked.

"Seems like it."

As the Principle Druid shambled forward, he glowed like he was casting a spell. Trees and vines began to emerge from cracks in the floor and walls, wrapping around the many shelves in the room. They slithered toward us, so I launched a Wildfire spell at the growing foliage. They flared up, and thick smoke filled the room. I think this was the first time that I saw smoke pool in an enclosed area from my flames.

Brock nocked an arrow but then squinted, looking around the room in confusion. "He's hiding in the smoke!"

"I think I know what to do."

Suddenly all I could hear was what sounded like the ringing of bells above us. I swung my arm and used Cyclone to clear away the smoke, revealing the old man standing above us on top of one of the shelves, conjuring a mountainous iceberg.

"Dodge!" I called. We both dive-rolled out of the way as the iceberg dropped and shattered against the floor, the explosion causing sharp shards of ice to fly toward us.

A shard took away a decent chunk of my Hit Points, and considering the earth spell he had used, I could only assume the Druid was using the third level spells I didn't yet possess. It was almost like the boss read my list of spells, saw what ones I was lacking, and then used them against me, knowing I wouldn't be able to predict their effects. It made me wonder what it would do against Spellcasters who had every spell upgrade.

Tough, but I guess this is *a Tertiatier boss.*

Water began to pour into the room from the cracks in the walls created by the vines, pooling at our feet. I recalled how I had used an Ice Wall to get over the gap in the bridges in Pirate Cove. Rubbing my hands in a circular motion, I cast one below me.

"Get on!" I called to Brock.

He did, and we balanced on the Ice Wall together like it was a raft. We floated up to the top of the shelf where the Principle Druid was perched. Brock nocked an explosive arrow and I equipped my Sapphire Edge. With a myriad of arrows and Shockwaves, we cut down half of the Principle Druid's health in a matter of seconds.

As though triggered when its health went into the red, the Principle Druid cast a spell I hadn't even heard of before. His hand glowed and a book from one of the upper shelves flew up into his hand.

The druid then called in a raspy voice, "You have made it this far; let's see how you fare against my Light Pillar."

Suddenly a force of blinding light hit us from the dome of the stained glass window in the roof. The impact of the blow broke through us and then the Ice Wall I had been using to keep us afloat. Brock and I both sank into the cold water beneath, the terribly powerful spell taking out more than half of our Hit Points. To make it worse, neither of us had the Aqua Lungs ability in our Key Triggers. The inability to breathe brought on a sudden panic.

I went to look at what spells I could use next, but saw that after the level two and three spells I had used—along with my

Shockwaves—I had no Mana to do anything that would get us out of this situation. We would lose all of the armor we had collected if we died here, which would set us back to square one.

Panic ripped through me until I felt a hand grab my arm. I opened my eyes to see Brock stab a glowing arrow into my shoulder. I flinched but then saw my Mana bar refill. It was one of his Mana Arrows. I grinned and nodded to him. I spun my arm around and around in the water and then pushed it out in front of me. My Vacuum spell turned the water into a whirlpool around us.

I equipped my Boomstick and cast a spell that I hadn't used much since I had learned it back when Brock had helped me complete the Lucineer Glacier. The second level water spell: Water Hose. In any other situation it wouldn't have done much, but with how much water was swirling around us—and me having enough Mana to use it repetitively—I eventually knocked the Druid into his own pool.

He hit the water with a splash, waving his arms around in panic. I used up the last of my Mana to cast another Vacuum that blasted Brock and me out of the water, and just as we were hurtling through the air, Brock fired a single arrow into the soaked druid—a specialty lightning arrow. Like it had cut through the Water Sprites during our first outing, it electrified the Principle Druid, zapping him of his final hit points.

Unlike other bosses that exploded on defeat, the Druid seemed to melt into the water that then drained through cracks in the stone walls and floor; the foliage vanished with it. Eventually we were lowered to the floor, breathing heavily and looking up at the high ceiling with light shining through the colorful dome on its roof.

—— DUNGEON COMPLETE ——

"You really need to learn that spell he did," Brock said.

I grinned and nodded exaggeratedly and we started to laugh, wet and exhausted, but victorious.

It didn't take us long to get back to our feet again. When I saw what was left in the room in the Druid's wake I couldn't help but laugh again. It was same gag vase that had been in one of the rooms without a Chaos Engine or piece of armor. But this time, the vase was filled with water.

We walked over to it. "Is this an item now?" I raised an eyebrow at Brock. "I got what I wanted. You take it."

Brock touched it and it disappeared into his inventory. "Pure Water… hah; apparently it restores you to full health."

I guess that answers my question for me. Pure water though, unlike the water from the Cursed Pool.

I couldn't help but see the connection between the two game elements.

"So, we have the armor. Now what?" he asked.

"Now we take it to Dice and have him program it into the Illusion spell. After that, I can cast it on us and see if that gets us through the Gateway Frank found."

"Alright. Message me when it's done. I'm ready to kick some butt in this debug room."

"You're finally speaking my language." I grinned and went to select the Wake-Up command when Brock stopped me.

"I …" He frowned, looking as though he was struggling to say something. "I want to say I forgive you, but …"

I looked at him in confusion but then shrugged, knowing it to be a guy thing, and suggested, "How about *I'll get over it?*"

Brock gave me that cheesy grin of his and pointed a finger at me. "That's much better. Alright, I'll see you later then."

I selected the option and woke up, feeling a little less like the bad guy than I had a week before. That's not to say that I didn't do the right thing. From everything that we had learned, from the Screamers being the missing beta testers to Malcolm's involvement, I thought that spoke for itself. Despite having a rocky beginning, it really felt like my relationship with Brock was on the road to recovery. Rising up out of my chair, I gave Dice the code for each item of armor.

"Now we can find out who the real bad guy is."

"What makes you think this will lead you to the *bad guy?*" Dice looked at me over his shoulder, his tone skeptical. "I mean, this *bad guy* has apparently been hidden away for years, and you just happen to think you've found a way to reach him? What if this is a misdirection? What if this is just another trap? You've been lured into one of those before."

I shrugged. "Well, we won't know until we get in there. Besides, unlike last time, I don't have much to lose."

"Don't be so sure." Dice smirked and shook his head. "There's always something to lose. It's just not until you've lost it that you realize what it is."

"I highly doubt it would be anything as serious as the risk of being put into a coma. Anything else I'm willing risk to get the answers we need."

Dice turned back to the wall monitor. "Just a suggestion."

As helpful as he was, sometimes I wished Dice would trust me a little bit more. *Trust might be the only thing that would get us through what would come next in one piece.*

Chapter 22
Open Sesame

With the code in place, you should be able to do the illusion spell and instead of a fake copy of your avatar appearing, the armor's item code will make it so that the armor will cover whoever you choose to cast it on," Dice explained slowly, like he hadn't told me this already.

"Perfect. Good work." I grabbed his shoulder. "Listen, I know I've been a bit of a cold bastard lately, but I can honestly say you've been more helpful on these missions than almost any other party member I've had in the past."

Dice's face didn't change. "Just doing my job. Not many people get to play computer games for a living, let alone Dream Games, and as long as you have a say in whether or not I get to keep doing that, I'll keep doing whatever you tell me."

"And after that?" I asked, trying to see where his loyalty lay.

Dice shrugged noncommittally and walked over to his recliner on the other end of the room. Around the room were Data, Brock, David, Vega, Chloe—and after hugging out their issues—Keri as well. Including Frank, Siena, and Tessa, the ten members of my Catastrophe team were ready and raring to go.

Can I really consider Siena, Frank, and Tessa a part of my team? Maybe they'll sign on if I change the name. Catastrophe doesn't really scream, "Here come the good guys."

"Alright, Keri. Considering this is your first time here, drink one of the vials on the wall, take a seat, and put on the helmet.

The setup will do the rest."

She nodded and I took my own dose of DSD.

Before it could kick in, I caught Chloe's eyes just as she was about to put on her Dream Engine and smiled. "Let's go find your brother."

She smiled back. "Thanks Noah. Even if this doesn't work, you're the best boyfriend in the world for going this far to help me find him."

David then called cheerfully, "Oh, she said it! It's official!"

I laughed and put my own helmet on. The buzzing of the recliner reminded me of being put under for major surgery at the dentist.

Official... did we really need to say it aloud to make it that way?

We all appeared on the Yarburn coast. Having not been there before, Data, Chloe, and Dice called their Bird's Eyes and carried us to Jossi Island, where we had agreed to meet the others. As we hovered to the top of the large hill, I could see Siena, Tessa, and Frank in her new fish-scale armor waving at us through the bushes. We landed in a clearing and then walked up to meet them.

"It's over here!" Siena called.

We followed her to the entrance of the well where Frank had claimed she had fallen through. The boards that covered it had obviously been broken through, and it made sense that only a Heavy like Frank would have found this Chaos Engine.

"Alright, I'll go first and message you when you can follow."

Siena's face went sour. "I should go first."

"You've already been down there," I said but then grinned. "But then again, no point in arguing about it."

Siena's smile faltered as I didn't hesitate to jump into the well. I fell and saw the churning cloud of the Chaos Engine move beneath me. However, instead of it teleporting me into a new area, I passed right through it. Panic hit me and I cast a Vacuum spell below me. The force of the air hit the bottom and then lifted me back up through the opening. When I landed back on the surface, I noticed that Siena was hacking away at a large tree monster called an Ent that had sprung out of the Chaos Engine.

I cast a Fire Weave on it, and its Hit Points quickly vanished. The others then looked at me in confusion.

"Did you not pass into the new area?" Frank asked.

I shook my head. "I passed right through the cloud without it taking me anywhere."

Tessa shrugged. "It worked for us."

Data nodded as though this made sense. "The portals must only be open to the debug room for a limited period of time."

"Alright, plan B then." I turned and looked around. "Vega, have you located where your Jade Edge is on the map?"

Suddenly Sirswift—no, Vega—appeared by my side and Siena jumped back, Color Blade raised. "Way ahead of you," he said.

Siena shook her head and pointed to Vega. "*You* are not allowed to do that."

"Says who?" Vega shook his head and returned his eyes to the map. "Alright, I've found him. He's appeared in the Toena City; there's an event going on there and he appeared there from a Chaos Engine in the hills."

My brow furrowed. "What kind of event?"

"It's the siege of Toena city," Data explained. "It's a monthly event where two sides are formed: the siege-soldiers and the besieged. Whoever's alive on the winning side at the end gets twenty minutes time added to any dungeon, which goes toward their Survival Record."

Another big gathering of players; the perfect place for another Screamer sabotage. I should have checked for that.

"One more event for them to ruin?" Chloe asked like she was reading my mind.

Keri looked down. "Just like in Heaven …"

"It doesn't matter." I pulled out a Transfer Orb. "Let's find this Chaos Engine and cut the Screamers off at the roots before things get too serious."

They drew near and together we selected the option to teleport into Toena city. In a flash, we appeared on the packed dirt of the busy street. The whole place was bustling with the number of the avatars getting ready for the siege. The sheer variety of armor styles and races in the Asian-inspired setting was baffling to the senses after having just been in such an empty open space. But I didn't have time to immerse myself in the impending battle.

The Screamer is around here somewhere. It doesn't matter. I need to focus on which Chaos Engine he came from.

"Chloe, Data, Dice, get out your Bird's Eyes and make your way into the hills."

I selected mine and it appeared, clearing a gap in the crowd for David and Brock to get on. Vega got on Dice's platform, Keri on Chloe's, and Siena, Frank, and Tessa jumped onto Data's. The platforms didn't seem to be affected by the weight of the avatars; having a Heavy on ours didn't change the speed at which we flew out of the city.

We passed over the guarded planks of the wooden walls where Range fighters were readying their bows and arrows, then the hundreds of avatars outside waiting for the main event of the siege to begin. We quickly flew over the fields, passed the Mishiji Temple, and rose up the hill into the Dragon's Wall that stretched over their slopes and peaks. I had seen this place many times before, but I never had time to explore it.

The place was essentially a Basetier dungeon, but one with a high difficulty because of how out of the way it was and the fact that it lacked a boss. It resembled the Great Wall of China, and like the dungeon in Penance Peak, other players would have needed a mount to get there if they didn't want to climb the foothills. We jumped off our Bird's Eyes and ran along the top of the wall as soon as we landed. Gargoyles and Stone Guards similar to the Terracotta Warriors that we had fought in the Mishiji Temple came to life all around us.

I looked over my shoulder. "Vega, how far away are we from the Chaos Engine now?"

Vega pointed ahead. "It should be just up there, below the barricade. It's—" He stopped and looked ahead. "Ah, should I take this?"

I turned back to see that there was a massive boulder rolling over the wall toward us. Siena bolted ahead of me and got out her

Color Blade. "Frank, Noah: Shockwaves, now!"

I smirked. "So you're giving the orders now?"

Frank and I both equipped our Color Blades and began slashing arcs of blue, purple, and red light toward the giant boulder. Chunks of rock flew from it with each beam of light that cut the air. Before long, the boulder had been cut to rubble and a few rolling stones. We turned around the see the backs of the others facing behind us, weapons equipped.

While we had taken the boulder out, the others had fought off the Stone Guards and Gargoyles that had attacked our rear. However, after they had finished them off, Data halted and eyed up Frank's Color Blade, raising a brow at Siena.

"Whoo! What a rush!" she called. "See that, Noah? That's what it looks like when your team trusts you unquestioningly!"

"Tsh, when did she get the Amethyst Edge, Siena?" Data inclined his head at her. "You didn't get rid of the ITS software I gave you, did you?"

"Of course I did," she lied. "Honestly, Data, she found the blade purely by accident in the Calandor Ruins."

"It's true," Frank said. "The guy wielding it dropped it when he died fighting the Fire Frog. Why else would she let someone like me keep such a weapon?"

Data nodded, as if to say Frank had a point.

Still, I couldn't help but remark, "Unquestioningly, huh?" triggering an unimpressed snort from Siena.

Vega ran ahead and was looking down between the crenulations on the wall. "Guys, I found it! The Chaos Engine should be just down there!"

I rushed to catch up with him and looked over the edge. There, at the base of the wall, was a shrine similar to the small flower shrine we had found over the swing bridge at the top of Mishiji Temple.

"Good work. Well, no time like the present to give it a try," I said and, deciding I didn't want to have another discussion about who would go first, grabbed the edge of the wall and vaulted over it.

The shrine came up at me quickly, the whirling cloud forming as I approached. I didn't have enough time to think about how I was plunging into the dark unknown, a churning, shadowy discord that only the name of the portal could accurately portray—an engine of chaos—before I hit.

Instead of landing on top of it, my body sank into it, and I fell for another seven feet before I landed on my backside on a metal floor. Wincing from the jarring sensation that took off a portion of my Hit Points, I sat up and gasped. All around me were glowing lights and metal walls. There were lines of neon blinking buttons, and layers of intricate ventilation. What it really reminded me of—with its small corridors and noisy pipes—was a cooler, futuristic version of The Engine Room.

Maybe this was an earlier design of the place.

Right as I stood up, I heard, "... out below!"

Siena dropped on top of me and I fell to one knee in order to catch her mid-fall. She looked up at me, eyebrows going up and down.

"Why Noah, my hero," she said sarcastically.

I set her down. "Is this the place you saw last time?"

Siena looked around and stuck out her bottom lip. "Seems the same."

Then I realized where Siena had come from and stepped forward with her just in time to avoid Brock, David, Chloe, and Keri as they came through. Where Chloe crashed into Brock, Keri was caught by David with a lot less effort than it took me to catch Siena.

Keri smiled. "Thanks, Davey."

"Anytime," he said, setting her down.

"I suggest you move forward," I said to Chloe and Brock, who were still groaning on the floor.

As soon as they did, Data, Dice, and Vega dropped through, landing casually and walking forward to meet us. Once they had moved, Frank and Tessa followed suit.

"Well, we made it," Tessa said with a grin.

I pointed to the ramp leading up to the large platform with

glowing rings at its base and asked Frank, "Is that the Gateway you couldn't use before?"

Frank nodded. "I was in full armor at the time. I thought that might've been the trick to getting inside, but it wouldn't work."

"Well, I have a feeling you had the right idea, just the wrong armor."

"What do you mean?"

"Let me show you." Turning, I made my way up the ramp onto the glowing platform. "My first suspicion arose when we found out the Screamers were using The Hall of Doors to go between areas using the Chaos Engines. I figured that, in order to access it, the players must have completed The Hall of Doors since they each had the armor you need to collect to get in to fight the final boss there."

"So?" Siena asked, rolling her wrist.

"So... that's how they do it."

Chloe rolled her eyes. "Are you saying we all have to complete that dungeon before we can get in?"

"No, I'm pretty sure they just used the same code to enter the boss room as they do to enter here. The armor, or the illusion of it at least, is their access key to get into the debug room."

David stuck out his bottom lip and nodded. "Pretty clever." He looked around self-consciously. "If it's true, I mean."

I studied the other ten avatars in my team. I felt like I could trust them.

"Everyone, unequip everything so you're only wearing your default gear."

After a moment of them looking into space, they all did so, wearing nothing but the rough starter garments that they began with when they first appeared in Galrinth. Looking at them like that, they all seemed like humble plebs, not the members of an elite VR group. I spun about once and then raised my arm. There was a flicker around me and suddenly I was wearing the same Silver Armor as the Screamers.

"Oh!" Vega murmured and then pointed. "I see. The Illusion spell was used to alter the code."

I nodded and beckoned them over. "Everyone, up here with me."

They each followed me up onto the platform and I cast the Illusion spell on each one of them. The armor fit to each of their avatars' sizes as it would if equipped normally. Considering the size of the average Screamer, I wasn't sure if the Heavies would be able to pass through, but after what they had done to help me find this place, I thought they at least deserved to give it a shot.

I cast it on Chloe last, and as I spun and raised my hand above her, the helmet covered a smile that warmed my heart. After all we had been through, we were finally back together with our friends, ready to fight for each other and for the game. As soon as the Illusion spell had changed us all to look like Screamers, the circle of light below us glowed brightly.

We huddled closer so that we could fit inside of the rings. Chloe was pushed closer to me with a Heavy at each of our backs. With a vibrating hum, the metal rings descended around us, and with a flash of light we were teleported into the debug room.

It worked!

We all appeared in a room similar in style to the dark corridor we had just been in, but this one was much larger.

Chloe looked up into my eyes from the slits in her helmet's visor and then to the rest of our surroundings. "Well, we made it."

I nodded and together we walked out onto the glowing floor.

Chapter 23

THE DEBUG ROOM

I f everything south of the Storm Wall was a pre-gunpowder era, and everything before Heaven was a pre-steam powered era, then the debug room could only be compared to a post-nuclear era.

Neo-Tokyo, Blade Runner, or better yet, the inside-a-computer world of Tron.

Our surroundings were blazing neon-lit, cold and dark streets with circuits for skies. Passive, featureless, white NPCs passed us, as though they were just waiting to have personalities and dialogue programmed into them.

We all walked through, past the buildings like giant capacitors that gave flickers of settings with snow, rain, and desert heat. The illusionary armor we wore flickered and then faded. We looked at each other in confusion, not saying a word. Ahead of us was the slope that led to several templated objects in an open space. It had springboards and ladders, empty chests, and Chaos Engine clouds that rotated slowly.

Data gazed up at the light surging above us. "This place is incredible. It's a completely closed off area. There are no rigs in this place, no leftover data packages. It's like a blank dungeon. Start with those tiles ahead and you could do anything to this place. There are endless possibilities."

I lifted my eyebrows at him in confusion. "What does that mean?"

Data's gaze caught mine. "It means that there are no rules here. Sure, we could insert our own parameters from what other game designers have created, but other than that, it's only what the programmer creates."

"So, someone's own virtual reality laboratory," Brock said, anger lacing his words. "But where are the Screamers?"

Siena moved forward and I strode to keep up with her. "What do you think?"

"I'm thinking that I've never been somewhere like this before and that we're probably way out of our depth." She shrugged. "That being said, I didn't die my first time trying the regular dungeons, either. This shouldn't be too different."

"Not too different?" Chloe exclaimed. "Did you just hear what Data said? They can do whatever they want here."

"Not precisely," Dice returned. "To kill us they first need to incorporate the parameters where death is a thing."

"Then how are we supposed to kill them?" Keri asked.

We stopped and looked at her, all considering how uncharacteristic it was for her to say something like that.

David shrugged his massive shoulders. "Find out the rules and use it against them?"

Vega laughed. "It shouldn't be too hard, so long as we still have our abilities from the game. With the magic, high jumping, and the generous health bars, we're pretty much immortals with a clock timer here anyway."

Siena blew out a raspberry. "You and I are really going to have to have another one-on-one after all this."

"Can I watch?" Tessa asked.

Siena glared back at her. "No."

I grinned. "Don't want anyone to see you ask for a best out of three after you lose the first round, hmm?"

Before Siena could respond to this, there were six flashes of light in front of us. With each flash, one of the Screamers appeared on the path we were on. We all stopped and waited, but they didn't advance on us.

They were all chanting, "Mal-colm, Mal-colm, Mal-colm."

Why are they chanting his name like that?

Siena rubbed her hands and looked back at us. "Alright, they want a brawl; who's in on this?"

To her chagrin, instead of charging toward us, they all turned. Behind each of the Screamers, there was another flash that silhouetted their armored forms. A doorway appeared behind each one of them. All six of them then walked through the doorways, disappearing into the shadows. Although the doors remained open, the Screamers did not return to face us.

"Aww," Siena moaned in disappointment.

"Are they expecting us to follow them?" Keri asked.

Vega raised his brow. "Was that meant to be rhetorical?"

"No, it's divide and conquer," Chloe said.

I recalled why Samuel had chosen Rubik's Castle as the dungeon to lure me in and steal my Transfer Orb. He had chosen it to separate us from one another until we weren't strong enough to fight his team. I was starting to think that maybe whoever was in command here told him of this tactic also.

"It's been confirmed that the Screamers can only force us to log off if we get within scanning range, right?" I asked.

Dice nodded. "We learned this when we found that the majority of players to report their teams' disappearances turned out to be Range avatars."

It made sense, really. If the scream could only affect those who could be scanned, Range players were less likely to be affected by it. It was the same reason Range characters were more prone to dish out friendly fire. Not being able to judge friend from foe at a distance could make their attacks indiscriminate.

"There are six doorways and there are eleven of us. We'll make groups so there's at least a Range or Spellcaster in each group."

Vega shrugged. "I'll go by myself. I've found I play new games better when I'm on my own anyhow."

I nodded. Vega's avatar was a hacked mix-Niche and he was a *master gamer,* so I had no reason to argue with him.

Siena put a hand on Frank's high, scaled shoulder. "Then I wanna go with Efty."

I shook my head. "You both have Color Blades that can use the Shockwave ability. We need to arrange the teams more balanced than that."

"Then I want to go with Keri!" she called.

I considered this. Keri may have been a Spellcaster with a few ranged attacks, but she was still a supporting mage at heart. I nodded, feeling that with Siena on offense and Keri on defense, they would be a pretty unstoppable team.

Dice looked at Data. "I think me and Datalent should be paired up. I'm a Range Niche and he's a warrior, and we both have good knowledge of the workings of the game's program. Even if we lose, together we'll be able to tell you more about its workings in there than anyone else."

I nodded again. "Frank, you and Chloe team up. You and Tessa both have the lowest accumulated Skill Points, and it wouldn't be smart to put the two most inexperienced people on the same team."

Frank nodded.

"Tessa and David, why don't you get more closely acquainted?"

Tessa screwed up her face. "What, I have to go with this big lummox?"

"Don't be mean, Tessa," Frank called. "David's a really nice guy!"

David shrugged and sighed. "I'm used to it, Frank."

I turned to Brock. "That leaves you and me."

Brock nodded, his face grim, and turned back to the doorway. His eyes suddenly narrowed at the numbers that were at the top of each frame.

"That's all well and good, but how do we decide what doorways we go through?" Siena swaggered toward one and grabbed it by its handle. "I mean, we won't know what's in there until we enter, so maybe we should just pick one at random and hope that—"

"No," Brock said as he drew closer, still peering up at what looked like coded numbers carved into the very top of the frame. "I recognize these numbers, somehow ..."

Data squinted. "They don't look like any code I recognize."

"No… I remember it from some time back before you joined Wona. I …" His eyes widened and he punched the side of his fist against his palm. "I know what these are! These are the project numbers of the dungeon submissions the beta testers did during Wona's qualifying tests!"

"Tsh, unused content, huh?" Data crossed his arms. "It's not so uncommon for unused levels and designs to be kept in the debug room and be played by people who enter them, but a lot of the times the levels are incomplete or glitchy, and most of the time they are removed from games before their release."

"So you know these dungeons?" Keri asked Brock.

"Not very well. But some of them were shown to me." He pointed to the middle door. "And I'll know that one like the back of my hand."

"Why's that?" I asked.

"Because *I* created it. That's the exact code of my dungeon design submission I sent to the Wona Company four years ago."

Vega grinned and patted him on the back. "Good spotting, Brockodile! And I thought I had a photographic memory. Remembering a long string of digits like that is rather impressive."

Brock scratched the back of his head while sporting his cheesy grin. "Well, I did obsess over the thing for nearly half a year."

I stepped forward. "Then we should do that one. If you know what it's like, there's a guarantee that at least one of our groups will succeed."

Siena raised her hands. "Hold your horses. You could at least tell us whatever you know about these other ones first."

Brock thought for a moment. "Well, a few of the other applicants did walk me through some of their submissions, but I can't say if I remember the numbers of them very well."

Chloe stepped up to him, eyes desperate. "Lucas didn't happen to show you his, did he?"

Brock shook his head but then looked up. "See how they all start with 01, 02, or 03? That means whoever created the different dungeons was either part of the 01, 02, or 03 beta groups. I was a part of the 03 beta group, the third group of people the DSD was tested on."

"Lucas was in the second lot of beta testers to try it, so he would be in one of the 02s." Chloe looked up at the other doors. "But there are three 02s here."

"Okay, so you take one and I'll take another," Keri said. "If either of us gets the dungeon Lucas is in, we'll have more of a chance to try and talk to him."

"If you get the one he's in …" Chloe bit her lip. "Just do your best to try and reach him, maybe find out where he's been hiding all this time."

Keri nodded. "I'll do my best, I swear."

Siena herself was looking at the numbers now, a cold focus in her eyes that I wasn't used to seeing. "The I.D. code I found on Jossi Island came from a girl called Kristie Tein. We both went to the same high school and applied to get into the beta program together. I might be a good player, but I wasn't good at game design like her, so she got in and I didn't. I want to see the dungeon she did that got her accepted and kick its ass." She shot Brock a glare. "Do you remember what round of tests she was a part of?"

"The second," Brock replied.

Keri's shoulders seemed to relax. "Well, that's handy."

Without another word, Siena picked one of the doors with the 02 code carved into the frame and walked inside.

Just like her not to hesitate to enter a dungeon. I'm foolish to think I could ever lead her. She takes commands from no one. I guess I'll have to disguise them as challenges and dares from now on.

"Alright, you two take another 02 dungeon," I said to Chloe and Frank. "We'll do Brock's dungeon and the rest of you …" I gestured to David and Data's groups. "Well, I'll let you decide for yourselves."

I watched as Chloe and Keri hugged each other one more time and whispered good luck in each other's ears before Keri followed Siena.

I moved to Chloe's side. "I hope you find him."

She shrugged. "One in three odds; better than the toss of a

die."

She leaned her forehead against my chest and I stroked her hair. "Good luck."

Chloe straightened and nodded to Frank. Together they moved to the other door with a code beginning in 02. Data and Dice simply chose the one closest to them, and Tessa led David through the remaining door. Seeing the tiny elf-like creature leading a tank was quite an amusing sight.

"Are you ready?" I asked Brock.

Brock raised his eyebrows at me. "Heck yeah! This was my baby, after all. I'm eager to see if they've changed anything in it."

I smiled. "I'm just interested to see what kind of dungeon you created."

He grinned at me. "Prepare to have your mind blown."

With that boast, we both stepped through into Brock's dungeon.

Chapter 24

GRAVITY MAZE

On the outset, Brock's dungeon looked very similar to The Catacombs of Sky Island, a kind of three-dimensional maze. However, when Brock showed me how we could use the yellow platforms to walk on the walls, I quickly had to re-think my opinion.

"Come on, try it!" Brock called as I hesitated to step off the platform and onto the wall. "The gravity of the whole room spins as soon as you put a foot on the wall."

I did so, and as he had explained, the whole maze spun so that I was now walking upright on the wall of the maze. My first reaction should have been that I was feeling strange from this, but with the sense of balance coming from the liquid in my inner ear, and the fact that my body was still lying down, the sensation was a little less terrifying than it would have been in real life.

"See?" Brock called as I caught up with him. "Wait until we get to the later parts of the dungeon where you can jump from gravity platform to gravity platform to access other areas of the maze. This is going to be awesome!"

I grinned. "And what kind of monsters did you put in here?"

Brock waved me off. "Just some lizards that can walk on walls. They're similar to those Salamanders in the Sulphur Pit."

We continued up the wall until we reached the next intersection. "How long did it take you to get this maze to make sense on so many levels?"

Brock shrugged. "I kind of took a shortcut with the maze itself."

"Let me guess: you stole it from some puzzle you already had?" I recalled how before Brock had started computer games he had been obsessed with puzzles.

"It's not that bad. I mean, I reversed it when I uploaded it into the 3D scanner."

I grinned. "I'm starting to see why they didn't use the dungeon after you submitted it."

"You can't file for copyright over a puzzle."

"Actually, I think you can. They probably took one look at this dungeon, thought *plagiarized,* took the gravity magic as an idea for one of their spells and brought you in to be their lab rat thinking it would serve you right."

Brock used another platform to swap his gravity so he could walk on what was the ceiling when we had first entered. "That's ridiculous. I wouldn't have been called up just because it was a similar maze. I changed the whole thing around. I mean, in my maze the goal is to get to the middle. The goal of the one I put in the scanner was to get to the other side of the cube."

"You just put a cavity in the middle of a maze cube you had, didn't you?"

He nodded guiltily but then raised a finger. "Only after I had flipped it, added lizard monsters, and made it so the gravity platforms in the center had to be used to get into the next area. I also made it so you have to collect items from the lizards to get into the boss room. I actually think they stole that idea to use in The Hall of Doors."

I shook my head. "Collecting items to get into a final room isn't an original idea either."

"But putting them together with lizards and gravity platforms was, okay?" He sighed. "All good things have to be inspired by something, Noah. You should know by looking at this world that nothing's purely original."

I decided to let him get away with it. "Speaking of lizards, I think we have our first one just up ahead."

A blue lizard skittered across the wall toward us. It stopped, its head turned, its tongue snapped at the air, and it skittered toward us again.

As it came crawling out over a gap, I summoned my Sapphire Edge.

"Wait, Noah, wait!"

He was too late. I had already used a Shockwave to cut it down, but as it died, its tail dropped down the gap in the maze it had been crawling over. I frowned and looked at Brock, who had grabbed his face in annoyance.

"What?"

Brock rubbed his forehead. "When the lizards die, the gravity magic no longer works on them. Now we have to work out a way to use the platforms to get us down there and collect its tail."

"Oh, whoops." I smiled awkwardly. "I think I'll leave the next lizards to you then."

It took us a good ten minutes to get the lizard's tail from the passage it had fallen down and continue on our way. We collected two more tails after he had used the platforms to get closer to the center. Without Brock, I would have easily been lost in the maze, and imagined that if the dungeon had been implemented in the Dream State, players would need some kind of map to help them find their way through.

One of the lizards snuck up behind me and zapped me with an electric shock. Although it didn't really hurt, I imagined the difficulty of this dungeon—if implemented—would've been Secotier or above.

"Nasty critters," I said as I jumped back and Brock shot it down with an arrow.

It fell onto the wall, which would have been the floor if gravity hadn't been tampered with.

Brock picked it up. "Yeah, we didn't have much to work with when it came to pain back then. A small electric shock was all we could really do to the player in-game unless we wanted to wake them up."

I rubbed my arm from the slight tingle it gave me. "Still, it's impressive they managed to do that much. The fact that now they have both hot and cold temperature pains, have separated the feelings of being bludgeoned or cut, and heck, even the feeling of being drowned, is a miracle."

Brock pointed ahead of us. "Okay, here's where the dungeon gets tricky. See how there are a few gaps in the maze coming up?"

I nodded. It looked like we were walking toward a junction in the regular maze, except that the turns were vertical rather than horizontal.

"This time we use the pad to get on the ceiling, and then use the pad on the ceiling to climb up the wall into the cavity at the center of the maze. You then kind of have to edge your way over to the next platform to make the wall the floor again. Does that make sense?"

I nodded and selected the platform to reorient myself and then shifted my weight down. I used the platform on the corner to lift myself up and into the opening. At first, I was hanging out in open space with the floor appearing to be a long way below me. Then I noticed the gravity platform across from me and edged my way over to it until I could press it to make the wall I was hanging from become the floor again. Hand over hand, I finally touched it and let go as gravity became normal for me once again.

I breathed out as Brock followed suit and we both sat there grinning.

"Man, that's a lot harder than I programmed it to be. Now, where's the—" He looked around the wide area and stopped.

Within the center cube was a collection of floating platforms, pillars, and runways, many of them with their own gravity orientation platforms. However, from the look Brock gave me, something in the dungeon seemed to be missing.

"Odd… there's supposed to be a boss lizard in this area. There's a barrier if you didn't collect enough lizard tails, but once you're in here you're supposed to …"

He looked up and trailed off again.

He then whispered, "Noah, look up!"

I did so, following his eyes. There, standing on the ceiling and looking down at us, was the silver-armored Screamer. When I saw him, I first expected him to run along the ceiling, walls, and platforms to get us in range of his scream. He didn't move sideways, but his body did shift slightly and seemed to become bigger. That's when I noticed the color of the floor beneath him. It had the same yellow color as one of the gravity platforms.

Brock called, "He's dropping toward us! Run!"

I started running just as I heard the Screamer begin to wail.

Chapter 25

MISTY LAKE

Frank and Chloe appeared in a misty glade. Behind them was a house that seemed to be only a part of the scenery, as it was inaccessible behind an invisible wall. From the way Chloe tried to get past the barrier—getting to the point of kicking and punching it—Frank figured the place was familiar to her.

"Have you been here before?" she asked.

Chloe stopped pounding on the barrier, stepped back, and nodded. "This is the lake house my family used to take us to when we were children. Lucas must have made this dungeon, inserting this image from an album we had."

"With this mist, it reminds me of a horror game I used to play as a kid." Frank squinted to see down the hill, which she could tell led to a lake through the mist. "Considering we can't go into the house, maybe we should explore this place a bit instead."

Chloe sighed and turned without a word. The beginning appeared to be the calmer part of the dungeon, for no monsters appeared from the mist to harm them as they made their way down to the lake.

"So, Chloe... you and Noah, huh?" she asked, trying to take Chloe's mind off her brother.

Chloe nodded. "It's been hard, though, while trying to convince myself that Lucas is alive after thinking for so long that he was dead. Noah's been patient with me; he knows it's hard, but he's also driven by his own goal of uncovering this mystery. I... I don't think he wants what we all think Malcolm achieved in this game to be true after what happened when his last girlfriend died."

Frank frowned. "Noah's girlfriend died?"

Chloe nodded. "And Catastrophe led him to believe she was still in the game. It's like he lost a little of himself when realizing Sue wasn't really alive in the game, and he's trying to help me because he knows how it feels to lose someone."

Frank shrugged, realizing the rabbit hole she had stumbled into, and decided to change the subject. "Didn't you say that your brother didn't recognize you? Are you sure he's the same Lucas you remember?"

"He had a similar problem when he was in the asylum." Chloe frowned in memory. "After the beta tests, he didn't always recognize me or my mother. But even before then, Lucas had become a bit different. He hid himself in his room playing games, and when he was working on designing this dungeon, I barely saw him. It was about the same time that he broke up with Keri."

They eventually made it down to the water. The base of the hill led to a wooden jetty that went out over the lake, the mist hovering above the calm water. Chloe walked along it, her boots loud against the wood, but Frank could see that it continued on much further into the mist than a regular dock.

"I don't remember it going on for this long," Chloe murmured.

There was a splash, and a large Piranha leaped over the bridge just in front of Chloe. It whipped its head, trying to bite her, but Frank pulled her back, allowing her to draw a gun and shoot the thing before it returned to the water. The fish vanished. There had been no music in the dungeon and the airy silence was suddenly filled with the echo of her gunshot.

Chloe looked around, drawing out her other gun, but no more Piranhas came out of the water.

Frank moved ahead. "I'm the Heavy here; maybe I should go first in case any enemies try to charge at us along the bridge. My defense is far higher than yours."

Chloe nodded, allowing Frank to pass. Her eyes were wide; clearly she had realized something about this dungeon that related to a memory.

"I remember… when we came here and went for swims in this lake, Lucas was always afraid of swimming too far out." She looked around at the massive lake surrounded by the creepy woods. "I think he turned the dock into a bridge that would allow him to explore the waters a bit more… or at least what he imagined was further out."

"And added an element of the fear he felt to share it with the other players, it seems," Frank said as they cautiously made their way over the bridge. "Still, I can see why this dungeon might not have been accepted by the company."

"What do you mean?"

Frank pulled out her Amethyst Edge, lighting the mists ahead of them with its purple radiance. "Well, the Dream State is a fantasy world. Sure, they have horror-themed dungeons, but having a place that exists in the real world may have taken away that fantasy a bit, you know?"

Another splash, another Piranha attack. It bit onto Frank's sharp shoulder armor, doing more damage to itself than it did to her. She cut it off with ease. Looking up, she jumped in fright upon seeing the transparent specters that had appeared in the distance, hovering around them over the water. They closed in on her, looking like elongated jellyfish.

Chloe grinned. "I did a similar ghost dungeon with Noah while searching for Siena's Ruby Edge, and I've equipped myself with bullets that work against their weakness."

"And that is?"

Chloe grinned. "Wind."

She shot at them, and each bullet created a wind blast that blew away the ghosts. Frank continued over the bridge, the population of ghosts becoming thicker with every step. Ahead of them, they saw an area where the monsters would not go. It wasn't until they approached the area that apprehension filled Frank's mind, for the area of the gap in ghosts was in a perfect circle.

The Screamer?

Chloe continued shooting through them, running as the ghosts vanished. She then stopped as the mist thinned around her and she saw what was in the center of the circle. Frank's suspicion was confirmed: it wasn't that ghosts wouldn't go near that area, it was more like the ghosts in the area had been destroyed.

The mist cleared, and the Screamer appeared before them in its armor, standing in the center of the clearing. The area of safety from the ghosts was a trap to lure them closer.

"Chloe, stop!" Frank called and she did. "Now, take this!"

Amethyst Edge glowing, Frank lashed out with three wide slashes around both of them, the beams of the Shockwaves blasting through the surrounding ghosts and blowing back the ones drawing near.

Their situation no longer felt as desperate, and Chloe stepped closer—into the circle but not close enough that she couldn't step out again if the Screamer started wailing.

"Lucas?" she asked.

The Screamer's helmet seemed to twitch slightly.

"You're Lucas, aren't you?" she continued. "That's why you chose this dungeon, right? It reminds you of the time when we were kids."

The Screamer went to walk forward then, and Chloe stepped back.

"Don't you remember me? I'm your sister …" Her face seemed to crumble. "Mom misses you, you know."

The armor-clad figure stopped and grabbed its head. Chloe's eyes widened, as though recognizing something in the player's movement.

"No, Lucas, please don't!" Chloe called.

Instead of a scream, there was a groan from under the armor. He shook violently, followed by a sudden stillness as he straightened himself.

He spoke, but given how low his voice was, the disembodied inflection didn't seem to belong to him. "Lucas is dead, he is no long—"

There was another fit of trembling and head pounding, as if someone else was trying to regain control of the avatar. Through the shaking, Frank could hear words.

"Help me disappear… Malcolm won't let me disappear… He said he would but doesn't let me …"

Chloe nodded and reached out a hand. "Just tell me where you are IRL and I can help you disappear from this place forever. I promise!"

"A… a warehouse. It is… dark. I hear… cars and a hum. There are others …" He grabbed his helmet. "No… So many wires, he must need …"

Lucas screamed, pulled off his helmet, and threw the flickering illusion into the lake. It made no effect on the water around them. They could see his face now, and Frank noticed how screwed up with pain it was in his effort to keep control. However, for just a moment his eyes changed and he seemed to recognize Chloe.

"Trace the signal that I leave in the game… find me… help me disappear!"

He then turned and sprinted into the mist. Chloe went to chase after him, but Frank held her back.

"What are you doing?" she cried.

"He's obviously not in control of himself. He's trying not to log us off so that we can continue!"

Chloe struggled and then pulled free of her grip. She ran after her brother, and the ghosts and piranhas flew up from the water to stop her. She shot through them, her guns blasting them back as her boots pounded along the bridge. Frank knew she couldn't keep up with a Range Niche but ran after her anyway, launching Shockwaves at the monsters.

The mist became thicker until she was running blindly after Chloe. She couldn't see her—she could barely see the bridge below her feet with the mist so thick. She heard Chloe let out a startled scream and then she saw there was no longer a bridge beneath her feet. She was moving too quickly to stop herself. She fell and darkness engulfed her.

Chapter 26

FAILURE

Brock and I jumped away from the falling Screamer, and I equipped my Boomstick, casting a Wind Blast so I didn't fall down a gap in the floor. On the other side, Brock rolled off the ledge, leaving the Screamer to face me. I raised my Boomstick and launched a Fire Ball from it like it was a cannon. The Screamer dodged to the side and started to run, jumping gaps in the floor to try and close the distance between us.

"Brock, get back up here!" I called.

I turned and bolted to the nearest wall, using the platforms that allowed me to change the gravity so I was running on the ceiling. My jumps could easily clear the distance between the runway and the pillars. Next to the wall was a floating platform, and I noticed another gravity sign on its surface.

I leaped up and touched it, which allowed me to run up the wall. The Screamer leaped up behind me, close on my tail. Instead of continuing to flee along its length, I ran to the side of the column and jumped. I gasped when seeing the distance between me and what was now the floor.

I cast a Cyclone spell as the Screamer followed me down. I glanced up, hearing the Screamer's wail as he came down on top of me, not slowed down by my wind like I was.

Crap!

He plummeted like an anvil toward me. However, before I could come within range, an explosive arrow struck him in the face, redirecting him from his path. I hit the floor and spun to see Brock nocking another of his arrows.

"Noah, use a gravity spell to slow him down!" he called.

I cursed, annoyed that I hadn't thought of this myself. I raised and lowered one arm while pointing my Boomstick in his direction. The warping animation appeared above him and he was instantly slowed, but not by much.

"Shouldn't he be going slower than that?" Brock asked. Then he facepalmed. "Oh yeah; the armor is only an illusion."

As he came closer, I saw that the explosive arrow had made the Screamer's helmet flicker, and the visor no longer covered his face. He looked to be my age and had strawberry-blond hair. I didn't recognize him. I cast a Wind Blast at him to slow him down and then cast Rush on Brock and myself. With our superior speed, we could back away and circle him so we were outside the diameter of his scream.

Seeing he couldn't get us in range, he stopped his cry and looked around. Without speed, he knew he couldn't reach both of us, and we knew that whomever he chased would kite him while the other attacked him from the flank.

Attacking while fleeing, I never knew I would get to use a Mongol strategy on these guys.

As long as we were faster than him, we would be able to win.

"Brock, can you see his face?" I called. "Do you recognize him?"

Brock nodded. "He's Maric Milano. He was one of the few people that we thought overdosed but survived the process."

Maric spun toward Brock, apparently recognizing his name. He rushed at him, but Brock fled toward the wall, knowing exactly where each platform was so he could run along the walls. Not only that, but he also knew what gaps in the wall had gravity orientation on their surface so he could take cover between them while firing arrows.

Maric stopped and looked around like a cornered animal. Something about seeing this made me feel pity for him. An idea came to me. Maybe the more we talked about his story the more

GHOST IN THE GAME

he would become aware of himself.

We're not here to fight him. We're here to find out who's commanding him and the other Screamers.

"Wouldn't it have been smarter for him to be sent to his own dungeon? Why is Maric in yours?" I asked.

"I don't know!"

"What *do* you remember of him?"

Brock shook his head. "Well… I think Maric didn't complete his dungeon in time."

"Is there a reason he's so good at doing your dungeon?"

"I guess it's because I let him play it a few times …" Brock seemed to pick up on my plan and began shouting back, "He only got into the beta tests because he was the son of the head game designer, Erik Milano."

"Why didn't he manage to complete his dungeon?"

Brock flipped up onto the ceiling and ran along the wall so that he was further away from the Screamer and allowed his voice to carry easier. "I heard he fell out due to stress. He wasn't very good with code or spatial recognition. I think I recall him saying that coding was like banging his head against a brick wall."

"Quiet."

It was just a whisper, but I could have sworn it came from Maric. Whatever we were doing, it was working.

"So, he decided to skip the whole thing and cried to his daddy to let him in; that's pathetic."

"Quiet …"

Maric spun and ran at me. He used the platform to jump onto the ceiling I was standing on. I cast a Cyclone between us to keep him at a distance and backed away as Brock fired another arrow at him, a metal one that stuck from his shoulder just in case I needed to finish him with a Plasma Beam. But I decided to keep talking. I wanted to see what information we could get from him.

"Now that I think about it, even though he couldn't make his own dungeon, he was obsessed with everyone else's. He must have tried out mine several times. He was definitely more a gamer than a designer."

"Quiet!"

A golden glitter rained down around the Screamer as he turned back toward Brock. I gasped. Maric was a Spellcaster.

"Brock, look out! He just used Speed Amp!" I called while pulling out my Boomstick to cast Rush on Brock again.

Suddenly there was the sound of ringing bells, and the same mountain of ice the Principle Druid had used launched toward me. I flicked my arm out and a wide gush of flame flew from my Boomstick. My Wildfire spell melted the ice, but the shards from it still flew at me. I quickly cast an Ice Wall to block them. I heard the ringing of bells again and reinforced my wall by casting the spell two more times. The mountain of ice crashed through both of them, but I had already thrown myself from its path.

As I recovered, a window appeared in my vision, saying:

—— ICE UPGRADE: "ICEBERG" ——

As fast as I could move my avatar, I copied the tutorial that appeared in my vision by instinct. I raised my arm in the palm circling motion that the blank avatar showed in the demonstration window. I saw then that the ringing sound I heard before the spell was the ice shards appearing and forming into the iceberg. I lowered my hand and launched the mountain of ice directly at him.

It hit Maric, taking his Hit Points down into the red, but he still chased after Brock and was quickly gaining. Using all that magic along with a level three spell had eliminated my Mana, stopping me from using Rush to help Brock get away. After letting it regenerate for a moment, I had just enough Mana to use the same spell Maric had used on himself. The glitter of my Speed Amp allowed Brock to keep pace, but Maric had already caught up enough to take him out.

"Brock, Mana Arrow!" I shouted.

Brock fired one as soon as Maric started to inhale for his scream. It hit me, my Mana shot up, and my Vacuum spell shot from my Boomstick toward them, pushing Maric back and expanding the distance between them.

Maric continued to scream, but through it, I could hear Brock yelling at him.

"Are you listening, Milano?" he shouted over the wail. "I wouldn't have passed the submission phase without you!"

The scream quieted and Brock continued. "That's right. When you played my game and gave me that feedback, like telling me to add more gravity platforms at the end to fight the boss lizard, it made the dungeon ten times better, man!"

Maric's face relaxed and his shoulders seemed to drop.

"The other betas told me the same. Your suggestions helped them, too. And you know what? I bet you got your father out of a jam when he was designing his dungeons as well!"

Silence filled the cavity. The atmosphere of the entire fight had changed.

"That might have been why he left Wona. Erik Milano was the lead designer for the Dream State. Without him, we wouldn't have half the dungeons we have here!" Brock continued. "And now you're trying sabotage all of the hard work he put into this game so that no one would see his masterpiece? Why, Maric?"

Maric stopped and seemed to shrink as he looked down.

I could see what Brock was doing, but I hoped he wasn't pushing Maric too far. We moved closer as he began to whisper, his voice almost inaudible over the distance we were from him.

"He was fired... just like Malcolm. Wona just used him... and threw him away." Maric began to shake. "Wona needs to pay... I must destroy his game... I must make all those playing it vanish!"

"No!" Brock shouted. "Don't you see? Your father was talented enough to continue creating on his own! I've played some of his newer games and they're great! By stopping people from playing this game, you're only stopping them from enjoying the very thing he put so much of his life into." Brock took a deep breath and continued. "So many gamers know his name. He will be remembered because of the Dream State. Why would you want to ruin his memory by stopping people from seeing it?"

"Who cares if he doesn't work for Wona anymore?" I yelled in support.

"Ice Castle, Dragon's Nest, Rubik's Castle, he was responsible for some of the best parts of the game!" Brock continued. It wasn't until now that I realized how much of a fan he was of the designer himself.

But then, Brock's always been a big VR fanboy.

"You really think ..." Maric trembled, so much that he seemed to blur. "People will remember him... because of the Dream State?"

Brock nodded. "There are shows where only a few episodes were directed by specific directors or animated by specific animators, and they were always the best episodes. True fans remember those episodes just like true fans will remember your father's legacy."

"Please Maric," I said, raising a hand. "If you tell us who's behind this, we can stop them from sabotaging your father's work."

Maric's trembling became shaking, the armor rattling like crazy. "You know him... if you know my father... you'll know him. Ah!"

Maric screamed and grabbed his head as the shaking continued until his form began to blur again.

"What's happening to him?" I asked.

Brock frowned. "*He* doesn't want him to tell us."

"Who?"

Maric looked up, his voice uneven as he said. "Ma—"

—— "You already know who I am." ——

Just like Sue had from Rubik's Castle, Maric vanished from the dungeon and an echoing whir suddenly filled the cavity. Brock looked at me as the different walls and sections in the maze began to move up and down, the textures spinning like tiles. Then they began to float apart, the gravity tipping us from the surface of the maze.

"No, we don't!" I yelled.

As we fell into the darkness surrounding the maze—the blank space of the debug room—text filled my vision:

—— **"Oh yes, you very much do."** ——

We continued to fall, our speed increasing until it ripped away at our senses. I wanted to scream, I wanted answers, but I didn't want to say the name that was forming on my lips. I thought I knew now why Windsor didn't want to say it.

—— **"Say my name!"** ——

Brock's voice became cold, but he finally said, "So, your experiment of twenty years paid off after all …"

"Malcolm Mirth," I finished.

—— **"That's correct."** ——

We suddenly hit a floor, or more accurately, the feeling of falling stopped as a floor appeared beneath us. Our health remained untouched as though the fall damage had been removed. The floor was squared off by more bright green tiles, and I could see that it wasn't just Brock and me in the space, but the rest of my team as well.

"Oh, everyone made it," Keri said, sounding surprised.

"Did anyone else find their dungeon too easy, even with the Screamer?" Siena asked.

We all slowly stood and stared around at the vacant, squared-off space.

"What the heck's that?" David asked, pointing to the back of the room.

We turned to see a black sphere hovering above the floor behind us. The cold feeling I felt from it was the same as every time I heard the whispers and saw the flecks of darkness in the corners of my vision.

This sphere must be where the darkness that Samuel and I saw comes from.

Like an upside-down and inverted whirlpool, a pillar lifted from the tiled floor under the black sphere, lifting it high above us. As though a spell had been cast on the sphere, lines of glowing light began to stretch and slash out around it, extending and morphing its shape. Spinning as it changed, it eventually transformed into the shape of a tall blank avatar, similar to the white avatar in the tutorial screens, but black and stretched to become taller.

The same cloak that the Principle Druid had worn in the final room of The Hall of Doors covered the form, but it was fitted to his tall figure rather than the Druid's short stature. We all stared in awe at the transformation, confused and stunned by the sheer metamorphosis of the world and this avatar above us.

"Is that him?" Data asked. "The supposed Malcolm Mirth?"

"Something tells me it is," I said.

Chloe pointed, looking thoroughly unimpressed. "Really? That thing?"

Vega gave a bow. "Quite an honor."

Tessa looked around at us. "Is he an NPC or a monster?"

"He's a dead man," Brock growled.

I shook my head. "No… not yet."

"Correct again, Noah. Welcome players—" He raised a hand, his voice echoing. "—to *my* dream state."

Chapter 27

MALCOLM

Finally, the true villain had appeared—or at least the avatar that represented him. Yet, despite all signals pointing to him being responsible for everything that had happened, there was one crucial flaw with his grand reveal.

"Tsh, Malcolm Mirth is dead," Data said.

"Yeah …" David concurred, tone uncertain.

"He died, that is true," the robed avatar called. "But only his body. This, all around us, is his life now—*my* life. You are now inside me."

"Eww," Tessa said, as if she took him literally.

Chloe rolled her eyes. "So, you're the one who's been sabotaging the Dream State?"

"Correct," the voice replied.

She glared at him. "Alright, tell us where you're keeping the beta players. Tell me where you've been keeping my brother!"

"What makes you think I'm keeping them anywhere?"

"Don't give me that! Lucas told me you're keeping him in a warehouse!"

Malcolm raised one robed arm. "How could I possibly keep anyone anywhere? I don't have a physical body anymore."

"Are you saying you have nothing to do with the Screamers?" Keri asked.

His voice became amused. "I didn't say that."

"Then what are you saying?" Chloe shouted, her voice

straining with emotion.

Malcolm didn't answer; he just floated there, his warped laughter echoing lightly around the darkness.

Siena's Ruby Edge flashed into her hand. "He's saying that he's the final boss of this game and doesn't plan on answering our questions. Isn't that right?"

The laughter stopped. "Hmph. You will be the first to go."

"Is that so?" Siena smirked and charged forward.

"Siena, don't!" I called, although I knew she wouldn't listen.

Before she even came to the pillar, another one lifted from the floor beneath her and a third flew down from the ceiling. With the sound of crunching rubble, the two came together, crushing her between them. When the two pillars retracted, Siena_the_ Blade, the self-proclaimed best player in the game, had vanished.

Keri gasped, and I couldn't help but be a little surprised myself. Siena had seemed unbeatable, but it appeared that what she had said about us being out of our depth turned out to be true after all.

"Those were the template animations for Earth Punch, like combining Ice Coffin and Plasma Beam. Combining complementary level two spells has always been more powerful than individual level three spells. Unless prepared for it, a direct hit with this combination can kill any Warrior or Range Niche relatively easily." Malcolm's voice continued to sound amused. "Wona said that he wanted to make the Niches balanced, but one Niche being able to one-hit-combo two of the others so easily doesn't seem balanced to me."

"Siena …"

Frank and Tessa stepped forward. Siena had been their flamboyant guide in the Dream State since they had met her, and despite their mixed feelings for their leader, it appeared that they were still loyal.

"Range and Heavy?" Malcolm said ponderingly. "One has very little defense but lots of speed, so range spells can—"

Tessa screamed as Wildfire surrounded her, stopping her from running, and then a boulder of ice flew toward her, taking her out with a flash nearly as quickly as Siena.

"And Heavies are the opposite—lots of defense, but no speed."

Frank was suddenly frozen in a block of ice.

"But the armor that gives them this defense has its own weakness, and water defense doesn't stop lightning attacks."

Jagged lines of light, which I could envision as being the template for Plasma Beam, hit Frank's ice prison twice. The first one shattered the coffin, and the second one split her apart like a tree hit by a fork of lightning. She vanished, and Malcolm turned to face the last of us.

"Now, who's next?"

Vega stepped forward. "You seem to know the weakness of each Niche, but what of a mixed Niche character?"

The robed form raised his palms. "You are a broken character, not worth my time."

Suddenly the tiles below Vega opened up and he yelped as he dropped into the darkness.

If he can do that, why doesn't he just do it to the rest of us?

Data gritted his teeth. "If you cheat, what's the point of even trying to fight you?"

Malcolm spread his hands. "Because you all seemed to want to try. For instance …"

Suddenly both Data and Dice rose up into the air, and before they could respond, Malcolm clapped his hands together and the two crashed into each other once, twice, three times, and then vanished.

"Besides, it's more fun this way," Malcolm continued, despite Data not being around to hear him. "It doesn't matter. I was just trying to show that after how long it took for you come here, you were merely walking into a place where I had all the power. It was a foolish plan, really. Besides, you won't die; you'll merely rest in darkness until my creation wears off. If I really wanted to, I could turn up the pain threshold and make it feel like everything I'm doing to them is real." He shook his head, looking displeased with the idea. "You see, unlike what Windsor would have you believe, I'm not a sadist. Everything I do is for a reason, and I see no reason to make you suffer physically. Particularly when losing seems to do that well enough to you all emotionally."

"You like things too easy." David shook his head. "The way you talk, you don't sound like you were a gamer at all."

Malcolm's hands shot out and a blank blade shot from them toward us. David ran out and spread his arms to block it with his diamond armor. Suddenly the glass-like armor gained a tinge of orange and the flying blades went right through him.

"I was never a player of games—that's for children. I am a scientist. I merely see how things work and turn them to my advantage."

"Then why have you spent so much time learning everything you can in this world?" Brock asked.

"Good question. I used to think that gamers were obsessive and had no lives. Ironically, when your entire world is a game like mine is, you cannot help but learn to master your own domain. I bet, of all people, Noah can understand that." He pulled his hand back. "It is true that I designed some of the monsters. Without my errors in making the Wailing Wall boss, I wouldn't have been able to cause as many problems with my Screamers as I have."

David cringed as the sword stabbed him several more times, his Hit Points dropping into the red as quickly as if he didn't have any armor on at all.

"Davey!" Keri shouted. She began the hand movement that would heal him, but then yelped as her arm was lifted up above her head, followed by the rest of her.

David managed to look back at us with a baffled expression just before he, too, vanished.

Chloe ran forward, panic on her face as Keri rose higher. "Keri, no! Let her down!"

"Spellcasters…" Malcolm rumbled as his hands drew together. "Maybe if every player was given the same abilities you had, this game might have been a little more balanced. The entire game has mechanics that are focused on one Niche. Range attacks, when using the right specialty weapon, increase your stats temporarily for whatever you need… so much power. And yet it's still a waste if you don't know how to use it properly."

At first, nothing happened to Keri—she just seemed to squeeze into a vertical position and then shrink.

"I'm being crushed!" she yelled. She tried to say something else, but it was incomprehensible as her body became a thin line and then vanished.

"Damn you!" Chloe uttered and pulled out her guns. She then unequipped them, knowing they would be of little use against him. "No, this isn't real! I'm going to find a way to destroy the real you!'"

"'There is no real me—only this version of me—but considering you drew on me first, turnabout is fair play."

Suddenly the template of several different guns appeared and fired. The bullets shot into Chloe's stomach, bringing her to her knees as another hit her in the head and made her vanish in a wink. Like we had been in the gravity maze, only Brock and I were left standing. Despite what I had seen, I remained silent, seeing that only those who had spoken became his targets. Brock appeared to have noticed this as well, for he simply raised his brow at Malcolm.

"And then there were two," the robed avatar said, taunting us.

Brock started laughing.

"What's so funny?" Malcolm asked, sounding affronted.

"Oh, nothing." Brock waved at him. "I just think it's funny, you throwing about your killing power like you think it's something impressive."

"Bah. Another Range fighter," Malcolm said. "Let's see how fast you move under a gravity spell."

A warping animation went over Brock's head, pushing him to the floor. However, where the spell would normally stop affecting a player, it continued to crush him against the square tiles.

"What would be... really impressive ..." Brock wheezed as his face was pushed into the tile. "Would be... to bring all of them... back."

As the force drove him further down, Brock winked at me and then let out a breath, his body collapsing and vanishing in front of me.

What is this? Did we come all the way here just to die?

"Do you know why I left you for last, Noah?" Malcolm finally asked me, his voice low.

I shrugged.

"Because you know what it feels like to be turned on by a friend when you know yourself to be doing the right thing. I watched it all: how you sought the power to search for the truth, those you trusted turning against you despite doing your best to explain yourself to them." The robed form shook his head. "I didn't get that chance. They didn't even listen to my reasons. They just threw me out of the company, called the authorities, and thought that would be the end of me. My resolve was never that weak… and neither is yours. I can respect that."

He… he thinks we're the same?

"It was Sue that did it, I'm sure. Her ideas made you suspicious of the game, pushed you to discover more, to find out for yourself how wrong it is. Well …" The robed form looked around. "Lies, corruption, and death! Was she wrong?"

I just stared at him, not answering, trying to keep that grin off my face but failing.

Malcolm appeared taken aback. "What's with you? Why are you just staring at me like that? Are you so eager to die as well?"

I continued to stare up at him, grinning. I couldn't help it once I saw the text of the Key Trigger that had shown up in my vision, and I suddenly remembered what had happened at the Broken Clock Tower against Sirswift and his team. I recalled clearly the despair it had made me feel after seeing what he could do. It made me happy to imagine that I would soon be giving that same despair to Malcolm. After all, *I* was the leader of Catastrophe now.

"It's your turn, Noah," Malcolm demanded. "Say something!"

I cocked an eyebrow at him. "Okay then, Instant Respawn."

Malcolm pulled back. "What?"

With ten flashes of light around me, every single one of my teammates reappeared at my side, weapons equipped and raised.

Brock stood beside me with that cheesy grin of his. "See, I told you it would be more impressive."

Chapter 28

NEW NICHE

Y ou are all just sheep following a blind wolf!" Malcolm
said in agitation. "I'll have to kill the wolf to save the
sheep."

Suddenly tiles around us spun, and the debug room gained the
skin of the Barrens, with the raining sky above us, and wasteland
hardpan at our feet. It brought me back to when I had fought
Brock on Peragon: the desperation to survive, the emotional
trepidation. But despite the rain, the drops of water didn't hit us,
as though the code for that effect had been removed.

The pillar Malcolm stood on now looked like one of the black
Claw Plateaus where I had met Data, staring down at us from
under his hood.

"Sheep? If you say so." I grinned up at him. "But my flock are
wolves at heart."

Malcolm's voice became a growl and he pointed down in
frustration. "Then let's see how they last against a real wolf." ·

I caught Siena's gaze and grinned. "Let's; Siena, would you
like to go first, or should I?"

Without answering, Siena charged in and I cast a Vacuum
spell at her feet. Keri cast a bubble protection around us as forks
of a Perfect Storm spell rained down. A blade flew toward me
but was cut away by Frank's Color Blade. Another blank sword
impaled her but David took her place as Chloe and Brock ran to
Malcolm's flanks and began firing.

Malcolm sent a tidal wave down on us, but Vega and I cast Ice Walls to split it, and then Dice leaped over the wall, firing shots from a rifle that Malcolm blocked with another pillar resembling an Earth Mold spell. He then waved his hands, and Shockwaves ripped through the rain toward my party.

I triggered Instant Respawn as Siena cut through one of the waves, and Frank flashed back to life and split another before they were both struck by Icebergs. Data drew his golden dual swords and threw them, their spinning blades flying up at Malcolm, but he bashed them away with a floating warhammer and then blew off more projectiles from Chloe with Cyclones on either side of him.

Dice summoned his Black Dragon and flew it up to meet him, using the Firebreath attack that made my Wildfire look like a level two spell. Malcolm blasted it away with Vacuum and then summoned several bows and arrows, piercing him with specialty arrows similar to how Brock had defeated him above Sky Island.

They may be able to lift us up to him, but it seems even mount attacks are useless.

The battle quickened in pace as I continued to use the Instant Respawn ability to revive my friends. Keri went down from a Fire Weave that swept through everyone like a scythe and then reappeared to cast a protection spell to prevent the damage from an oncoming Plasma Beam.

"Maybe we should run. We're not getting anywhere here," Keri said.

Siena was at my side, grinning after having run in to die three times already. "Run away? Hah, my mother used to tell me it was better to lose than to run away!"

Frank jumped in front of a Fire Weave rushing at me, having equipped her old Dragon Armor to block it. "Wait, I thought it was the other way around?"

Siena laughed. "How do you know my mother?"

Flicking out her Ruby Edge, she ran forward, cutting through two more Shockwaves that were rushing toward me.

"Why doesn't he just kill Noah?" Vega asked as he dodged a

few attacks and then ran in with Siena.

Siena shrugged. "Maybe he's having fun; I know I am."

"That's the point!" Data called before I was forced to respawn him after taking a summoned axe to the face. "Maybe he wants to challenge us on equal footing, to show us how pointless it is!"

"From up there?" Siena exclaimed. "It's like he thinks he's better than us or something."

I ground my teeth. "Let's show him how wrong he is."

"You don't need to tell me." Siena grinned and ran in again.

However, as she did, Malcolm raised a hand above him, and the blank template of a book floated from the changing tiles below him into his hand.

Brock shouted, "He's using Light Pill—"

He was cut off as the dark clouds above transformed into a source of light that threw us all to our knees with a devastating flash. My team fell back, and Keri was forced to heal me after my Hit Points went into the red. I was lucky that every time she was revived her Mana regenerated also.

I looked up, seeing Malcolm once again on his pillar above us, arms crossed and completely unharmed by our combined attacks.

"This isn't working!" David shouted.

I revived Tessa again and she cried, "We're getting nowhere with this," ignorant of what David had just said.

They're right. Even with Instant Respawn, we're only just barely staying alive against him.

Vega shook his head. "I still don't get it. Why isn't he just opening the floor to kill Noah like he did with me? That would stop us from respawning."

Frank's Amethyst Edge vanished from her hand and was replaced with her massive cannon. There was a deafening blast from it, and the animation for a smoke cloud appeared around Malcolm's hooded form. I couldn't believe it—she had actually hit him. We stopped and watched as the white particle effect vanished to show his robed form completely unharmed.

That attack knocked me right off of Apollo's Lookout, and yet it didn't even phase him.

"Hit him again!" Tessa cried.

Desperately, Frank fired another cannonball. This time, instead of it hitting, Malcolm seemed to blur to one side, dodging as the metal ball flew past him and struck one of the large pillars in the distance with an explosion of rubble. Several of us gasped and we all went still as his attacks on us ceased as well.

Frank was lucky to hit him once, and even then it did nothing. But with that speed, I doubt we'll hit him again. Unless ...

"You asked the question," Malcolm finally called. "Why don't I make Noah fall through the floor like I did with you, didn't you Sirswift?"

Vega raised a finger. "It's Vega, act—. You know what? Never mind."

"Datalent's right. I want to make my victory so obvious that it shows you who this world truly belongs to. I want to make it clear how pointless it is to—"

"I think there's another reason!" a familiar low voice called up from behind us. "Maybe it's because you know that if you succeed in sabotaging this game entirely, you will be left all alone. Malcolm, my old friend, I didn't want to believe it, but now that I see it with my own eyes, I'm honestly amazed."

We all turned as an avatar none of us had seen before appeared on the tiles and walked out in front of us to face Malcolm. I knew I recognized his voice, but it wasn't until he turned to look back at me that I knew where I had seen this avatar before. It was exactly the same as the statue of the rifle-wielding hunter from Heaven, the one that I had already thought resembled Windsor.

And that voice... it is Windsor!

"Sorry it took me so long, but I finally found a path from my own beta room into this one," Windsor Wona announced. "And now that I see that the main boss has taken his form, I believe it's time to show you all the new Niche I've been working on for so long. So everyone... wanna see?"

Along with the same scarf, long jacket, goggles, and single leather shoulder guard as the statue, Windsor's avatar also had what looked to be a dog companion—a cross between a husky and a curly-tailed Akita that moved with him, the likes of which I had never seen before in the Dream State.

Is that supposed to be a pet?

Suddenly, the massive rock pillar Malcolm's avatar was standing on lowered and his robed avatar walked out to face us on the hardpan. It seemed he was finally willing to come down and fight us on our own level. As he did this, the titles in the debug room spun again, and suddenly we were standing in a grassy field surrounded by hundreds of avatars: two motley armies fighting desperately against each other. I turned around and saw a feudal Japanese-like city behind us, its gates opening as more avatars flooded out to fight.

"Toena?" David asked. "How did we arrive in Toena?"

"This is a skin, idiot," Chloe said. But then she looked around as the players who had just run through us stopped to stare. "But they can see us... uh, is this like some kind of layer effect?"

It was the Toena siege event. Chloe's guess made sense; it seemed they could only see us. They couldn't interact with us, as if we were holograms that were there just so everyone could watch the fight between Wona and Mirth. Despite the two layers not being able to interact, the nearby players backed away as though unsettled by having to walk through us. Those around them also stopped their fighting to watch the anomaly.

Malcolm stopped as he came within scanning range of Windsor. "My old *friend...* have you come to show me yet another unbalanced class for me to eliminate?"

"Come on, Malcolm." Windsor grinned and hefted his ancient looking staff. "Don't ruin it before you even know what it is. Humor me. After all, it's been a long time and I want to show off."

Malcolm walked forward and raised a hand to the hundreds of avatars watching around us. "Well, now's your chance. For old time's sake, I'll bite. Show me what this new Niche can do."

Windsor grinned and lifted his weapon. Upon closer inspection, it looked more like a gunstaff similar to my own Boomstick, but older and more refined; the wooden grip of its barrel reminded me of an old hunting rifle. He pointed the gnarled staff-end of the rifle out in front of him.

"What do you call it, a Huntsman?" Malcolm asked. "Or something just as stupid?"

Windsor shook his head, eyes flicking to the many female avatars around them. "Huntsman is too gendered. I simply call it the *Tamer*."

As he said this, a cloud formed from the staff-end of his rifle that looked similar to a churning Chaos Engine. From it, a large clawed fist emerged. Malcolm recoiled for a second, as did the players around us, clearly shocked by it.

"You see," Windsor started. "Like the Chaos Engines drawing random monsters from the debug room, I thought, wouldn't it be cool to have a class where a player could have their own room in which they can catch the monsters they've fought?"

A blazing, brown arm came from the cloud, and then a fiery chest and a foot until the monster's horned form revealed its whole self. I could hear whispers of confusion and trepidation from the crowd.

"And then I thought that, instead of fighting with magic and weapons, what if the player could call these monsters from their rooms and fight with them in their stead like they can with mounts? Of course, the monster and player are linked, so the more Hit Points the monster has, the more damage the player takes when it's defeated, but I couldn't help thinking how fun it would be."

The thing was similar to the demon I had fought atop Apollo's Lookout, but sharper, without wings, and fire blazing all around it. I didn't recognize the monster, but I could see similarities between it and Windsor's pet, which had suddenly vanished.

From his wide eyes, it seemed Data was the only one who recognized the beast. "Oh man, that's an Ifrit, one of the strongest monsters in the game," he murmured. "He's the boss of the toughest Tertiatier dungeon in Heaven, the thing that keeps the whole island afloat with his power."

I whirled on him. "Wait, this is the boss of The Engine Room?"

Data nodded and turned back in awe.

Dice gritted his teeth. "I'd argue that he's the strongest. You need to be in a guild just to fight this thing!"

"Really? A summoner class? *How original,*" Malcolm said sarcastically, raising his hands. "For someone who's supposed to be a genius, you can be a real moron sometimes. Wouldn't summoning such monsters make a player too powerful? How does the player even control such a beast?"

"I was waiting for you to ask just that, but first—" Windsor glanced my way. "Noah, does my old friend sound a bit angry to you?"

I raised an eyebrow, not catching on to why he was asking me. "More like frustrated."

"Remember what I told you about my new attack?" Windsor tilted his head in Malcolm's direction, brow raised. "Why not use your magic to help him chill out a bit."

I immediately understood what he meant and rubbed my palms in front of me, casting an Ice Wall first behind and then to either side of him. Malcolm made no attempt to escape my spell. He knew as well as I did that any fire magic could tear through the walls faster than I could create them, making trapping him inside impossible. But after what Windsor had already shown me of his new Niche, I knew that wasn't the point.

As soon as the last wall of ice appeared in front of him, I reinforced the walls and ceiling, covering him in a thick layer of ice. As though he had grown impatient, Malcolm blasted open a doorway with a Fire Weave spell and made to casually exit the prison I'd made. Before he could, Windsor spun his rifle so that the barrel was pointing at Malcolm and fired it with a loud *pop!*

A red tag flew through the air with the force of a spud gun, arcing in a short parabola through the opening in my prison, and then hitting Malcolm's robe. Utilizing his speed, he could have easily dodged the shot, but with walls to his sides and rear, there was no room to evade or even cast a spell in time to escape it.

"Tag, you're it!" Windsor called.

Malcolm looked down at the tag, appearing confused, but

as soon as he did, the Ifrit punched the grass beneath itself and roared. Baring its fangs, it charged at him.

Everyone watched speechlessly as the massive, demonic beast hurtled across the grass toward Malcolm. It took only a second to cover the distance, but in that time Malcolm summoned a blade from the template of the debug room and made his way toward it. Through the bulk of the Ifrit, none of us could see what was happening to him, but flames erupted from the battlefield, and the entire plain seemed to shake from the impact of their collision, shattering what was left of my ice prison.

For a good hundred meters around us, players had stopped fighting and were staring in awe of the battle going on between Malcolm and the Ifrit. Gasps could be heard as Malcolm slashed off, using a protection spell as a river of fire rushed at him. He ran in and engaged with the monster again, the noise of the impact drawing more attention from the surrounding armies. From the way each army joined one side or the other of the battleground, it was reminiscent of the civil war depicted in Heaven's Museum.

As though hearing it in our heads, we could still make out Malcolm's voice during the fight. "Hmm, high Hit Points... argh! And even higher defenses. Very well then, let's see how quickly those Hit Points go down when I remove that defense."

A rotating yellow light covered the Ifrit's back, turning the monster's brown skin a sickly fluorescent orange, just as he had done to David's Crystal Armor.

"Let's see how many max-strength multi-attacks this big guy can take now!"

Hundreds of quick-fire flashes from white swords, axes, and spears flickered in and out of the Ifrit. The same blitz of weapons appeared around it, hitting its back and sides, each flurry of blades cutting away at its Hit Points. Malcolm's robed form then flew out from the Ifrit's back, the blade he first summoned attacking in a wide, sweeping slash before vanishing from his hand. An artificial wind roared from the blow—apparently the default reaction to his attack—and the crowd gasped once more.

Behind him, the Ifrit slumped forward, its limbs exploding and its body disintegrating into the darkness. The erupting animation signaled the end of a great boss fight. As though thinking it was a show for their amusement, a thunderous applause filled the Toena Valley but was cut short as the tiles spun once more and we returned to the debug room. After the noise, the silence in the green-tiled room was deafening. None of us spoke, although I was speechless not because of the display, but the ease with which Malcolm had beaten Windsor's new creation.

His hit points fell into the red and then to the zero percent mark. However, instead of vanishing, Windsor's avatar merely flickered slightly and became transparent, as though programed to linger in the debug room even after death.

"Impressive, even with a boss like that. Oh well... a Niche wouldn't be balanced if it couldn't be beaten by someone... like you, eh Maou?" He looked up, seeing the red tag still pinned to Malcolm's avatar. "Luckily for me, the Ifrit wasn't the... *real* surprise. The restraining program in that tag should've uploaded... into your avatar by now."

"Restraining program?" Malcolm asked, sounding unconcerned. He stalked forward, almost like he intended to pass right through Windsor, looking dismissive in his clear victory. "No program can touch me here."

"True... but when 'here' is one server and the Dream State is another..." Windsor just grinned at him as his avatar's flickering became more violent, his voice jarring with each disappearance. "I hope... being a god... doesn't get boring... even when... you're trapped... in a place... like this."

Malcolm moved through him but then stopped, faltering in his step. "Trapped?"

Without getting an answer, Windsor vanished from the debug room, leaving us alone with Malcolm. I was stunned. We all were.

"Wait, did Windsor just cut him off from the rest of the game?" Keri asked.

Chloe smirked as she, too, realized what Windsor had done. "I think he did."

No wonder he wanted me to wall him up. It made absolutely sure

Malcolm couldn't dodge the tag containing his restraining program.

Although taking pause at this turn of events, Malcolm appeared to quickly regain his composure. "That you gained access to this place at all shows your tenacity, but it will not happen again. Just as you've locked me out of your world, I can easily lock you out of mine." Malcolm waved his hand below him. "But as a parting gift for making it this far… here's something for those who still don't believe I truly am Malcolm Mirth."

I looked at his now visible stats, his in-game name—*Maou,* of course—striking in the red border. However, by walking forward I knew that this wasn't just to see his in-game name and his barely touched Hit Points, but also so we could record his user I.D. code.

"Remember it; see for yourself."

There were several flashes of light in front of him, and suddenly standing before us were the six Screamers. Three of the Screamers were no longer wearing helmets: Maric, Lucas, and the sullen face of a pretty blonde girl that I assumed was Kristie. Chloe's grin from knowing Malcolm was locked out of Dream State faded as soon as she saw Lucas.

"I will exist so long as the Dream State exists, and as long as I have this room, I can do whatever I want here." Malcolm turned his back on us and began walking. "As I said before, this is *my* dream."

Before the other three Screamers started wailing, I could see Lucas staring at Chloe and Maric glaring at Brock. I couldn't read their lips, but they seemed to be saying something followed by, "Find us." I cringed as the wails began, but the second time their lips moved, I made out another two words.

Clues… game… Find us.

The last thing I heard before I woke up was Chloe calling, "I will! I will find you!"

Chapter 29

JUSTICE

Once again, I heard the whirring of gears as the recliner lifted me into a sitting position. Brock, David, Keri, Chloe, Data, Dice, and Vega were with me in the GC. As we all sat up, the majority of us leaned forward and planted our heads in our hands from the discomforting remnants of the Screamers' wails.

"We died again," Keri sighed. "How many times has that been now, Noah?"

I shrugged. "I guess you could say I'm getting used to it."

"So now what?" David asked.

"Now that Malcolm's power is limited to his debug room, he's not our real problem," Chloe said. "It's the Screamers under him that are the issue. If we could find them and take them out of the equation, he would have no power in the game itself."

Keri looked down. "But how do we find them?"

The door slid up and Windsor suddenly strode in, his eyes wide with excitement.

"That was by far the best constructive criticism I've had in years!" He gave us all a bewildered look. "Why does everyone look so down? Cheer up! You should all be thrilled! Ecstatic even!"

"Why?" Brock asked, sounding agitated.

Windsor shook his head, eyes bulging as if he thought we were crazy. "You're joking, right? I just ran the I.D. code you all picked up before you got taken out. The guy we were fighting really was Malcolm Mirth!"

Chloe frowned up at him. "So? We already knew that."

"So? *So!* Don't you know what this means?" He screamed and grabbed his head, the most emotion I had ever seen from him. "If that's true, and he is alive in the game, it means that when my company created the Dream Engine, we didn't just create the first dream-based, virtual reality gaming system, but a device that can make a person's consciousness immortal!" He leaned back on the wall, clutching his chest. "I'm going to get a Nobel Prize for this. I'm going to go down in history as the man responsible for ending death as we know it!" He stopped and looked around, eyes narrowing at us as though afraid we would steal his idea. "I have to find out how he did it!"

Is that really what he's focusing on?

I rubbed the back of my head. "So, you're not going to help us find the locations of the Screamers?"

Windsor seemed to wake up at this question. "Good point. I must keep up appearances. Noah, your team is relegated to that task. Now, I must get to work."

With the same pace that he ran into the GC, he exited again, nearly hitting his head on the sliding door that wouldn't open fast enough. We still heard his footfalls echoing through the corridor as it shut again behind him.

Data stood and walked to the door. "Well, at least *he's* looking at the big picture."

Dice followed suit. "Maybe there's a bonus in sticking around here after all. If I can be included in the team that discovered digital immortality, this job might just be worth it."

They both left the GC, leaving us to hear Vega's raucous laughter.

"And what do you find so funny?" Chloe asked, still sounding bitter.

Vega just shook his head. "I just have the feeling he's going to want to extend my contract. While you guys are going to be looking to find the Screamers, Windsor's probably going to try and make me find out Malcolm's secrets. Hah, why not?" He shrugged. "How can I call myself the greatest gamer of all time if I don't live forever, eh?"

I raised my eyebrows at him. "I thought you said you didn't like to play the same game for too long a period of time?"

He stretched. "Are you really trying to tell me that playing in that debug room was anything like obeying the rules of the Dream State?"

Keri nodded. "Yeah, it kind of does make it into a sandbox."

"We're probably all going to get our own rooms like that to try and find a weakness in Malcolm's armor." He shrugged and the door opened. "With a rivalry that surpasses death going on between them, I can't think of any other way Windsor's going to uncover his secrets."

He exited the GC as well, leaving just us five youngsters to stare at each other. It felt like the world had been turned upside-down.

"Lucas said that he would give us clues in the game to help us find the place they're keeping him." Chloe linked her hands in front of her face. "All I have to do is find the warehouse in a city next to a big power source. I think that's what he meant by *humming*. If he manages to find out more about where he is, I'm sure he'll tell me."

Brock lay back again, raising his hands to his eyes. "So, while Windsor and his team are going after Malcolm and the secrets of his immortality, we're going to be hunting this immortal's in-game slave soldiers?"

I nodded. "Sounds about right."

Brock rubbed his hands and sat back up. "Alright then, where do we start?"

We all went quiet. David raised his hand excitedly but then lowered it again, as though second-guessing his idea.

There was a moment of silence before Keri looked up and finally said, "Maybe... in the game?"

A week passed, and the day of Colban and Samuel's murder trial finally arrived. It took three whole days in court for the prosecutor to go through all of the evidence in front of a jury, along with hours of pointless deliberation on the part of Samuel's lawyer.

Despite having documents showing motive, proof of intent, and footage of the murder itself, the judge was lenient and only gave Samuel twenty years in prison. Colban was given thirty to life simply because he was behind the wheel of the truck that had been the true cause of the crash. It felt like an injustice, but I was just relieved everything was finally over.

Being a part of the prosecution team, I had a front row seat as the security guards came and took both of them away. The courtroom was small. Most of the jury, and the judge herself, were only shown over monitors—they weren't even willing to show up for a murder case. However, as Samuel passed me, he stopped and looked in my direction with a familiar sinister grin on his face.

"You know, Noah, I didn't tell you everything I know about Malcolm... and these Screamers of his."

I raised my brow at him. "Believe me, the mystery of the Screamers will be solved *long* before you get out."

Despite the confidence in my words, the grin didn't leave his face.

"We'll see. You won't be able to catch Malcolm like you caught me. He's like the air, Noah. Try to snatch him, and he'll slip right through your fingers." He turned away and continued to walk. "But I'm sure you already know how that feels."

His words suddenly brought me back to the anxiety I had felt when my mother had told me Sue was dead. How, at the exact same time, Samuel's letters had made me believe that her consciousness was somehow still lingering in the Dream State and that I could save her.

Even then, I thought I was going out of my mind.

The memory of realizing she was gone only made Malcolm's accomplishment in the game all the more poignant. Where the Dream State had failed to keep Sue alive, it had somehow made

Malcolm immortal.

Malcolm succeeded where Sue failed; where's the justice in that?

The people around me murmured as the courtroom began to empty out. Before I left, I noticed that Sue's parents were still in their seats, grieving for their daughter even now that her killers had faced justice. I could understand that. The coldness of my old life was quickly replaced with the warmth of the present when I saw Chloe walk through the crowd. Like Brock arriving to save me from slipping into a coma while in the game, Chloe took my hand and saved me from lamenting my losses.

She smiled. "Come on. You know I can't do this without you."

I smiled back as she pulled me through the masses. "Same here. We've still got to find your brother."

"I think I know the first place we should look."

One case closed, another case opened.

We left the courtroom hand in hand, ready for more work in the Dream State. It took us less than an hour to take a cab back to Wona's facility, enter the GC, ingest some DSD, and delve into the Dream State. I closed my eyes to a dark world and opened them again in a bright, shiny new one.

Appearing on Heaven's floating city with a flash, I breathed in the cool-but-fake air in the cool-but-fake world and made my way over the bridges to the Gateways to start trying out some of Heaven's new dungeons. I hadn't returned since the grand re-opening after confronting Malcolm. I was surprised to hear that it went off without a hitch and there hadn't been any more Screamer sabotages since. Things appeared to have finally calmed down a bit.

However, I noticed there were a few messages waiting for me in my comms. The very first message was from Frank. It made sense that she was trying to contact me in-game since she had no other way of reaching me. But when I read her message, I had to stop walking. As my eyes scanned the words again after skimming it once, it felt like my heart was slowly creeping up into my throat.

FranktheTank: "Noah, I'm sorry. I honestly don't know how it happened, and trust me, after the promise I made you, this is as hard for me to write as it will be for you to read. After fighting Malcolm in the debug room, I noticed that some of the items in my inventory list had been shifted around and I knew something was missing ..."

I couldn't breathe as I read the final sentence.

"... It's the Wakizashi, Noah. It's gone."

ACKNOWLEDGEMENTS

This was the first book in the Dream State Saga that wasn't triggered by a car accident but, ironically, the idea that made it work did come to me while I was in a car that was about to be worked on. By the third book, I thought I should introduce some deeper concepts and being an agency in a machine at the time brought forward the Ghost in the Machine idea that ended up becoming the key concept in the story. This idea wouldn't have gotten as far as it did without having many back and forth conversations with Hayley and Liam, who the book is dedicated to. Thanks to Emma Hoggan for picking up and working with this continuation.

About the Author

Growing up in the small town of Timaru, New Zealand, Christopher Keene broke the family trend of becoming an accountant by becoming a writer instead. While studying for his Bachelor of Arts in English Literature from the University of Canterbury, he took the school's creative writing course in the hopes of someday seeing his own book on the shelf in his favorite bookstores.

He is now the published author of the Dream State Saga, as well as his new epic fantasy trilogy, A Cycle of Blades. In his spare time, he writes a blog to share his love of the fantasy and science fiction genres in novels, films, comics, games, and anime (fantasyandanime.wordpress.com).

To learn more about LitRPG, talk to authors including Christopher, and just to have an awesome time, please join the LitRPG Group.